THE MYSTERY DEEPENS

THE MYSTERY DEEPENS

JOHN CHAMBERS™ BOOK TWO

MICHAEL ANDERLE

DISRUPTIVE IMAGINATION®

THE MYSTERY DEEPENS TEAM

Thanks to the Beta Team
Larry Omans, Jim Caplan, Mary Morris, Kelly O'Donnell, Rachel Beckford, John Ashmore

Thanks to the JIT Readers
Dorothy Lloyd
Dave Hicks
Debi Sateren
Deb Mader
Jeff Goode
Diane L. Smith
Micky Cocker

If I've missed anyone, please let me know!

Editor
The Skyhunter Editing Team

Copyright © 2020 by Michael Anderle
Cover Art by Jake @ J Caleb Design
http://jcalebdesign.com / jcalebdesign@gmail.com
Cover copyright © LMBPN Publishing
A Michael Anderle Production

LMBPN Publishing
PMB 196, 2540 South Maryland Pkwy
Las Vegas, NV 89109

First US Edition, January 2021
Version 1.01, July 2021
ebook ISBN: 978-1-64971-404-6
Print ISBN: 978-1-64971-405-3

DEDICATION

To Family, Friends and
Those Who Love
to Read.
May We All Enjoy Grace
to Live the Life We Are
Called.

— Michael

CHAPTER ONE

Dick buzzed through to the apartment and waited for an answer.

"Hello?" Terra's tinny and distorted voice replied.

Driverless cabs, but they still can't upgrade the audio setup not to sound like you're speaking to R2-D2.

"It's me." Dick pinched his tired eyes.

There was a moment's pause before another buzzer sounded and the door unlocked.

Terra met him at her door. "You look like shit."

"I don't feel so hot right now, either." Dick motioned inside. "Mind if I come in?"

Terra wore comfortable night shorts and a black tank top. Her hair was twisted into a ponytail and her face stripped of makeup. "You got my gun?"

Dick handed her the GLOCK 99.

She gave an approving nod and stepped aside. "Good boy. Come on in."

She followed him with her eyes as he made for her couch and sat. After grabbing a steaming mug from the counter, she examined him closely. "Are you going to tell me what this is about, or should I presume that you're looking to stay here again, Dick? We can't make a habit of this, you know. People will talk."

"Fuck people."

Terra smiled. "That's why *I'm* with the public office of protection, and *you're* a private investigator. I care about people. It's why I do my job. Speaking of, I've just come off a twelve-hour shift. I'd like to know what's going on here so I can get some shut-eye."

Dick sat up and leaned his elbows on his knees. "I need somewhere to crash, Terra."

Terra sighed. "I thought that's where this was going. Look, I can't have you crashing here every time you get into a rough spot. First, I don't trust you. Second, I'm a lone wolf. I like my personal space. I gave you some wiggle room the other night, but this can't become a habit."

Dick stared at her levelly. "I'm not asking to stay here, Terra. I'm asking you to find somewhere for me to crash. I'm in something of a tight spot, and the people who are involved know my circle well enough that they'll likely figure that I'd stay at a friend's house or somewhere familiar."

"We're not friends," Terra reiterated.

Dick placated her with his hands. "I know. Don't think I didn't get that dig. To be honest, I'm not all that fond of you, either. But I'm in a situation, and I need to disappear."

"Disappear?" Terra sipped her drink. "What kind of shit are you in, Dick? This sounds serious."

Dick's mind flashed to the note that had been left at his apartment. He saw a montage of his fights with the Russians who had invaded his home, and the bitch who had stolen Santana's pendant and happened to have been one step ahead along most of the way of his former investigation.

"You know I can't say," Dick replied.

Terra shrugged. "Was worth an ask. Look, the AJS will be more than happy to assist you if you head down to the precinct and make a formal report. Our witness protection scheme can do what you're asking, if you truly wish to become invisible. Although let's be honest, both of us know that invisibility isn't possible in Atlantica. One way or another, your body will be found. Whether you're alive or dead when that happens, that's entirely up to you."

"I'm not looking to disappear entirely," Dick clarified. "I'm looking for a safe house. An unassigned apartment. Somewhere I can set up shop while I figure this shit out. The people that are after me thrive on technology. You think that if I file an AJS report and go into witness protection that they won't hack the system and find me?"

"Hold on, who's hacking the system?" Terra asked.

Dick ignored her, not wanting to open that can of worms. He knew a handful of people who were doing just that, and he had used every single one of them at some point in his career. Was he any better than they were?

"Terra, please. You must know of *somewhere*. A few days to a week tops. A safe place where they can't find me. Free from technology and prying eyes."

Terra considered this as she clutched her cup with both hands and narrowed her eyes at Dick. She took a long sip and finished the drink before setting the cup aside, then propped a hand on her hip. "I'll ask one more time: what the hell have you gotten yourself into, Dick?"

Dick shrugged. "When I find out, I'll let you know. Please, Terra. I'll give you the one thing you've always wanted."

Terra's eyebrow raised. "Your head on a pike?"

Dick laughed, then shook his head. "Leverage over me. I'll owe you a favor. You know as well as I do that I'm true to my word."

Terra's shoulders softened. "Fine."

"Fine?"

"Fine," she confirmed. "I know a place. Hold on, let me get

dressed and I'll take you there."

They drove in relative silence until they pulled up outside the AJS precinct. Morning had come, and the building was a hive of activity. Civilians walked into and out of the building, presumably filing their cases, AJS officers wandered to vehicles in metallic-blue bodysuits, armed and ready for action, and the constant wail of sirens added a dissonant orchestra to this side of town.

Dick wore dark glasses and kept his head low the entire journey there. He peeked through the windows of Terra's blue Jaguar F-Type, hunting for anyone who might be following them, or any suspicious activity that indicated they were in any danger.

There was nothing of note that he could detect.

Still, when Terra exited the vehicle and left him sitting inside behind the tinted windows, Dick couldn't help but feel as though time moved slowly and he was being watched.

Terra returned a few minutes later. "Sorry that took so long. I had to find a way to sign out the keys without arousing suspicion." She gave Dick a hard look where he'd ducked in his seat. "You know the windows are tinted?"

"You can never be too careful. I know a guy who dishes out tech that can see through these kinds of shields."

Once again, Terra asked, "Dick, what are you up against?"

Dick remained tight-lipped.

Terra pulled out of the AJS parking lot and sped out onto the streets. The radio was silent, and the Jaguar's engine was loud. She stop-started at the traffic lights and navigated her way to the edge of the city proper until they reached a part where the buildings weren't so tall, and apartment buildings were interspersed with large production factories and warehouses. The neatly kept roads of the main city became simple grey strips of tarmac, and foot traffic all but ceased.

Dick glimpsed Atlantica's coastline in the distance, a white strip of sand veiled thinly by the fog. Beyond that, the sea was a murky blue.

Terra parked beside an abandoned warehouse, the corrugated sheeting of its walls covered in an array of graffiti. Its windows were boarded up, and a "Sold" sign stood crooked on the corner by the road.

Terra exited the vehicle and gave a cursory glance around. Satisfied, she ushered Dick out of the car.

Dick closely followed as they walked up a small ramp that led to a door. It might once have been an office, but it had done nothing but collect dust ever since its closure. Terra unlocked three separate mechanisms, threw a final glance behind, then entered the building.

Dick drew a deep breath. "It stinks."

"It's your new home. Don't knock it until you've seen it."

They passed a reception counter and stopped at a door near the back of the room. Terra thumbed in a four-digit code, and a light turned green. "Three, four, seven, two. Remember that."

Dick followed Terra into the dark and down a set of stone steps.

This didn't feel good to him. The whole experience of walking in the dark reminded him of his descent into The Warehouse a few nights ago. He half-expected to hear the sound of music playing, to suddenly be attacked by light, and discover that he was in the underground gambling circuit where he had met Sadie Turnberry for the first time.

What he found, however, was quite different.

The stairs went down to a sunken floor below. Terra opened the door and clapped twice. Lights kicked into action, illuminating a living room. The space was ample, there were plush couches in an L-shape pointing toward the TV, and fresh carpet laid beneath their feet.

"Take your shoes off before you enter," Terra commanded. "A lot of this is brand new. Fully refurbished."

Dick gave an appreciative nod. "You really know how to treat your guests, don't you?"

Terra shrugged. "Victims of crime in need of being hidden shouldn't be kept in a shit situation, you know? As much as the AJS is hated by many, we're here for the people. There are bunkers like this all across town. Places where people can hopefully hide and remain undetected while we figure out the shit that got them in trouble."

"Hopefully?"

"We can only protect those who are smart." Terra's face straightened. "If someone heads into the city and causes a ruckus, then gets tailed back to this place? Well… We're not responsible for what comes after."

Dick kicked off his shoes. "You mean this place is also subject to the residential rules of the law? I thought you said this is a safe house?"

"Oh, no." Terra chuckled. "You miss my meaning. Although a residential place, this falls under the AJS's jurisdiction. It isn't a true residential property. This is a purchase of the AJS and is a necessity to conduct our work. If someone dies in here, you can bet your ass we're getting involved."

Dick narrowed his eyes as he investigated the property. It was nice. Much nicer than some of the places he had seen in the city. "Maybe the AJS should go into residential lettings. I bet there are people in the city who would kill for that kind of protection."

"Don't think we haven't thought about that." Terra sighed.

Dick gave her a questioning look. Terra simply replied, "Politics."

She showed Dick around the place, giving him a guided tour of the bedroom, a separate kitchen, and a bathroom with a shower. Everything was clean and tidy, which was a stark contrast to the reception area.

Heading to the kettle to fix himself a hot drink, Dick asked, "What did this place use to be? I assume the 'Sold' sign is part of the props holding up this illusion?"

Terra nodded. "Can't slip anything past a private investigator, eh? It was one of the original power units holding up the island's power grid, way back when. There are a host of derelict generators in the main hub of this building. The units around here are all similar. A few have been purchased by shitheads trying to hide their drug operations or traffickers who think they're smart enough to smuggle their cargo. But we catch them all in the end."

Dick shook his head in disbelief. "On an island where people can get away with anything in the comfort of their homes, why do they bother doing this shit in public?"

Terra shrugged. "Old habits die hard. People miss the excitement. Half the thrill of doing the bad shit is wondering if you're going to get caught. It adds an extra layer of adrenaline. It's not a bad thing, anyway. Most scum stay away from this part of the island, knowing that there are often AJS roaming around on the hunt for raids."

"People are idiots," Dick scoffed.

"Can't argue with that." Terra yawned. "Is there anything else you need before I go on my merry way? Know that I can't provide you transport and there's only enough in this place to last a few days in terms of food and drink. I recommend not ordering takeout to this address. Or hookers." She raised her eyebrows.

Dick laughed. "Was that really necessary?"

Terra smirked. "I don't know what you're into. Just keep this place safe and tidy. Remember, it's AJS property."

Dick nodded, then scanned the walls. "Any hidden cameras I should know about?"

This time, Terra laughed. "Come on, Dick. No one wants to watch footage of you jerking off."

CHAPTER TWO

Dick slept uneasily, his unconscious mind working through the unfinished business that had come from Santana's case.

They had won the pendant back, but that was the least of the battle. There were still threads that Dick couldn't explain, and they ate away at his peace.

Sadie Turnberry was still at large. Probably in the hospital, but she would no doubt be looking for Dick. She didn't seem the type to let things go.

Something we have in common.

The larger question remained: why? What was so precious about Santana's pendant that Sadie felt the need to steal it? What about that piece of jewelry kept the trail so cloudy and induced a family of Russian mobsters to get involved, twist the arms of Dick's associate Ricardo, and try to hush people?

And the larger question, who the hell was Dexter Lockhart?

In Dick's sleeping mind, he saw the note signed "DL" that someone had left in Sadie's apartment. It floated before him like a leaf caught in a gust of wind and flew away every time Dick reached for it. The words of the Russian he had thrown down the garbage chute reverberated in his head. "Dexter Lockhart."

Dick tossed in his sleep. The bed was surprisingly comfortable but did little to bring him peace. He wondered about his apartment, suspicious that people might now find their way inside to raid his communications. He thought of Santana, probably out there in the wilds somewhere and wondering if she was safe. If they had come for the pendant once, they would try again.

He had to warn her.

Dick awoke an unknown time later. In his groggy state, he searched for his window but found only bare walls. The memory of where he was sleeping came back to him slowly, and he prepared himself a stiff black coffee.

As it brewed, he thumbed through his cell phone and hoped to high hell that Valentina's anti-hack methods were secure enough that no one had used his device to follow him here. He looked for Santana's number and typed a message. "Keep safe. Their eyes may be on you. Avoid your house for a while."

When he sent the message, it failed. There was no signal in the bunker.

"I guess that answers my question of whether people can hack into my phone down here."

When the coffee had brewed, he filled a mug and walked up the stairs. He found his way through the dusty reception area and stood by the boarded-up windows. The only piece of glass remaining was in the front door, and even that was only a small square. Dick glanced outside at the empty street, the sun setting somewhere overhead through the fog.

The message sent.

Dick waited a few minutes for a reply while sipping his coffee. When nothing came back, he assumed that Santana must be out somewhere, doing whatever she did. He headed back down inside the bunker and made some breakfast.

Dick strolled out of the industrial estate as night descended. Shaded by the darkness, he locked up the three locks on the front door and headed out into the night.

It was a twenty-minute walk before he found civilization again. Navigating around the buildings was tedious, but he was glad of the cover. Along the way, he overheard the less than careful conversation of a nearby drug deal, and in the distance, someone screamed. AJS sirens wailed somewhere in the city.

Dick made his way along the streets, his collar high and a hat low over his brow. He found a phone booth on the corner of the block and was about to tap his phone against the wireless receiver to pay when he realized that might lead a paper trail to his location. Instead, he fumbled through his pocket for some coins and placed them in the slots. A dial tone met his ears, and he tapped in the number.

"Ace? It's Pitbull. I need something." Dick waited for the response.

An overexcited voice called so loudly through the receiver that Dick had to pull it away from his ear. He glanced out the phone booth to check that no one was watching him. "Yo, Pitbull! Been some time, man. How you living?"

Music blared, and women laughed in the background. Dick growled, "Is this a bad time?"

"Nah, man," Ace replied enthusiastically. "It's an amazing time. You should join the party, bro! We need more peeps like you to bring the thunder. Y'all need to loosen up, y'hear?"

Dick ran a hand down his face. "Ace, can you go somewhere private? I need your services. I'm prepared to pay. Big."

That caught his attention. "Ite, ite. Hold on." The music grew louder before it grew quiet, then faded to a dull thud as Ace found somewhere where he could speak. "Shoot."

"Are you alone?" Dick asked.

"For now," Ace replied, a hint of mirth in his tone. "Until these bitches get four down the hole, then they common sense gonna be out the door, ya feel? Gimme an hour, and I'll be cocooned by bitches—"

"Ace!" Dick shouted, regretting putting in the call. He was wary of how long he had before his coins ran out and the line went dead. "I need you to surveil someone for me, okay? Do your magic and keep an eye on this address." Dick read Sadie's address, unsure if Ace was writing it down or committing it to memory. He had no reason to doubt him since he had never failed before. "You got that?"

Ace told him he did. "So, what? You want me just to buzz you with her location? Tail the bitch and give you regular updates? What we talking? Five minutes? Ten minutes? An hour?"

"As often as you deem necessary," Dick replied. Another thought hit him. "Hey, Ace...You aware of anyone by the name of Dexter Lockhart?"

"Nah, man. No one I can think of." A woman's voice shouted in the background. The sound of a door opening and the music growing louder came through the receiver. "You sure you don't want to come, Pitbull? I'm telling ya, there's plenty for everyone. These bitches are powdered, pissed, and ready to plough, nahmean?"

"I'm fine, thanks," Dick replied. "Maybe another night."

Ace laughed. "That's gotta be yo catchphrase, Pitbull. Peace out."

Dick explored the area surrounding his new warehouse after ensuring that his collar was high and his face was shadowed. He always did his best thinking when he was walking, and the steady night breeze allowed him a chance to consider his next steps.

What were the open loops? Where were the areas of investigation that Dick had yet to explore? He knew that Sadie Turnberry was a cog in the machine, and he knew there was a tie-in to the Russian family he had encountered. Dexter Lockhart fit somewhere into the equation and the fact that he had no idea where drove him crazy.

Dick stopped at a 7-Eleven and was about to buy himself some coffee when he realized that any financial transaction would leave a paper trail. He needed to get cash, but how could he manage that without revealing his location to anyone who might be tracking him?

Just go to the bank. You're acting paranoid.

Paranoia was an investigator's best friend. A paranoid mind opened up hidden possibilities and kept you guarded. As long as he was careful, he'd be okay. He'd be stupid to think that Sadie wasn't out there looking for him right now.

Dick settled on a bench by the coast and looked out over the sands and the dark fog covering the sea. He thought back to the note he found in his apartment and wondered if he had been hasty in tossing it in the trashcan. Was there any possibility of fingerprints somewhere on the paper?

"Couldn't hurt to look," he muttered around the cigarette hanging from his lips. "But how to get back without causing problems?"

Dick turned over his shoulder and watched the night's thinning foot traffic. This area was a far cry from his central city apartment. Right about now, his streets would be alive with people heading through the city and going about their business. In the quiet borders, there was less activity than Dick had expected.

He took a risk and turned on his phone, then thumbed across the map screen for his next location. He found it only three miles from where he sat. It was a little close to home for his comfort, but he hoped that it would turn out to be worth the risk.

Dick rose from the bench and walked through the night.

CHAPTER THREE

Sadie Turnberry lay in the darkened hospital ward with her headache drumming a regular beat.

She had barely slept a wink. Despite all the painkillers the doctors had given her, and the numerous stitches holding together the gash at the back of her head, she couldn't sleep. She was fuming.

Flashes of the previous night whirled through her head in a violent montage. She had been blindsided, caught off-guard by the detective and the bitch. While Sadie had been operating The Warehouse and ensuring that the gambling ring continued its operation in a brand-new location, the detective had broken into her goddamn house.

And the only reason she had to move The Warehouse's location was because of the goddamn detective in the first place.

She growled, eyes narrowed as a nurse walked past her ward, the staccato clack of her hard shoes on the laminate floor too loud for Sadie's sensitive head.

What was the point in paying thousands for security when her cameras and guards could be compromised so easily? Why should she pay a company to guard her property when she was absent, to protect her prized possessions, creatures, and plants, if two assholes could break in without so much as a whisper?

That was the part that hurt her the most. She had no idea how they had managed it. The wall at the back of the house was difficult to scale. If someone had leaped over, the guards should have picked it up. If someone had broken inside the house, the cameras should have alerted the guards. The guards should have been able to eliminate the intruders, no problem. Anything was legal on her property, and a simple, well-placed bullet would have ended her problems.

What was worse was that they stole back the pendant. The tiny piece of jewelry that she had worked so hard to recover. The flashy bit of gold that she had hidden behind layers of misdirection and scumbags who should have been able to deal with the problem. That was the part that irked her the most. It wasn't merely that it was gone, it was that she'd have to explain to Lockhart exactly what went wrong.

Sadie closed her eyes, knowing sleep wouldn't come. When the ward reached its quietest, she tore out her IV drip, climbed out of bed, then padded out of the hospital. A couple of nurses tried to stop her exit, but Sadie was tenacious, and no one was going to tell her "no."

She arrived at her house thirty minutes later, in pain and angry.

For a minute, she simply sat in the driverless cab and stared at the iron gates. Her heart fluttered, her confidence shaken. If Dick had broken in before, who was to say that someone wasn't waiting in there now? She hadn't had a chance to give the security team a tongue-lashing—that would come—but what if someone was hiding in the shadows of her house?

Don't be stupid. You're Sadie Turnberry. Arm yourself and get ready to shoot. If another person breaks into this place, I'll turn their brain to pâte.

The house was quiet. A smattering of guards remained with the dogs in the courtyard, but Sadie ignored them and made her way through the house to her room. Her private space felt infected, as though a virus had passed through. She didn't trust a thing she saw, and when Sabrina careened around the corner, Sadie yelped in surprise as her hand moved to her chest.

The ocelot rubbed her head into the cup of Sadie's hand. Sadie gave a weak smile, hating how violated she felt in her home. The bitch who had broken in had controlled Sabrina, somehow. What the hell had that been about? They'd turned everything had Sadie against her.

Who the hell were these people?

Sadie entered her room and sat on her bed in the darkness for some time. Her thoughts turned poisonous as she considered the path before her. The painkillers would wear off soon, and she would have to fight through the pain.

Pain is the fuel. Pain is the power source that drives the greats.

She leaned over to the phone on the bedside table and thumbed in the extension for the security manager's office. Dwayne kept his business on the first floor of the apartment, a grid of screens in front of him at all times. He and his team should have spotted something last night, yet they didn't.

Sadie waited for Dwayne to pick up. When he did, she didn't allow him a chance to speak. Two minutes later, he muttered a weak apology and hung up. Sadie considered trying to get some rest, but then an idea struck her. She scrolled through her phone, hunting for the right number. She found it, dialed it, then waited for the answer on the other end.

A man with a deep, growling voice answered. "Yes?"

Sadie drew a breath as pain flared in her head. "I have a job for you. No questions asked. Triple your usual rate. Are you in?"

There was a pause on the other end before the reply came. "Give me the details."

Sadie did.

CHAPTER FOUR

The alleyway was dark.

Dick had been walking for twenty minutes when he first encountered the ink-heads. He navigated the alleys and did whatever he could to remain out of the public eye as he traveled across the city. The rumble of souped-up vehicles passed on a few occasions and forced Dick into the shadows. He didn't know if the Russians were involved in street racing or had kitted out their cars to stream through the city and hunt for him, but he didn't want to take any risks.

A PI hunts in the shadows. If you find one, he's already lost.

When he turned down the labyrinth of alleys surrounding a series of quaint DIY and textile stores, Dick knew he'd come down the wrong passage.

There were at least twelve of them gathered in a circle around a trashcan lit on fire. They huddled closely, fingerless gloves rubbing together for warmth, and dark lines covering their bodies. Although ink was still relatively misunderstood in Atlantica, Dick knew enough to identify the dark substance staining their bloodstreams as it twisted the fabric of their reality and took them far from the world they all hated.

As Dick slowed down and tried to sneak past, he only hoped they were far enough down the inky void that they would be blind to his passage. When the first ink-head shouted, he knew it was far too late.

"Wahey!" A woman with a row of missing teeth and an eye that seemed unable to open called with unrequited enthusiasm. "Another guest for our merry gathering! How about it? Free ink for all!"

She laughed as her words echoed around the alley. From where they sat, it was impossible to see the wider streets, and judging by the burn marks scorching the ground, this wasn't the first time this location had been used for this kind of gathering.

To Dick's surprise, the man sitting beside her clenched his fist and punched her in the face. She gave a pathetic yelp as she fell off the box she sat on and hit the ground. "Shut the fuck up. You're going to get the AJS on us, bitch."

Three men stood and wobbled uncertainly on their feet. "Oi, don't fucking hit her," one cried.

"That was uncalled for," another said.

The third remained silent and merely glowered.

The man who punched her grinned. "Oh, sit your asses down. You're too fucked up to bring it to the big dog."

Dick remained where he stood, hands deep in his pockets as he watched with morbid fascination. As they broke into arguing, Dick moved to slip away.

"Oi. Sunshine," one of the ink-heads called to Dick. "Where do you think you're going?"

The woman sat up slowly, dizzied from the punch, but with the smile somehow still on her face. A swollen lump appeared on her cheek.

"She's right," the inkhead continued. "There's plenty to go around. What do you say?"

Although their words were inviting, there was a menace in the expressions. Dick knew the model: invite another inker into the group and you have someone to share the costs. If you're also a dealer, then you automatically accrue a new client when the addiction hits. It's the ultimate pyramid scheme. Give a little for free, get a lot in the long run when your client becomes putty in your hands.

Dick smirked. "I'd rather fuck a scarecrow."

The man's smile dropped, as did the smiles of the others standing around the flaming trashcan. "You what?"

Dick sighed, hands coming out of his pockets. "I said, I'd rather fuck a scarecrow. Do you know what that shit does to your bodies? There's a whole world out here where you can excel and make cash in ways that the rest of the world could only dream of. And here you are pumping your veins with a second-rate product to get a momentary high—while out in the streets, too!" Dick shook his head. "Don't even have the common decency to go to someone's house and fuck yourselves up in private."

The man scowled. "Second-rate product?" He glanced at the other ink-heads. "My shit is the finest you'll find, prick."

"*That's* the part you took offense to?" Dick asked in disbelief. He waved a hand. "As you were, gentlemen. Have a good evening."

He turned to leave and discovered his way barred by two women who appeared as though they were set to join the circle. They gave him a strange look then turned to the big man for reassurance.

The man laughed. "Ah, Breanne. Taylor. Good timing. We've got a new member of our gang. Would you be so kind as to bring him over to us? I'll warn you. He's going to put up a fight."

Dick flexed his fingers as a moment passed between the three. The girls took in their leader's words and adjusted their stances, holding up their fists ready to fight.

Really? Even the alleys aren't safe anymore? Dick thought sarcastically.

"I'll have you know," Dick warned, "I don't hold back. No matter what's between your private parts, if you start it, you'll get it. Are you sure you want to go ahead with this?"

The women stared levelly at him, his way barred. Dick couldn't help but notice that their veins weren't half as dark as the others, meaning that they probably still had their faculties and could likely put up a fight.

"Very well," Dick muttered.

He closed the gap toward them, and the woman on the right struck like a viper, her fist lashing out with a sharp jab. Dick dodged out of the way, but barely. The second woman threw a punch and caught Dick off-balance, catching him on the shoulder. Dick brought his fists up and jabbed at the woman's chest, sending her a couple of feet backward.

The first woman came at him, kicking at his stomach. Dick blocked the strike and twisted out of harm's reach. As he spun, he noticed the ink-heads getting to their feet, ready to join the fray.

Gotta make this quick, Dick. Make an opening and get the fuck out of here. You're never going to look like a hero taking down ink-heads.

The first woman returned a strike, using the heel of her other foot. She had some martial arts training, judging by her technique. Dick felt the brunt of the kick in his recovering hip and winced. The woman noticed this, smirked, then went for the same place.

Her foot caught the wound again. Dick's hand came to his side. It felt like he was bleeding beneath his clothes, but he wouldn't give her the satisfaction of seeing it for herself. Adrenaline raced through his body as he went for her.

He blocked a kick, then a second. The other woman saw the oncoming attack and rushed to her comrade's side. Dick stopped a punch and grabbed her wrist, then sharply twisted her to one side. It sounded like something broke.

The kicking woman drew closer to the wall. She punched, used her knees, and flailed as she retreated against the brick.

Dick grabbed one wrist and twisted it behind her back, then spun the woman so she was in front of him and blocked the others like a human shield.

The woman tried to back-kick into his crotch, but Dick braced himself and countered it. The woman groaned under his wrist lock.

The ink-heads paused, backlit by the flaming fire until they were all silhouetted as menacing shadows. The lead ink-head drew a gun and aimed it at Dick's head.

Dick shook his head in disbelief. "I'm holding one of yours hostage, and you're fucked off your head on drugs. If you take the shot now, who do you think you're going to hit? Her, or me?"

The woman tried to wrestle out of Dick's hold, but he only gripped her tighter.

"Like I give a shit," the man replied, no emotion on his face. "If I hit her, I hit you both. Win-win."

The woman with the broken wrist gasped in disgust. "You asshole. You kill her, and you may as well kill me, too."

The ink-head turned the gun on her, eyes flashing. Sound exploded around the alley as the shot fired. The woman Dick was holding screamed for her friend, and Dick let her go to her.

"Taylor! Taylor... No!" Breanne screamed.

Taylor had turned a ghostly white and stared up at Breanna. She clutched her broken wrist and looked on her body for the bullet wound, but found nothing.

They turned to the ink-head, who stood with his mouth hanging open, gun arm pointed at the ground as blood spilled from a wound in his stomach. Dick holstered his pistol, the tip still warm from the shot. He approached the injured ink-head, and the others retreated. "You threaten the life of an innocent woman for the sake of a few measly dollars in your pocket, and you're going to feel the wrath of God. In this case, that's me."

The ink-head folded to his knees, hands trying to stem the flow of blood.

Dick turned to the others. "You call a hospital, and he stands a chance at living. I missed his vital organs. It's on you to decide if this fucker lives or dies." He knelt by the man. "I don't fancy your chances."

Dick rose to his feet once more, muttering, "All I wanted to do was walk peacefully through a fucking alleyway."

Dick stopped across the road from Louie's Florist and sat on the bench.

The incident in the alleyway hadn't been pretty. Not for the last time, it made him question his decision to live in Atlantica. When a grown man couldn't walk through the back alleys of the big city without fear of death, was it safe for anyone to live here? Where was the justice?

I'm the justice. There is good in the world, fighting against evil. Sometimes good isn't as pretty as the movies show you.

He finished his cigarette and approached the darkened store. The flower arrangements were all packed away inside and crowded the entrance. Dick cupped his hands to the glass and peered inside.

There was no one around. He hadn't expected there to be. He took a step back and checked that no one watched him, then turned to the apartments above the store. A few lights were still on, including the room he assumed to be Jessica Jackson's. He looked at his phone and debated calling her, then decided against it. Instead, he took a pebble from the ground and hurled it up at her window.

The first two tries were way off base. The strain of throwing the stone caused pain to flare in his hip. The third found its mark. After a minute of silence, he threw a fourth that hit the window square in the center.

An old man's face appeared at the glass. Dick recognized

Louie instantly.

Louie slid open the window, and a puff of smoke escaped into the night. He groggily examined the street and found Dick standing below.

"What do you want?" Louie asked, exasperation in his voice.

"Jessica." Dick didn't need to say more than that.

Louie sighed and disappeared into the room. A few minutes later, the door at the back of the store opened, and Louie emerged. He fumbled with keys and let Dick inside. "You know that late-night visits are going to start costing you?"

Dick told Louie that he was good for it as Louie led him upstairs and into the apartment lounge.

Dick expected to find Jessica in the armchair from before but instead saw her lying on the couch in a black satin slip that barely covered her legs.

"I'll leave you two to it," Louie remarked, slowly closing the door as he left the room.

"It's been years since we've had two late-night booty calls in a week," Jessica crooned. "Can't get enough of me, baby?"

Dick removed his hat and opened his jacket before he sat in the armchair. Smoke poured out of Jessica's lips as she spoke, a cigarette hanging loosely in her hand. "You want one?"

Dick shook his head. "I'm cutting down."

Jessica shrugged. "More for me. What is it I can do for you, Dick? I'm assuming that you want something. Otherwise why would you hunt me in the darkness?"

Dick grinned. "As you say, I'm ready for another booty call."

Jessica's eyebrows raised. "You know, in my business, it's my job to be able to read people. To spot the things that people aren't saying. You think I'm stupid enough to believe that you came here only for sex? Every Dick encounter always comes with conditions. I've learned that the hard way." She glanced at Dick's crotch as she finished her sentence.

Dick relaxed into the chair. His hip throbbed. "You know me

too well. I need someone to do me a favor. I need a burglar, of sorts. Someone who can break into a property and retrieve something of value to me. I'm happy to pay, but I need it done quickly. Are you in?"

Jessica considered this with a bite of her lip. She sat upright and crossed her legs. Dick tried to resist glancing at her bare flesh. "And there was me thinking that *you* were the prize burglar, Mr. Chambers. Have you finally found a property that has you stumped? I never thought I'd see the day Dick couldn't enter wherever he wanted."

Their eyes met. Dick's throat went dry. He composed himself. "The target is my apartment. I can't say why, but I can't be there right now. I need to get something back, but I can't be seen near the place."

Jessica narrowed her eyes. "What kind of trouble are you in, Dick?"

Dick grinned. "I'll provide my usual answer: the less you know, the better."

Jessica took a drag of her cigarette and thought deeply. After a minute, she rose to her feet. She padded gently across the room and stopped in front of Dick.

"For the record," Dick warned, "if you're thinking about any of that good stuff, just know that I can't right now." He moved his jacket aside to show where the blood from his hip had stuck to his top. "I'm in a bit of pain."

Jessica leaned forward and placed her hands on the arms of the armchair, a confident grin on her face. "Oh, I'm sure we can find other ways to have some fun. What do you say, Dick? A favor for a favor?"

CHAPTER FIVE

By the time the sun was rising, Dick had exited Louie's Florist with a smile on his face, and the note back in his possession.

Jessica's report had been disturbing. According to her recount, Dick's place, while not trashed and destroyed, had been tampered with. Muddy footprints stained the carpets, and cushions and objects had been moved to positions that made it clear someone had rooted around his place.

This was both good and bad news for Dick. On the one hand, it was nice to know that his paranoia wasn't unfounded. On the other, it meant that people were looking for him. He had to play his cards close to the chest and be careful.

"Be careful out there, Dick," Jessica cautioned.

Dick thanked Jessica and left her naked in bed. With the note in his hand, he examined the scrap of paper and read the message once more. For the first time since he had found it, something struck his attention.

"Mr. Chambers. You can run, but you can't hide. I play to win."

There was no signature on the bottom. The first note Dick had found in Sadie's decoy apartment had been signed with the letters "DL." This note had no signature. Was that because a different person left it, or because the author presumed that Dick would know who had left it and what it meant?

Deciding not to wrack his brains in trying to decipher something he couldn't answer without evidence, Dick made his way down the block and headed back toward the city.

He had only gone a mile when his stomach rumbled. Remembering that he had no cash, he found the nearest bank branch and drew out a wad of notes that raised the clerk's eyebrows high. Dick placed the money inside his jacket and walked out briskly, knowing how many eyes would be following him to get their hands on that kind of money.

When he was clear of public view, Dick found a quiet recess between buildings and sorted the cash into smaller piles he could access easily without arousing so much attention. He made a note to place some back in his safe house soon so he wouldn't be carrying so much on his person.

Dick found a small cafe and grabbed a black coffee and some toast. He sat at the back, facing the door, watching everyone who passed the restaurant or came inside. At this time of the morning, the clientele was thin, and Dick left shortly after, satisfied and sufficiently fueled on caffeine.

The pharmacy was half an hour away from the cafe on a usual trip, but Dick made the walk in twenty-five minutes. He opened the door and found another twenty-something woman behind the counter. She had a bright smile and a head of fiery auburn hair. "Hello, sir. How may I help you?"

Knowing the result, Dick tried his luck. "Lisinopril for Charlie Porter, please."

"One moment, please." The woman turned to a stack of prescriptions in the corner and thumbed through them, mumbling to herself as she read the labels. "I'm sorry, sir. No Charlie Porter is on my record."

Dick wiped a hand down his face and sighed. "Can you get Chuck out here? I need to have a word with him."

"Chuck is busy at the moment," the woman replied. Her pleasant demeanor faded. "I can make you an appointment to see him."

Dick strode to the side of the counter. "Don't worry. I'll get him out." He made for the back door. "Chuck! You have a visitor."

The woman rushed to his side in alarm. "I'm sorry, sir. You can't go that way. It's for staff only."

Dick found little resistance from the pretty young thing and opened the door. He banged his fist on Chuck's entry in the back area. While the new clerk tried her best to usher him back out, the old man's face appeared around the door.

Chuck sighed. "It's okay, Christine. This man is a client. You may return to the front desk."

Flustered and confused, Christine tried to reply. She was breathless, her neat appearance out of sorts after the sudden struggle. Dick gave her a pitying look. "Sorry, sweetheart. This is bigger than you."

Chuck tutted and guided Dick down into his lab.

If it was at all possible, Chuck looked even more tired than before. His glasses were crooked, and the lab was slowly falling out of order. Bottles and paper bags and instruments littered the tabletops, and there was a smell of ammonia in the air.

Dick narrowed his eyes at Chuck. "You know there wouldn't be so many problems if you told your staff the goddamn password. Remember the password? The thing *you* invented specifically for clients? I didn't make it, Chuck. You did."

Chuck waved a hand. "Oh, simmer down, would you? I'm all out of sorts. Like there's not enough to do around here without worrying about the extra pressure you bring to my business."

"Why would you have all this equipment if you didn't mean to use it?" Dick asked. "Our work pays your bills, Chuck. Don't you forget that shit, okay?"

Chuck turned on Dick and looked out from over his glasses. "What do you want, Dick? I haven't got all day. I usually don't see you for months at a time, and now it's twice in a week? Must be some juicy case you've got your jaws clamped onto."

Dick took out the note. "Analyze this."

Chuck snatched the paper, tearing a tiny fragment of the corner. He brought it close to his face. "'Mr. Chambers. You can run, but you can't hide. I play to win.' It's a note. From someone who's not very fond of you, I'd wager." He passed it back to Dick. "There you go, now get out."

Dick laughed. "Since when did you become so hostile? I was once your favorite customer, remember?"

"Oh, get a grip," Chuck replied. "I say that to all my customers." He stared at Dick, then sighed. "Look, the AJS is bringing up the heat across the city. Do you know how many people like me there are out there? Folks trying to make a living by providing premium services and praying every day that we don't get caught? This is a public business, Dick. I can't have these machines down here anymore. How I've lasted this long is ludicrous. I need this crap moved, and I need it done soon before the AJS descends on me like vultures and picks my bones."

"You paint quite a picture."

Chuck waved a hand. "Ah, what do you know? You're out there all the time. You're a moving target. No one can reach you. That's why you use people like me to keep your hands clean while mine grow redder by the minute."

Dick moved over to one of the large white machines that looked similar to a train ticket booth you'd find at the station. "Why is this such a job? Just unplug the machines and move them."

Chuck let out an exasperated laugh. "Easy for you. You're a man in your prime. You have connections. You could move this shit in a night and have it set up somewhere safe. I'm sure with the millions you have in your account you could buy a private residence and offer this shit out of a mid-city apartment. I'm not that fortunate. One man goes on vacation, and I'm running this place into the ground trying to cover staff costs while serving customers."

Dick raised a hand. "First of all, I don't have millions." His mind flashed to the wads of cash hidden in his jacket. It wasn't millions, but it was a lot. "Second, if it means that you have somewhere to operate more safely, I'll fund your goddamn lab."

Chuck's thick grey eyebrows raised. He twisted a finger in his ear. "What did you say?"

"I'll fund your lab," Dick repeated. "For a fixed term. I'll pay three months of a place where you can run this hidden operation, and after that, you pay your way. Get the customers to come in, pay more staff to help, and you'll be on your feet and well underway."

Chuck frowned, and a dozen more wrinkle lines appeared. "Why would you be complicit in something like this? You're a PI. Doesn't this put you in the shit?"

Dick shook his head. "Because I was never a part of this, okay? I get you set up as an invisible angel investor, and you tell no one that you saw me or that I was involved, got it?"

Chuck slowly nodded. "Of course."

Dick continued. "I need you, Chuck. I'm not raking the pieces of shit from this loamy soil to find another person who does what you do. I trust you, as rare as that is in this city, and I need you to keep doing what you're doing. I'm not paying *you*, per se. I'm paying for a secure means for me to get what I need when I need it. Capisce?"

Chuck nodded again. "Capisce."

Dick narrowed his eyes and handed the paper back to Chuck. "Analyze this. Let me know when the results are in. I'll come back to discuss the operation with you when the store's closed and we can speak in peace."

Chuck ran a hand through his wispy hair, the strands like

grey silk threads. "I don't know… I usually leave at 6:00 p.m., then I grab some food, and I hit the hay by…"

His words trailed off when he saw the look Dick gave him.

"I suppose I could make an exception on this occasion," he corrected.

"Good boy." Dick strode toward the door, only pausing to point at the paper in Chuck's hand and instruct, "Get to work. That's an important piece of my puzzle."

As the door swung closed behind him, he was almost certain that he heard Chuck mutter, "Always a goddamn puzzle. What the hell is going on out there?"

CHAPTER SIX

It didn't take Dick too long to get used to new things. When he awoke in the safe house for the second time in his life, there was no disorientation whatsoever. In fact, he liked being somewhere new.

His life had taken him in many directions he'd never dreamed he'd take. As a kid, his parents hopped around a lot, traveling alongside his dad's ever-shifting career. When he joined the military, he didn't have the luxury of personal comforts and spent most of his time focused on the job at hand. Even since he'd first landed in Atlantica, he'd been forced to move every few years at least. In some cases, the moves came every few months.

Life as a private investigator had its hazards, and Dick was more than prepared to face them head-on. This safe house was simply another step forward in the case, and it was beginning to feel like home.

Dick cooked himself some eggs over-easy and coffee and decided to chance the news on the TV as he ate. There was the usual never-ending ticker tape of crime, homicide, drugs, and politicians at each other's throats. Dick thumbed the controller and switched channels to a TV series about high school teens that he'd seen glimpses of through store windows.

After five minutes of trying to understand the plotline and the reasons behind the teens' anguish, he flicked the TV off. Silence had always been a good friend, and it kept him company now.

When he had finished eating, Dick looked at his phone screen and was about to turn it on when he remembered that there was no signal in his little bunker. He dressed and got himself ready, then headed outside into the chill night breeze. He glanced at the milky orb of the moon through the fog and smirked. "Sleeping all day and partying all night. If my mama could see me now."

His phone was only on for a minute or so, giving Dick enough time to read a message from Chuck to tell him that the analysis was ready. Dick sighed and started his walk. He missed his reliable sedan and made a mental note to ensure he picked it up when this was over.

The walk was good for Dick, and although he was a little breathless when he arrived at the pharmacy, he noted that his legs felt stronger and his muscles ached less. His hip was still a little sore, but he had cleaned his wound and wrapped it before bed and hoped that all would be better in a few days.

Dick approached through the back door. Chuck waited eagerly for him, clearly exhausted and wanting to go home. Dick followed him to the lab, where Chuck leaned against a table and read aloud from a printed piece of paper.

"Sergei Petrov. Forty-four-year-old male, nine charges of battery and assault, three cases of soliciting prostitution, fifteen accusations of homicide with only one proven. Battered the head of a rival gang with a sconce he tore from the wall and turned his brain to mush. The feud leaked into the street, which is why he was caught. Convicted in 2017 with a thirty-year sentence. Let out on good behavior in 2024."

"Sounds like my kind of guy." Dick's heart sank.

Chuck handed Dick the paper while informing him, "It wasn't easy. They were careful with this one. Hardly any prints, and those I've found I'm not a hundred percent certain of. Your DNA is all over that scrap, of course. Didn't help that you screwed the damn thing up and tossed it in the trash. I can tell you there were coffee stains, apple residue, and…"

"Yeah, I get it." Dick waved a hand as he read the paper. "No sign of Sadie whatsoever? Nothing at all?"

"Zilch." Chuck yawned. "So there you go. I hope that's useful to you. Now, if you don't mind, I have an appointment with my bed, and I'd really like to get some shut-eye ahead of tomorrow's open. Beth has already called in sick so I have Gillian running a double-shift and she ain't too happy about it."

Dick wasn't listening. In his mind he could see Sadie Turnberry smiling at him, giving him that wicked "I'm one step ahead" grin that he had witnessed at The Warehouse when he first confronted her. Somehow, this Russian convict was tied into the whole damn thing. Had she upped her bodyguards? Had she gone from thugs to criminals on her personnel roster? So many questions and so few answers. What was certain was that Dick didn't like the idea of going toe-to-toe with this Sergei until he knew a hell of a lot more about him.

"You got his rap sheet?" Dick asked.

Chuck whirled and took a stack of papers he had printed, which looked like AJS records. Dick gave an approving nod. "Thanks. And don't forget that I made a promise to you. Here." Dick took a wad of Atlantican bills he had kept aside after storing the rest at the safe house and tossed them onto the table. Chuck's eyes lit up.

"That should be enough to get you someplace nice," Dick informed him. "You find a space, and you rent it. Effective as soon as humanly possible, got that?"

Chuck nodded.

Dick continued. "When that space is secure, you let me know, and we arrange the transportation of your goods. I want proof of purchase. I want to know the plan. I want timelines. I want the damn thing wrapped up in the next seventy-two hours, maximum. Understand?"

Chuck raised an eyebrow. "That's a tall order, Dick. I'll do what I can."

"You will make it happen," Dick corrected. "Don't think I won't watch you. Don't think I won't keep my beady little eye on where every cent of that cash is going. And, who knows? Maybe at some point, you won't have to scramble around this drug dealer's paradise looking for staff cover when you have your empire running."

Chuck remained silent as he weighed the bills in his hands and gave an approving nod.

"Chuck?" Dick nudged. "I'm not talking into the void here. Give me answers."

Chuck looked up at Dick. "Your investment is safe. Thanks."

"Good. Now get out of here and get some sleep. You look like shit."

Dick walked through the city with his hands in his pockets, lost deep in thought.

Sergei could be trouble. If there's one bad egg, the rest are likely going to be shits, too. Who does a guy like Sergei hang out with? Bad people. Bad people beget bad people, and the cycle continues.

He felt around for his cell and grasped it in his hands. He hated the mistrust he felt for technology. Although Valentina had secured his cell with her brand of tech that should prevent anyone from infiltrating the software, Dick couldn't help but remember Ringo's words.

"Technology always evolves, and so does the counter-tech department. Every device has frequencies and signals. Think of them as digital fingerprints. You have to keep moving and changing things up."

How long would it be until someone could *hack into my cell*?

Knowing that he needed to take some risks to flush out the enemy, Dick turned on his phone and dialed Ringo's number. After a few rings, Ringo answered with an enthusiastic lilt. Dick arranged to meet the man at a bar across from where he stood, a little place called Turners. When he hung up, Dick entered the bar and found himself a seat.

Turners was a far cry from the bar where Dick had met Santana. Soft jazz played over the speakers, and the lights were low. The clientele were all older, in their middle ages and upwards, and thin strips of neon illuminated old instruments pinned to the walls. It was soon obvious that Dick missed the memo on the dress code in this place when he spotted the men in cleanly pressed shirts and the women in fine dresses that showed off slender legs.

Dick removed his jacket to reserve his seat at a small table in the corner, then approached the bar.

"Whiskey. Neat," he ordered.

The barman gave an approving nod before turning to the rack of amber-filled bottles behind the bar. "Any preference?"

Dick narrowed his eyes at the bottles. They had an impressive selection, that was for sure. He settled on a drink from an egg-shaped bottle with a label that read Fireman's Bane. He paid with cash.

"What brings you out here tonight?" The barman studied Dick's clothing. "Don't see many of your type out here. Not on a weekday night."

Dick arched an eyebrow. "My type?"

"Officials," the barman clarified. He sported a thick black

handlebar mustache that looked absurd on his thin face. "Officers, detectives, that kind of thing."

Dick gave an impressed exhalation. "You have a good eye."

"I have to. It's my job to know my customers, and when someone comes in who stands out from the crowd, it's my job to know what's going on." He raised a finger to a customer, indicating he wouldn't be long. "So, what is it? Got a suspect in this bar you're trying to scope? Meeting some people about some bad news? I'll give you a heads-up that our security is ready to deal with any mishaps."

"Are you threatening me?"

The man held up his hands. "Not at all. I'm saying that my security will be there to help you if things get rough. The last thing I need is to scare away customers and pay to replace broken glasses and tables if you get my drift."

Dick smiled. "I get you. Don't worry. It's only a meeting with a friend. That's all."

"Very well." The barman moved to the waiting customers and started fixing their orders.

Dick went back to his table and sipped his drink. From where he sat, he could make out the main portion of the bar and its clientele. He couldn't imagine there being too many barroom brawls in this kind of establishment, but then again, he had learned in his business that the world only showed its best side. Once you started digging a little deeper, you found the scars and warts that society tried to hide.

Dick had finished his first drink when Ringo arrived.

He spotted him at the door, the strange man uncertain that he was in the right place. Like Dick, Ringo stood out a lot more than he had hoped. He spotted Dick and rushed inside with his bag clutched tightly to his chest. His hair was messy, and there was a frenzied aspect to his walk.

He placed the bag on the table and shook Dick's hand. "Nice joint. Don't suppose they serve pancakes too, do you?"

Dick grinned. "No. I don't suppose they do." He studied the bag. "Why do you clutch that thing like a bomb's going to detonate in your hands? If there's anything that's going to arouse more suspicion that you have something valuable in there, it's holding your gear like a five-year-old girl who's afraid someone's going to snatch their Cabbage Patch Doll."

Ringo shrugged. "When your entire life work lives with you in a rucksack, you learn to be protective."

"You learned to make it obvious," Dick replied. His brows knitted together. "That's your entire life's work?"

Ringo grinned. "Nah, not really. Only a handful of my latest gear. I'm meeting a client after this in need of something to... Well, I probably shouldn't tell a PI."

Dick returned the smile and offered Ringo a drink. He politely declined, but Dick went to the bar and bought himself another. The barman raised his eyebrows and looked over at Ringo.

"Nothing to worry about," Dick soothed. "A friend of mine. He couldn't swat a mosquito off his arm."

Dick returned to the table and drank from his whiskey. Ringo leaned back in his chair and stretched. "So what brings me to you, Dick? You sounded pretty urgent on the phone. I assume you're up to no good, as usual."

Dick tossed his phone on the table. "I need this examined."

Ringo weighed it in his palms. "It's a cell phone."

"Haha." Dick shook his head. "My last cell phone was hacked. I need to ensure that this one is unhackable. A friend of mine worked some magic on the gear, but I want to test it. You offer that service, correct?"

Ringo raised an eyebrow. "I've told you before that no digital device is, as you say, unhackable."

Dick stayed silent. Across the bar, a man was setting up a double-bass on a small stage.

Ringo sighed. "Fine, let me have a look." He fished into his rucksack and took a laptop from the pocket. It wasn't a model that Dick had ever seen before. There was no brand, and the keys on the keyboard all looked as though they belonged to a different set. Ringo fired it up and rapidly tapped in a password to open the main interface. He drew out several cables and wires from his rucksack and plugged them into various ports, crudely handling Dick's phone as he ensured it was also plugged in.

Dick's phone turned on without Ringo touching it.

"That's not a good sign," Dick muttered.

Ringo let out a small laugh. "Technophone. That's initiating the boot-up sequence. Cell phones can be triggered by more than thumbprints and on-off switches."

The phone screen demanded a passcode. Ringo played with a few commands and buttons to break it open but had no luck. As Dick sipped from his whiskey in silence, Ringo turned the phone over in his hands, hunting for things that Dick could only imagine. He removed the back casing and studied the electronics, occasionally prodding with a metal needle that emitted sparks from its tip.

The double-bass player was half an hour into his set when Ringo resigned and handed the phone to Dick. "It passed the physical break-in. Can you unlock it so I can check out what's going on?"

Dick gave a satisfied nod. "That's a good sign, right?"

Ringo shook his head. "I wouldn't get your hopes up. Most of the damage comes from unseen signals when you're accessing media and content on your device. It's when you enter the password that the damage can begin."

Dick got himself another drink and grew bored with watching Ringo testing his methods. He observed the double-bass player who played his bassy licks alongside the music on the speakers, improvising his jazz melodies to a music-hungry audience. After an hour of his set, the player sat back and thanked the crowd, who demanded an encore. Dick wondered if he should purchase the man's album from a wicker basket at the front of the stage.

He was about to rise for another drink when Ringo threw his hands in the air in exasperation.

"Bad news?" Dick asked.

"Great news for you," Ringo replied. His hair was all over the place after so much head rubbing, and his face was wrinkled from frowning. "I'm not sure who you've got working for you, but whatever has been done to this cell phone is impressive as all hell. I've managed to find one exploit that allows me to power your cell phone down remotely, but the rest of it is currently untouchable."

"Are you sure?" Dick asked.

Ringo gave Dick a level stare. "Are you kidding me? Am *I* sure? Dick, the coding levels and layers on this thing are profound, unique, sophisticated. This phone *can* be hacked, but it'd take an expert days to work through what's on here. The whole coding has been written from scratch, foregoing the usual formats that make the damn things vulnerable." He grabbed Dick's hands in his own. "You have to tell me who did this. I need to meet this mystery person."

Dick pulled his hands away. "I'd rather not, thanks." He imagined Valentina coming for him in the night, pissed and armed to the nines. "It's not worth the aggro."

Ringo looked hurt by this response. "Please, Dick. I'll forego my usual fee."

Dick laughed. "What fee? I buy you breakfast and pay you a pittance. Besides, you already owe me, remember?"

Ringo sulked as Dick took his cell phone back and placed it in his pocket, this time not bothering to turn it off. Ringo packed away his wires and computer, then checked his watch. "Shit."

"Late for your next meeting?" Dick asked.

Ringo sighed. "It's halfway across town. I'm already ten minutes late."

"Better get hopping, then." Dick drained the contents of his drink.

Ringo stood, torn between leaving and staying. "Please, Dick. A name. That's all I want. That phone is a piece of modern genius."

Dick shook his head. "Not for all the money in the world."

CHAPTER SEVEN

When Ringo was gone, Dick spent the next half an hour looking through the phone and examining it himself.

The phone was a basic thing. He couldn't understand how something so simple could be so sophisticated. Valentina had only spent a few minutes handling the device as she worked to secure it for Dick, so how could she have performed such magic?

Not only that, but how could Dick not have trusted her?

Simple. Rule number one: trust no one. Especially ridiculously sexy mercenaries who have the ability to appear out of nowhere and kill you without you realizing they were there.

Dick opened the explorer app and typed in the name, Sergei Petrov. Thousands of hits sprang up at once, with links to the most recent articles regarding Petrov's homicide and his exit from jail. There was little in the way of what Dick would consider "true journalism" since his release, and very little of interest that might help Dick locate his whereabouts.

It wasn't until Dick was at least six pages into the search results when he found something that pricked his attention. There was a picture of Sergei standing beside a gleaming red Nissan Skyline with glowing rims and neon lighting beneath the vehicle. The windows were tinted, and the hood was gleaming black carbon fiber.

Dick gave an impressed nod and read the article, gleaning that Sergei had recently gotten involved in the editorial side of a supercar magazine, "Atlanti-CAR," as one of their "Ridealong" columnists. Through this column, Sergei documented his night rides through the city of Atlantica, talking about the behind-the-scenes of Atlantica's night-time racing scene.

Dick scrutinized the article and was able to find the editor of the magazine, a large woman by the name of Kirsty Hunter. Dick noted that on his notepad and continued his search, discovering the location of the Atlanti-CAR offices. He jotted that down and looked up the offices on the map.

After more digging, the most he could find was a smattering of other articles that linked Sergei to the racing scene. While Dick knew that drag racing was illegal in Atlantica, particularly on the streets, he couldn't find anything that tied Sergei to criminal activity in that space. From what he could find, Sergei raced within the speed limits and had evaded all clashes with the law up until that point.

Dick packed up his things and brought his glass back to the bar. He thanked the mustached barman with a nod of the head. The barman replied with a, "Hope to see you around."

"You know, I may come back," Dick replied. "This is my kinda place."

"Maybe dress more like it." The barman winked and returned to his customers.

The man stood outside the apartment and stared up at the window with scrutinous eyes.

Civilians passed, oblivious to his presence. His coat was dark, collar turned up high, a hat low over his brow. If anyone even thought to look down the alleyway, they might have spotted the beetle-like glint of his eyes, but they would quickly scurry away. He waited patiently, standing in the same position he had used for the past twenty-four hours. Waiting to see if the scumbag was brave enough to return.

Unlikely, if he knows what's good for him.

The man had rooted through the apartment earlier that day, knowing that Dick would either be asleep or out somewhere on the job. His car was nowhere in sight, and breaking into the PI's home was surprisingly easy.

Unfortunately, as much as he had searched for some indication of a location, nothing had shown up. Dick was a private investigator, and as such, had learned to leave little in the way of clues behind him. He worked in secrecy, knew the tricks of the trade, and pressed his advantage whenever he could.

Yessiree, Dick Chambers was officially in hiding, which only meant one thing: he was afraid.

The man stared levelly out at the street and watched a woman stumbling down the block in a skirt too short to be out in public, and a booze-addled swagger to her stride. She paused at a nearby tree, planted into the concrete to give the illusion that the city hadn't forgotten about nature, and hurled a healthy stream of vomit at its base. With a wipe of her hand against her mouth, she continued on her way.

This woman wasn't the first one he'd seen arrive near the apartment. A pretty young thing with white hair parked some time ago and entered Dick's apartment. If she was there for a late-night booty call, she was barking up the wrong tree. He waited for her to knock on the door and return with her hands empty, but was surprised to find she had a key to his place. The lights in his living room turned on, and he watched her silhouette scurrying around the apartment as she searched for something.

Ten minutes later, the woman returned to the street. She entered her car and drove away, giving the man a full view of her license plate. He would be able to track her down sooner or later. License plates and their owner's addresses were surprisingly easy to access online. When he was ready, he'd find her if he needed to. She was one of many possible leads to follow.

And the man was in no rush. While his employer had stressed how important this mission was to her, the man would not rush. Dick was the mouse, and he was the cat. The longer the game spun out, the more exciting it would be for him.

An hour or so after exiting the bar, Dick was trying to stare up at the thirtieth floor of the Jameson Building, a towering skyscraper that reached toward the clouds and lost itself in the fog.

A handful of lights were on inside the offices. In his research, Dick discovered that this building didn't belong entirely to Atlanti-CAR. It hosted a wealth of media outlets, IT services, and other office-based industries who rented the space and shoveled their cash into Monique Jameson's pocket.

Dick studied the people still walking in and out of the building. News never slept, and it seemed that neither did the people who wrote it and provided twenty-four-hour coverage to the city of Atlantica.

Dick finished his cigarette, stomped it out, and headed inside.

The lobby was brightly lit. An office guide was printed on the marble walls. Dick walked over and confirmed his findings, glad to see Atlanti-CAR listed in bold next to "30F." He wandered over to the desk clerk.

"Excuse me." He waited until the clerk finished typing on the computer. "I was wondering what the operational hours are for the Atlanti-CAR offices? Only, I'm hoping to make an appointment with the editor, Kirsty Hunter."

The clerk silently typed something into her computer. "Mrs. Hunter is currently out of office. Her calendar is pretty tightly booked until later this year. Can I put you down for an appointment then?"

Dick gave his sweetest smile. "I'm afraid I'd prefer to see her as soon as possible. Can that be managed at all?"

The clerk shook his head. "Mrs. Hunter is a very busy woman, I'm afraid. Appointments are much sought-after, and she's very particular with her schedule. If you want her, you'll have to wait in line."

Dick debated flashing his badge and trying to muscle his way in, but he knew it would be no use. He'd encountered women like Kirsty Hunter before, high-powered executives who believed they were invincible. If he wanted to get to Kirsty, he'd have to find another way to get her attention.

Dick thanked the clerk and left the building. Standing outside, he scanned the surrounding buildings and hunted for a place to set up shop.

Dick sat in the comfort of the La-Z-boy and stared out at the window.

The apartment had been a cinch to break into. The building across the road from the Jameson Building was cast in darkness, with a side door that's security protocol was easily scrambled. As he hunted through the corridors, Dick was able to ascertain an apartment that had yet to be leased and broke his way inside, glad to find that the place offered a view of the front door of the Jameson Building.

The apartment was silent, the darkness comforting. For the first time in days, Dick felt truly safe. As he waited for any sign of Kirsty Hunter, he worked his way through a coffee and a croissant that he had acquired from the corner store before breaking inside. He scratched a hand across the rash of stubble on his face and bided his time.

Hours passed with no sign of Hunter.

Cars drove by, some more flashy than others. Every time the roar of an engine approached, Dick sat up straighter and hunted for its source. He couldn't imagine the top editor of a magazine revolving around supercars would drive something subpar and ordinary. No, she would be among the vehicles whose roar rivaled that of the lion's.

It was closing on 4:00 a.m. when Dick finally got his first peek.

The car careened around the corner, difficult to miss with its bright green neon illuminating the undercarriage. Heavy bass thudded from the speaker system as the car—a Lamborghini Successor, by the look of it—skidded around the ninety-degree corner and slowed when it approached the parking lot.

Dick waited patiently, pleased to see Kirsty Hunter striding out of the lot. A man accompanied her, his thick muscles making his neck the width of his head. He wore a dark suit while she wore a shimmering green cocktail dress. They walked arm-in-arm toward the offices, where she disappeared inside.

Dick took his opportunity and left the apartment building. He snuck across the street and headed toward the parking lot. Her car wasn't difficult to spot among the half-dozen parked vehicles. Dick strode over to the Lamborghini and casually checked for the security cameras. When he spotted one nearby, he continued walking and found a location outside the camera's range before he clicked the button on his circuit scrambler.

Satisfied that he was out of sight, Dick crept over to the car. It was a beautiful piece of machinery. He couldn't imagine how much the standard issue of this vehicle would cost, let alone all the custom-fitted extras. He stroked a hand across the smooth metal of the hood and allowed a moment of admiration.

Footsteps came from nearby, echoing around the concrete lot. Dick ducked behind the car.

Two men approached a kitted-out Tesla parked across the

way. As they neared, Dick remained in the Lamborghini's shadow. They wore leather jackets with the zip only done halfway up to reveal bare chests beneath. They stumbled a little as they walked, their voices raised and rowdy. Dick assumed they'd perhaps had a few drinks beforehand, and when one of the men placed a can of beer on top of the car, his assumption was realized.

They howled with laughter as the driver twisted the ignition and set the music on blast. Dick clapped his hands over his ears, the music far too loud for him, let alone the guys sitting in the car. The custom engine purred to life, and the car reversed with a screech, then they drove from the lot in a flurry of speed.

Dick waited for silence to return, but the car could be heard from miles away. When he was finally able to listen to his breath, he examined the lock of the Lamborghini and wondered if he'd be able to work his magic on the latest model of machinery.

CHAPTER EIGHT

Kirsty Hunter laughed as she exited the Jameson Building.

The night had been a whirlwind of fun, adrenaline, and drugs. Her head spun, the borders of her vision were foggy, and the man on her arm was everything she'd ever dreamed of as a kid.

Toby made a joke. Kirsty would forget it by morning, but that didn't stop her from belting out her laughter and slapping him playfully on the arm. They stopped on the corner, and their lips met. She bit her lip.

"Back to mine, cowboy?" she cooed.

Toby's eyes lit up, saying everything so that his lips didn't need to. They stumbled across the road and almost collided with a driverless cab that swerved dutifully at the last minute and beeped its horn as it drove away. The pair of them laughed again, then ran the remainder of the way across the blacktop.

Kirsty caressed Toby's muscular arms with every stride, unable to wait until they made it back to her place and got down and dirty. They had been going steady for a few weeks now, and Kirsty didn't want to jinx things by saying they were a couple, but she hoped that tonight would seal the deal. She was preparing her game plan for their tumble in the dark when she opened the scissor doors of her Lambo and climbed inside.

Toby hopped in the passenger side and placed a meaty hand on her bare thigh, the dress slipping up as she thumbed the ignition and caused the engine to rumble. They kissed again before she firmly moved his hand back to his lap. "Eager much? The waiting makes it hotter."

Toby grinned, a moment of indecision crossing his face as he decided whether or not to push the subject. He decided against it.

Music blared from the speakers. Kirsty's cheeks were flushed. The drive home blurred by and had the AJS pulled her over, they likely would have taken her into custody for the amount of illegal substances in her system. Luckily, the roads were empty, and the adrenaline sharpened the fuzzier edges. Soon enough, she passed through the gates of her manor. She found her parking spot next to an array of other gleaming souped-up vehicles and hushed the car by switching off the ignition.

She rested her head back on the headrest and turned a coy eye to Toby. "Are you ready?"

Toby was practically foaming at the mouth. The tent in his pants wasn't subtle. "Baby, I was born ready."

Neither of them expected the man to jump up from the back seat. "I'll be honest, can you hold back a few seconds? I have a couple of questions for you."

Kirsty screamed, eyes pulling so wide it appeared that her eyelids had fled. The muscular man responded in the same way that Dick had assumed he would, and turned in his seat, reacting by lashing out with a meaty fist.

Dick had accounted for this and reached around the other side of the man's seat. He held the hand-taser to the little bit of exposed skin that had come from the man's maneuver, slightly above the belt where his shirt had untucked from the strain and held the button.

The man's momentum sapped as his body grew rigid and shook violently. Dick watched with a slightly confused expression on his face. The taser was the size of a AA battery, the voltage relatively low. He had used this on frailer people in the past, and they hadn't shown as much drama as this guy did. The woman's screams turned into shouting Toby's name. Dick clicked off the button.

"What the hell?" The woman reared back against the door as though she'd seen a spider running across the floor. "What are you doing? I should warn you that I have a gun!"

She scrambled a hand to the glovebox and opened it. There was nothing inside.

Dick held the pistol with his other hand, gripping it by the barrel to show that he meant no harm. "Miss Hunter, I only want to ask you a few questions. I'm not here to hurt you."

Kirsty glanced at Toby's unconscious face. "Are you fucking kidding me?"

The faint smell of urine filled the car as Toby's bladder released. She turned her nose up in disgust.

"In all honesty," Dick continued, "I'm not sure why he's making such a big deal. He'll be fine in a few minutes, I'm certain of it. No lasting damage. I'm sorry to ambush you like this, but your schedule is packed, and I need answers and fast."

Kirsty replied so quickly that it was clearly a reflex to lie. "I don't know anything. I promise. I'm innocent."

"Not you." Dick sighed. "I need information on one of your columnists, a driver by the name of Sergei Petrov."

"I don't know a Sergei," Kirsty snapped back, hand clawing at Toby's pants before she remembered the urine.

Dick rubbed his eye. "I promise this can be easy. *You're* not in trouble. I'm not the cops. Give me straight answers, and I can get out of here and leave you to your evening."

Kirsty considered this, visibly calming down as she eased away from the door and returned to her seat. "You won't hurt us?"

"I won't." Dick waited.

"You know that if you're a cop, you have to tell us, right?" Kirsty frowned. "It's the law."

Not in Atlantica. Try every other country in the goddamn world.

"Sure," Dick replied. "I'm not a cop, though."

Kirsty ran a hand through her hair and drew a deep breath. "What is it you want to know?"

"Sergei," Dick stated. "What do you know?"

Toby snorted, then grew slack. Kirsty gave a disapproving look. "Sergei is an asshole, that's what I know. He's great to have for the column, but he's one of the most unreliable writers we have. He saunters around the office like he owns the goddamn place, then disappears for weeks on end without a trace. We've had to bring in ghostwriters a few times to fill his columns because he's too busy speeding around the streets competing against the Dead Devils." She paused and examined Toby. "Are you sure he'll be okay?"

Dick rolled his eyes. "He'll be fine. Continue. Who are the Dead Devils?"

"They're a rival speedster gang. Don't get me started on them. They've been a pain in my ass since I first brought Sergei onto the team. Every chance they get, they pitch one of theirs to write as if they're entitled to having another column to themselves because I hired someone from the opposing team. It's not my goddamn gang war." She smacked her lips together, distracted. "Is the air dry in here?"

Dick clicked his fingers. "Stay with me. Where can I find Sergei?"

Kirsty looked at Dick as if seeing him for the first time, her pupils extremely dilated. "Huh?"

"Where can I find Sergei Petrov?" Dick repeated.

"Oh." Kirsty laughed. "Hell if I know. If we knew that, we'd have a reliable columnist. You want to get to Sergei? You gotta find where the race is happening. He misses deadlines like crazy, but he's never missed a race in his life." She shook her head, talking to herself now. "All I wanted to do was share my love for supercars. Who knew there'd be politics in underground racing?" She reached into her clutch purse and pulled out a needle.

Dick raised an eyebrow, watching with alarm. "What are you doing?"

"Topping up the tank." Kirsty laughed as the needle hit her arm. For the first time, Dick noticed the other red marks on her skin. "I have a hot date, remember?" She sprayed mouth spray and shook Toby as though she'd forgotten his little nap. "Come on, baby is horny."

Toby's eyelids fluttered, and his head rolled.

Dick cleared his throat. "Well, that's my cue to leave. Thanks for your cooperation, Miss Hunter."

"Yeah, yeah." Kirsty waved a hand and straddled Toby's lap. "Why is he wet?"

Dick didn't answer. Instead, he levered himself out from behind Kirsty's seat and exited the vehicle. His last view of the couple was Kirsty kissing Toby's mouth as he wrestled with coming to consciousness, the pair of them lit only by the interior light on the ceiling.

Dick gave a small chuckle. "No hope of them remembering any of this shit come morning. Now, to find out more about these Dead Devils."

The man stared levelly at the woman, relishing the control he had over her at that moment.

The room was hazy, and the remnants of smoke stung his eyes. Even with the window open it did little to alleviate the residue built up from years of smoking indoors. The walls were yellowed from nicotine, yet somehow the disgusting habit hadn't stained the pretty young thing tied to the plush armchair.

The woman coughed and spluttered as her head rolled back, and her eyelids fluttered. A small stain of blood was on her chin.

"Are you ready to talk?" the man asked, his voice gruff, his face hidden by a black covering that only showed his eyes.

The woman shook her head. "You'll never get it out of me. Louie will know you're here. He'll call the AJS. He probably already has. You only have a few short minutes before the sirens come blaring—"

The man's slap echoed around the room. "You didn't answer my question, Miss Jackson. Tell me where he went."

She growled at him, her delicate features tortured into a shrewd mask. "I don't know what you're talking about."

The man sighed and pushed himself to his feet. He strolled around the room, moving out of the woman's line of sight. She was the very definition of vulnerable right now. The man had found her sitting idly in her chair in only a skimpy negligee designed to torture a weaker man. It was no wonder the old bag hung around the pretty young girl. Even if they didn't fuck, he'd get more than his share of personal material to store in his mental spank bank. It was sickening, but so were many strange symbiotic relationships that arose as a necessity in this city.

The man stopped behind the chair and gripped the back with his hands. "If we're going to start playing games, you're going to lose. I only have so much patience, and I'm already nearing my limit. Tell me where Dick Chambers has gone."

"I don't know." Jessica struggled against her bonds. "I don't even know a Dick Chambers."

The man tilted her chair back, which elicited a yelp from her ruby lips. "Do not lie to me. Your car was parked outside his apartment. You entered with a key. You searched inside for something *for* him. You exited and drove away. You were there. Do not bullshit me."

He let go of the chair, and the feet slapped against the wooden floor. Jessica's face hardened. "Well done. You can follow someone based on public information. What do you want, a medal?"

"I want Chambers," the man snapped.

Surprisingly, Jessica laughed. "You want the man of smoke, do you? The man who only appears whenever *he* wills it? Do you have any idea who you're dealing with? Chambers is the best PI in all of Atlantica, even if he doesn't know it. Catching him is like trying to catch water with your bare hands. You don't stand a fucking chance—"

He slapped her again, moving so quickly to face her that she was lost for breath. He gripped both sides of the armchair and held his face an inch from hers. "*You* have no idea who you're dealing with. Dick may have gained a reputation for morality, but I assure you I have no morals. I wouldn't think twice about jamming a dagger in your thighs or popping a cap into the skull of your creepy geriatric friend. We're inside your house, remember? Ain't nothing public about where we are right now. You'd think a woman of your...profession would have better security. Who knows who's going to break in and scar that pretty porcelain skin of yours?" His hand traced up her bare leg, and she struggled against the bonds again.

"Spill the beans, Miss Jackson," he ordered.

She opened her mouth to speak when the door opened, and Louie's head peeked through. "Everything okay down here, Jess? I thought I heard some—"

His eyes found the man's. The color drained from his face. Jessica wrestled in her chair. "Call the AJS, Louie. Do something. Get this man out of my house—"

The report was loud, the gunshot leaving a painful ringing in Jessica's ears. The man kept his pistol trained on the old man, who looked down at the blood blossoming on his chest in stunned silence. Louie's mouth flapped before he sank to his knees and collapsed to the floor.

Jessica's mouth formed a perfect "O," but no sound came out. It was to her benefit that she couldn't spin to face the old man. It might only have fueled a scream from her lips.

Not that the gunshot wouldn't have awoken the neighbors.

The man turned the gun on Jessica so slowly that he might as well have been moving underwater. "Speak, or you're next."

Jessica closed her eyes as a single tear rolled down her cheek. AJS sirens wailed somewhere in the distance, although the man knew they wouldn't be for him.

Not yet, anyway.

CHAPTER NINE

Dick spent the next day searching online for any mention of the Dead Devils and possible locations for their upcoming races.

He knew from experience that these kinds of events, while noisy and garish when they were underway, were shrouded in secrecy. Those who rode lived by the same rules as those who gambled at The Warehouse, and it would take a person who was in the know to tell Dick what they knew.

Dick scoured the internet, made some calls, and managed to yield a single result. A fleabag named Monique who used to drive the circuits way back before she had been caught joyriding under the influence back in '25 gave Dick the crumb he was looking for.

"The only time they ever meet at the same location, for the same race, is the anniversary event for the Soupe-lympics." Monique clicked her tongue as she spoke, evidence of the tongue bar that had always seemed too large for her mouth. "They go nuts for that shit."

"The Soupe-lympics?" Dick responded. "Who names this shit? Sounds like a free food event for the homeless. All you can eat soup."

Monique gave her signature chesty laugh. "I wouldn't say that shit to those guys. They're prouder than punch of that kinda shit. You're in luck, too. If nothing has changed, the Soupe-lympics is tonight. Head out to East and Third, and you should find a glaring display of neon lights, meatheads, skanks, and a whole host of other characters with heads so far up they ass that they should all permanently have pink eye."

Dick laughed. "Aren't you one of those characters?"

"Former characters," Monique clarified. "I ain't have no ego now. I was one of the best of them, though. The greatest there was until the AJS fucked me up."

Dick shook his head. "You can't blame the AJS for the fight you started in prison. If your driving leg is busted, you only have yourself to blame."

Monique feigned offense. "I don't know why I help guys like you out. Straight and narrow, my ass. You PIs are as crooked as the rest of us."

"Welcome to Atlantica," Dick announced.

Monique chuckled. "You're goddamn right."

Dick hung up the phone and looked at the pinkening sky. Morning had come, and the city was waking up. Dick yawned and ran a hand through his hair, wondering if there'd ever be a time in his life where he could return to sleeping at "normal" hours. He knew it wouldn't be soon, not with night providing the best cover to do the work he did, but it was nice to have a dream.

"One day, when I retire, I'ma leave this shit-rock and live somewhere away from all of these problems," he told himself. "Just me, sun, sand, and surf."

He laughed and shook his head, knowing the ludicrousness of his promise. He could have retired years ago. He had enough money to do great things. He could live a simple life, yet he kept going.

Dick grabbed a cream cheese bagel and a Coke from the corner store, then strode back to the safe house, taking extra precaution to go the long way and shake off anyone who might be on his tail.

He wasn't sure why, but he couldn't shift the feeling that something bad was coming his way.

Dick entered the pharmacy a little past 5:00 p.m. There were only a few final customers, and he waited for these to leave before approaching Gillian at the counter.

She gave Dick a warm smile and brushed a lock of hair behind her ear. "Mr. Chambers. How can I help you today? Am I to assume that you're here to see Chuck?"

Dick told her he was and moved to the side of the counter.

Gillian raised a hand. "Wait. No need to barge in today. We're on it. Hold on." She pressed a buzzer beneath the counter and called, "Chuck, Mr. Chambers is here for you."

Her smile broadened as she held the door open for him. "There you go, sir."

Dick thanked her and handed her a $50 bill.

Chuck opened the door to the lab and, to Dick's surprise, smiled.

"Service around here has improved," Dick commented. "May have to change my Yelp review from a three-star to a five-star."

Chuck raised a thick eyebrow. "What's Yelp?"

Dick chuckled, remembering the difference in Atlantican and US culture. "Doesn't matter. Nice to see a smile on your face."

Dick wasn't lying. It looked as though Chuck had reversed in age by at least five years. The bags beneath his eyes weren't as prevalent, the wrinkles had smoothed out, and he had even dragged a comb through what remained of his hair.

"You offered me an opportunity, Dick." Chuck made his way inside the lab. "I'm not one to waste it, not one as good as this."

Dick scanned the room. All of the usual apparatus located around the room was in boxes, packaged and ready to ship.

"There's a van out back," Chuck informed him. "We've got to get these packages to the top. Then we'll be ready to move to the new locale."

"That's great." Dick smiled. "I'll be honest. I'm surprised you pulled it together so quickly. Didn't know you had it in you to follow through. I would have bet my bottom dollar you'd run off into the sunset with the cash."

Chuck's cheeks flushed. "You're a good guy, Dick. Atlantica deserves some good. That's the only reason I do what I do."

Dick moved over to the first few boxes and weighed them in his hands. They were manageable, but the stairs would be an issue. Whoever had moved this stuff into the store's basement originally had the better deal. Gravity was a useful moving body.

Dick put a foot on the first stair and turned to Chuck. "Hey, can't the moving guys lend a hand? You're paying to get this shit shipped. Bring them down here and let's get them involved. Make them work for their money. It's not like you're going to be any help, is it?" Dick studied Chuck's thin arms and the pitiful contents of the single box he carried.

Chuck nodded. "Sure. I'll follow you up."

Dick made it to the top and shouldered the door open. He glanced out the back door at the moving van and stopped in his tracks. His eyes lowered, and he sighed. "Chuck?"

"Yes?" Chuck couldn't hide the slight warble in his voice.

Dick gritted his teeth. "Those moving guys you spoke of. What are they planning on doing with me when they take me captive?"

Chuck stammered, "I don't know what you're talking about."

"Don't bullshit me." Dick tried to keep his voice quiet and calm. He could make out Gillian locking up and closing the store down through the door to the main pharmacy. "How much have you paid them?"

"Dick...I..." Chuck answered weakly.

"Or have they paid *you*?" Dick prodded.

Chuck muttered. Dick lowered the box to the floor, not taking his eyes off the back door. When he was doubled over, Chuck let out a loud, "Now!"

Dick dove to the side, his shoulder clattering against the wall. The back doors burst open, and an athletic woman in a dirty white tank top and combat trousers came into view. She triggered an assault rifle and sprayed the lab doorway, only narrowly missing Chuck who had ducked out of sight on the stairs.

Dick reacted quickly and tossed what appeared to be two ball bearings joined together by a thin piece of wire at the woman's feet. They rolled toward her, the string growing taut and bringing the balls together as they spun around her ankles and bound them together.

She turned the gun on Dick but was too slow as her legs clamped and she lost her balance. She kept the weapon tight in her hands, although Dick used the moment to push off the floor and run to her despite that.

She squeezed off a single shot that soared between his legs and hit the stone wall behind. Dick kicked the gun and sent it tumbling out of her hands. He went for another kick to her face, but she grabbed the sole of his boot in both hands and twisted.

She was strong. Her muscles flexed as Dick's body corkscrewed in the air. He landed flat on his back with the woman straddling him, sending blow after blow at his face.

Dick bucked his hips and threw her off-kilter, absorbing a punch with his chest as he shoved at hers and tossed her onto her back.

They were tangled on the floor, writhing around and wrestling for dominance when Chuck appeared at the top of the stairwell. He had climbed the stairs on his belly, and now his eyes found the forgotten assault rifle. He slithered toward it, arms reaching to grab the firearm.

His fingers grazed the barrel. He pulled it toward him and held it in his hands, then triumphantly pushed himself to his feet. His hair was askew and his eyes crazed. He pointed the gun at the writhing mass and shouted, "Enough! Stop before I shoot."

The woman's smile stretched across her face. Dick paused, his stomach sinking. He remained in a crouch while the woman pushed herself to her feet and brushed herself down.

Dick met Chuck's eyes. "Come on, Chuck. We can talk about this. I'm offering you an opportunity, remember? What the hell do you gain by threatening me or selling me out to this whack-job?"

The woman kicked Dick in the face. He spat blood.

"You should be careful with your dollars." Chuck's chest heaved with each breath. "Flashing that kind of cash in Atlantica is a surefire way to get you kissing the dirt. You know who carries that amount of money? Someone on the run. Someone trying to hide in the city. Which means there's a very strong probability that you have more, don't you? I can see it in your eyes. Where's the money, Dick?"

The woman remained silent but reached for the rifle.

Chuck stepped back and held the gun closer to his chest. "This is my chance. You'll get your pay. Let me have this moment."

The woman growled and wrestled with his command, but relented nonetheless.

"So, what do you say, Dick?" Chuck continued. "Are you going to hand it over easily? Or do we have to drag it out of you?"

Something moved in the glass window behind Chuck's head. Dick turned to the woman. "How come she's so silent? You'd think that a hired goon would still have something to say to a man who kicked her ass."

The woman's lip curled.

"Hired goon?" Chuck laughed. "Dick, you leave a trail of enemies wherever you go. I didn't have to look. This glorious bag

61

of muscles came to me and offered me this deal. I tell you, with enemies of yours like this, who needs to be your friend?"

Dick narrowed his eyes at the woman. "Vy russkiy, ne tak li?"

The woman cocked an eyebrow.

Russian.

Dick adjusted himself on the floor, which caused Chuck to jab the gun his way. "Stay still!"

"I'm getting comfortable. Damn." He raised his hands. The shadow moved behind the door again.

"Show me where the money is," Chuck commanded.

Dick shook his head. "No thank you."

Chuck stepped forward, mouth twisted into a grimace. "Now!"

Dick took that moment to roll a full revolution to the side as the door slammed open and caught Chuck in the back. It shoved his body sideways, and the weapon skittered across the floor. Gillian appeared, her head a glowing beacon of fiery red as she shoved the door once more into Chuck and dodged out of the way of the Russian woman's blows.

Dick pounced across the floor and grabbed the gun. He twisted to aim at the pair but found that only Chuck and Gillian remained. He turned to the open back door where he saw the woman running away into the darkness.

"Shit," Dick exclaimed. Chuck, whose body was pressed between the doorway and the wall, groaned. He muttered apologies and whined as Dick asked Gillian to remove her weight from the frail man.

Chuck spun and slid to his ass, looking careworn and weary once again. "I'm sorry, Dick. I'm so, so sorry."

Dick fired a shot at Chuck's feet. The bullet found the space between his legs and caused the man to leap in fright and whimper. "You ever pull some shit like that again, I'll make certain that you never see the light of another day."

He held out his hand. Chuck glanced at him cautiously, relief flooding his face as he reached for Dick to help him up. Dick pulled away at the last minute and frowned. "My money, Chuck. Give me back my fucking coin. I hope you didn't spend a single cent of it."

Chuck couldn't hold his gaze. "Well... You see..."

Dick shot again. This time, the bullet scraped the flesh of his thigh. "All right! All right! I'll get it. Hold on..."

Chuck rose unsteadily to his feet and headed into his lab. Dick waited as he hobbled down the stairs. He turned to Gillian. "Thank you. You know there's going to be hell to pay for what you did?"

Gillian gave a solemn nod. "I'll find a new job. He wasn't that great an employer anyway." She smiled. "You might want to follow him. I'm pretty sure he has a shotgun down there."

Dick returned the smile. "You have a good heart. Don't let this city steal it from you."

"I won't," Gillian returned.

Dick caught up with Chuck halfway down the stairs.

CHAPTER TEN

"Just drop me off around here, please." Dick kept his eyes peeled on the streets, hunting for any sign of the Dead Devils and their coming anniversary celebrations. East and Third was a couple of blocks away, and Dick didn't want to risk Gillian getting too close to the action.

She signaled to a space at the side of the road. "Are you sure I can't help more? I know that private investigation is usually a solo sport, but even Holmes leaned on Watson from time to time. Actually, Watson was sometimes the brains of the whole damn thing."

Dick smiled. Gillian was fresh-faced, beautiful, smart, and kind. She had proven all of those things tonight, and Dick had been glad of her company. He had been even more thankful when she had offered a lift, knowing that he was getting tired of walking and that at least her car shouldn't be tracked and traced like his.

"You read Arthur Conan Doyle?" Dick asked.

"*Sir* Arthur Conan Doyle," Gillian corrected. "Almost exclusively." She smirked. "I'm kidding. I read pretty widely, but he's up there with my favorites."

Dick nodded. "Why do the Brits care so much about the 'Sir' moniker? Just because some ancient piece of royalty taps a knife to their shoulder, doesn't mean the world owes them favors."

Gillian looked offended. "Are you kidding? Knighthoods are the symbol of greatness. I'd give anything to get the equivalent of a knighthood someday. Maybe it won't happen in this city, but somewhere. Maybe."

Dick studied her carefully. Gillian caught the intensity of his look. "Oh, no."

"What?"

"You're giving me the 'I want to take you to bed eyes.'" She shook her head. "Sorry. I'm not your type, nor am I available."

Dick stammered slightly.

"I'm kidding!" Gillian broke into laughter. "Man, you old guys are easy to fuck with."

Dick returned the grin. "You take care, Gillian. Thanks for the ride, and good luck with the job hunt."

"Oh, yeah." Her face turned serious. "For a moment, I almost forgot I was complicit in attacking my boss and stealing his money."

Dick raised a finger while standing outside the car but leaning in to speak to her. "*Returning* money that was already mine, and stopping your boss committing homicide."

Gillian considered this. "That does sound better."

"Here." Dick took the notes he had given Chuck—minus a couple of hundred that Chuck had already spent on God knew what—and threw them on the passenger seat. "Consider it a startup on your new venture."

Gillian's face lit up as her jaw dropped. "You can't be serious."

She got no reply. Dick had closed the door and was heading down the darkened street with his hands in his pocket.

Dick stalked around the blocks, performing figure eights and hunting through all the nooks and crannies of the areas surrounding East and Third. Inner-city hotels, diners, and broker firms filled the bulk of the area, which seemed an odd space for the anniversary rally to take place.

He checked his watch and saw that it was nearing 10:00 p.m. From what he knew about rallies, many of them took place in the dead of night, so he would likely be an early guest at the party.

Deciding he had some time to kill, Dick beelined for a dingy pub on the corner of the block, its facade painted in dark green with the corners peeling. He wondered if looks like this were deliberately rustic, given the amount of cash that flowed through the city. Judging by the types of barkeeps he'd met, he wouldn't put it past the owners to pocket every last dime they squeezed through their patrons' pockets.

The bar was quaint and quiet, with dark wooden beams and a smell of stale beer and vomit in the air.

My kinda place.

Dick made his way to the bar and ordered himself a Blue Moon beer. The bottle was chilled, and he paid in cash. He thanked the bartender, then noticed a flyer on the wall advertising something that caught his eye.

Dick nodded to the flyer. "Am I too late to get started?"

The bartender looked over her shoulder. The flyer sported a stack of multi-colored chips and a large bold legend that read, "Big games, big bucks."

She looked at the clock on the till. "I should think you're cutting it fine, sweetie. Doors closed two minutes ago."

Dick handed her a fifty. "Will that open them again?"

She led him up a set of stairs and through a door at the back of the room. The game room was larger than some of the ones he'd previously been in, and he was surprised to find that half of the table was empty.

A familiar face looked up at him. "Mr. Chambers. Haven't seen you in a few days. I thought you'd gone off on one of your adventures."

Connie Broughton smiled up at him with her grey hair combed tight to her skull. She wore a silver fox around her neck, and her nails were as sharp and manicured as ever. At a distance, it looked as though she had daggers fixed to her fingertips.

"I've been around," Dick replied. "Just because I'm not playing with you, doesn't mean I'm not playing somewhere. May I join?"

Connie looked across the table to a woman with dark hair and ocean blue eyes. She wore a hooded sweatshirt with the sleeves rolled up and had a cigar hanging from the corner of her mouth.

The woman shrugged.

"That's all the confirmation I need." Dick pulled up a chair and sat.

The sullen woman dealt Dick a hand. An older gentleman tossed some chips his way, and the game got started. As they played, Dick couldn't glean too much information on the man and the woman, but he got the impression that they were an item. Occasionally he would glimpse her hand moving to his thigh, and he would shift in his seat, although with the dismal lighting Dick might have been imagining this.

He drank his beer, and he played well. He knew Connie's tells and signs as easily as if he had a mirror set up behind her, and soon her pile started to dwindle. The other two... They were harder to read, notably more so because of the shadows that covered their faces.

"I should have warned you about Mr. Chambers," Connie announced to the table a few rounds in. "He has something of a third eye for this kind of activity."

"Have you ever beaten him?" the woman, whose name Dick had discovered was Darla, asked.

"Rarely," Connie replied. "Makes it all the sweeter when I do."

The man, Hugo, whispered something in Darla's ear. She gave a confirming nod. "I have that feeling too, hun. I feel as though we've been set up." She leaned on the table. "How much of the winnings is he going to give you? You two planned this, didn't you?"

Connie looked offended. "I'll have you know that my honor is all that I have. I wouldn't dream of cheating in a game as sacred as this. I'm a woman of my word, and that's all you need to know." She tossed the rest of her chips into the pile. "All in."

Dick shook his head and laughed. He held a pair of aces in his hand, and there was another ace on the table. He glanced at the couple and once again noticed the movement of hands beneath the table.

Dick kept his lips tight, knowing not to antagonize the dealer when you're sitting in their house. Connie lost the hand and left the game. She spent the remainder sulking with a rum and coke in her hands.

The game was more back and forth than Dick had experienced in some time. Every time he was about to pull away and take the lead, Hugo or Darla would claw the comeback and even the game out. By the time midnight struck, the game was level-pegged, and Dick's suspicions were confirmed.

Hugo revealed his hand. The ace of hearts was showcased for the fourth time in as many rounds. He hadn't dismissed the glances between the couple and the constant shifting beneath the table, and now he called them on it. "Bullshit. I call collusion."

Darla's mouth fell open. "Excuse me?"

Dick grinned. "You're a fantastic actress, but you're a terrible cheat. I've seen your movements under the table since I first sat down. At first, I thought you two were getting your kinks on, but when you draw the same card four times in a row, suspicions start to rise. Tell me, how threatened are you of losing that you feel the need to cheat?"

Hugo glared at him. Darla slapped the table with one hand. "Get out! How dare you accuse a host of cheating? How dare you?"

Connie pushed her chair back and placated the group with her hands. "Easy now. Tensions are high, but let's remember that this is a game."

"A game that this man can't stand losing," Darla accused. "Get out! Get out!"

Dick stood up resignedly, resting his knuckles on the table. "If that's what you wish. I do have somewhere I need to be right now, anyway, so I'll thank you for your hospitality and leave."

He paused before leaving and touched his chin. "Oh. One more thing…"

He struck so quickly that Hugo didn't have a chance to defend himself. Grabbing Hugo's wrist, he pulled the man to his feet, and a series of cards slipped down his sleeves and floated to the floor. Darla curled her lip in disgust and shouted, "Out! Now!"

Dick shoved Hugo back into his seat. "With pleasure." He drained his bottle, then told Connie, "You'd think you would vet the people you play with. No wonder your luck is so damn bad."

He left before Connie had a chance to respond.

Dick had only walked three blocks away when his search for the Dead Devils ended. He rounded the corner and discovered a roadblock of AJS vehicles, their blue and red lights flashing atop their sleek cars. Officers stood outside them, pistols in their hands, ready for something to go down.

Dick ducked around the corner and spotted a few familiar faces among the police lineup. Terry Yayanovich looked authoritative in his uniform, and gun trained ahead for anything that might speed around the corner.

Somewhere in the distance, engines roared and rumbled.

"Shit," Dick mused. "Looks like a futuristic Western. Swap the cars for horses and the rumble of engines for dust storms and approaching bandits, and you've got yourself a good old-fashioned showdown."

He hugged the shadows as an idea sprang to his mind. If he could somehow warn the Devils that the AJS was waiting for them, surrounding them like lions around a herd of wildebeest, then maybe he could earn some credit with them and boost his access to the top. Gangs like the Dead Devils usually sported a strict hierarchy of access. Start at the bottom; work your way to the top. Dick didn't have the time to play those sorts of games.

He walked in the direction of the rumbling engines and found the cars a few blocks ahead. There were at least two dozen vehicles, sporting an array of bold metallic colors as neon lights glowed around the rims. Now that he was closer, music thumped from inside the cars, joining the tremendous roar as the cars drove at speed up and down the empty strips of road.

Not half as many as I thought. Isn't this supposed to be an anniversary celebration? Maybe only the stupid and the bold were out tonight.

Dick checked his surroundings, performing a scan for possible AJS intervention. When he saw that he was safe, he crossed the street and headed toward the vehicles.

A car screeched its tires as it careened around a corner and raced at Dick. He had just enough time to leap out of the way before the bright red vehicle streamed past him, leaving a sour taste of burned rubber in the air.

Dick picked himself up off the ground and dusted off his jacket. His hand moved unconsciously to his hip. He followed the trajectory of the red car as it disappeared around the corner, although he could hear where it was heading when it was long out of sight.

Dick crossed the remainder of the road and beelined for the stationary vehicles. There were only a few parked at the sides of the road while the others performed their laps. He found a buff-looking man standing outside his car talking to another jacked-up man, the pair deep in conversation, and beelined toward them.

Before he could open his mouth, a hand clapped on his shoulder, gripping tightly into the hollow of his neck.

CHAPTER ELEVEN

Dick smirked, expecting the interruption, and grabbed the man's calloused hand as he spun around and placed the guy in an arm lock, twisting the arm behind his back. "I could hear you coming from miles away. You want to sneak up on a detective, find a quieter pair of shoes than those thick leather things."

The other two men caught the action and started toward Dick. The man who he had spotted by the car wore a black tank top with a leather jacket over the top. Dick wasn't sure what was printed on the back of the coat, but he was pretty confident it would be a gang emblem. "Yo. You got a problem? You take it out on us."

Dick released the grabby man and stood in the middle of the three. "I haven't got a problem. I don't appreciate being fondled from the rear. Does that tactic ever work for you?"

"Most of the time," the second man explained. He wore dark aviator shades although there was no sun in the sky. "Pretty simple to get the drop on most people in this city. Nuts, really. You think people would be more careful in this town, but those who come to Atlantica grow cocky. That what you done, detective?"

"Detective?" Grabby asked.

"Yeah," Aviator replied. "He said it a second ago. Turn your hearing aid up."

To Dick's surprise, Grabby twisted something inside his eardrum. "Ah, that's better."

Tank Top raised an eyebrow. "What business does a detective have sneaking up on the Dead Devils? You snooping around our business?" He drew closer, towering over Dick in a feeble attempt to intimidate him.

Dick replied, "I have business with your boss. Can you show me to him?"

The three looked at each other in turn, then burst into laughter. Aviator smirked. "You want to get to the boss? I'm afraid you'll have to go through us, sunshine. We've got direct orders to keep the cops at bay. It's our birthday, after all."

"About that." Dick leaned around the towering figure toward the meager assembly of vehicles. "Did you forget to hand out the invites? Seems like a pretty shitty birthday party for a notorious rally gang."

Grabby laughed and grabbed his shoulder again, spinning Dick to face him. "Oh, detective. You clearly ain't that clued up, are you?"

Dick removed his hand forcefully and took Grabby's collar in his hands. "You lay a hand on me again, and I'll stick my foot so far up your ass that you'll be walking sideways for a week. Got it?"

Aviator and Tank Top dragged Dick away, pulling him back with such ferocity that Dick had to scramble with his feet to remain upright. Aviator pulled Dick close and wrapped a meaty arm around his throat, attempting to hold him in a headlock.

Before he could secure the lock, Dick stuck a foot between Aviator's legs and kicked upward. A yelp of pain came as Dick's foot connected with his crotch, and the grip loosened. Dick took the arm and spun it around behind Aviator until it was on the verge of snapping.

However, he couldn't hold it for long since Tank Top jumped to his comrade's aid and threw a punch that Dick avoided with ease. He ducked low, jabbed at Tank Top's side, then managed to hook a leg around the back of his enemy and bring him to the ground. Tank Top fell roughly to one knee.

Grabby returned, a smug expression on his face as he reared up before releasing what could have been a powerful kick to Dick's face. Dick jumped backward and held his stance ready for whatever the three threw next. Somewhere behind him, he could make out the commotion of the other gang members catching onto the fight.

Grabby growled and made to go for Dick, but Tank Top held him back. His expression turned from contempt to impressed as he stared at Dick.

"You fight well," Tank Top declared. "I'm impressed. That ain't no AJS fighting style you've got there. Where did you study?"

"Military." Dick chose to withhold any further information.

Grabby curled his lip. "You going to give him a fucking merit badge? The dude kicked our asses."

"Not as badly as he could have," Tank Top replied. "That gun on your hip, is it defunct?"

Dick shook his head.

Tank Top continued, "So, you chose not to use it. Bold. I like that." He moved close and waved a hand to slow down the group that sprinted across the road toward them. "You with the AJS?"

"No," Dick answered.

"You bullshitting, trying to get our people fucked up?" Tank Top added.

Dick shook his head.

Tank Top took another step closer. For a moment, Dick was prepared for a secret strike, for the man to catch him off-guard and send a blow to his cheek. Instead, the man offered a hand.

Dick took it in his and Tank Top tugged him closer. The man looked down at him, a seriousness coming over his expression. His eyes flickered back and forth, studying Dick. "I sense you're telling the truth."

"I'm an honest man." Dick held his gaze.

Tank Top's hardened expression softened. "The boss is looking for more men like you. Men who can fight. Men with honor. You think you've got what it takes to impress him and get him to answer your questions, by all means, be my guest. Just know that there are layers you'll have to pass through. The boss is diligent with the company he keeps. There's honor among thieves, and the Dead Devils are loyal to one another. It's how we operate. If someone enters who looks to compromise that, we band together and fight off that infection. You got that?"

"Absolutely," Dick agreed. "Where can I find him?" He turned his head over his shoulder, examining those who were standing and watching. With the engine roars mostly cut off, the silence was a looming presence. "These don't seem like the 'boss' type."

Tank Top grinned. "Observant, too. Look, here's the truth. You think that the Dead Devils would put themselves in a position where we'd get cornered by the AJS? Don't be fucking ridiculous. We're all sacrifices here, all of us." He spread his arms wide and spoke loud enough so that the others could hear. "We are mere children in the hierarchy. Bait, designed to draw in the AJS while the real party happens elsewhere. You think it'd be so simple to catch the Dead Devils?"

Dick shook his head.

"Good. Because it's not." Tank Top looked around, as if the AJS was going to be standing right behind him. "There's a dead spot in the city. A set of industrial buildings that have been defunct for years. Early works of the city, supposedly. A place where residents are less likely to complain and draw attention to them. Over by the—"

"The docks?" Dick finished, finding it impossible to believe that he could be so in luck that the Dead Devils would be cruising around near his temporary accommodation.

"Exactly." Tank Top closed the final distance between himself and Dick, their noses almost touching. "If that information slips, we'll know it was you. We'll come for you with all we have, and the Dead Devils won't rest until you're spatchcocked and tied to the hoods of our cars, you got that?"

"I do," Dick acknowledged. He offered another hand, which Tank Top shook. "Appreciate the intel."

"Don't mention it."

In the distance, an AJS siren sounded. The gang members glanced around, hunting for the source. To Dick's surprise, Tank Top grinned. "Looks like it's showtime, people. Time to draw away the Feds for the greater good." He whispered to Dick, "This is our initiation. Take one for the team, live in glory."

"Quite the test," Dick replied.

Tank Top smirked, "Now, get out of here. They're coming."

The AJS sirens formed the soundtrack to Dick's retreat. He only made it across the road when they screeched around the corner, and the gang fled to their vehicles. A few of them were speeding away in the opposite direction to the industrial estate before the others had a chance to catch up.

The AJS was swift, diving into action as they worked to blockade the group in and stop their flight. Dick smirked and disappeared into the shadows.

Walking was growing tedious as he made his way in the direction of his bunker. A driverless cab sped by on a few occasions, and he held back his temptation to hail a ride and hop in. In this day and age, everything left a trace. It was almost impossible to live off the grid without some concerted effort. Everything from phone calls to bank transfers, to walking into licensed premises with CCTV that automatically logged you into the system, and who knew which sharks fed on that data?

Over the years, Dick had learned the best ways to plan, but he wasn't foolproof from the invasive clutches of digital data mining. As much as he wished to believe that he could remain a specter in the city, it wasn't possible. Sooner or later, someone would find him.

Dick passed a bicycle chained up outside the front gates of an apartment complex and thought back to borrowing the boy's when he had ridden to Sadie's mansion. He was tempted to try again, but couldn't bring himself to do it. A borrow would mean a return. One job led to two, and he didn't need that right now.

He increased his pace as the milky moon arced over the sky. Almost an hour later and he finally came to some places that he recognized. There was the reassuring hum of engines in the distance.

Dick reached the end of a network of alleys and faced out to the industrial estate. The large, abandoned buildings were silhouetted monoliths, forgotten and abandoned. Dick had no doubt they'd soon be scooped up and renovated by some rich bitch with a billion burning a hole in her pocket but until then…

Until then, he'd try to worm his way into the Dead Devils and speak to their leader. They were the best lead he had to locating Sergei and finding out what he knew. If he could trace Sergei, maybe he could discover why there was a target on his back, and what his association with Sadie was.

There's always a bigger fish.

Dick strolled across the road, making a conscious effort to look both ways this time, as he melted into the shadows of the buildings and made his way to where the party was happening. Music boomed, people cheered and laughed, and neon lights decorated the coastline for a quarter-mile in each direction.

The first thing Dick noticed was that no one was driving. The cars were parked on the island shoreline's golden sand, the car doors open, trunks popped, and hoods raised as mirthful gang members strolled in tiny clusters and admired everyone's handiwork. Dick could make out the hierarchy almost instantly, with meatheads and babes leaning casually on the hoods of their cars, or sitting on the roofs as hawking admirers encircled them like hypnotized jackals. There were more people than vehicles by a clear mile. Dick guessed that three hundred or so strolled around the beach and laughed as clashing music blasted from hi-tech sound systems.

Nearly all of the crowd wore the same leather jacket that Tank Top had worn. Some wore cheap imitations, clearly wannabes working their way into the group. As Dick worked down a small slope to the beach, he fancied that he could spot a few pits, cordoned off into squares, where topless fighters were going at it in bare-knuckle fighting.

Dick paused and scanned the crowd to find some indication of a leader. Usually, there were telltale signs—a VIP area with more space and fewer people, one person sitting on a throne of sorts, sometimes people bundled around a single vehicle.

From what he could tell, there were no obvious signs, which meant only one thing. He would have to work his way through the crowd and figure things out by questioning the boozehounds.

The things I do to remove a bounty from my head. Dick immersed himself in the party.

CHAPTER TWELVE

"Oh, he's cute," the woman slurred while sauntering across the sand in little more than a bikini top beneath her jacket and a tiny, flowing sarong. She held onto her friend for support, a bottle of wine half-empty and hanging at a dangerous angle in her hand. "You from around here, sweetheart?"

Dick raised his eyebrows in surprise, then asked the question he'd asked at least a dozen individuals. So far, he'd managed to glean that there was a man named Hugo Evans who seemed to be the head honcho of this flock. "You know where I'd find Hugo Evans?"

The woman burped and laughed, her friend falling into fits of giggles beside her. "Come on, hun. There's an empty shack down the road. Why don't we jump in for a test drive?" She practically fell on Dick, holding onto him for support instead of her friend. Dick gently eased her upright and guided her back. "Maybe another night."

"Boo. No fun," the woman replied before someone behind Dick drew her attention. "Hey, you. How about a test drive?"

Dick rolled his eyes. It was almost impossible to navigate the crowd once you were inside. Most people were either reluctant to give information or too far gone to give him a straight answer.

The first somewhat sensical answer came to Dick from a makeshift drink vendor who stood by a steel barrel laden with beers. The owner was a large woman with a flirty smile and a twinkle in her eye. She called over to Dick as he passed. "I'd have you down as a Blue Moon kinda drinker. Am I right?"

Dick's ears pricked up. "That's right. How could you tell?"

"I have an eye for these things," the woman replied. "You're not from around here, are you?"

Dick took the offered beer and took a swig. "I'm from Atlantica if that's what you mean."

She raised her eyebrows.

"Okay." Dick chuckled. "Not originally, no."

"You ain't one of these either, are you?" She waved her arm with a flourish. She wore bright beads around her neck and sported the team leather jacket.

"Do I stand out that much?" Dick grinned.

The woman laughed. "Please. You've got the look of a cop about you. Someone snooping through the crowd. I'm surprised you haven't been picked up yet by one of our guards."

"I'm good at what I do," Dick replied. The beer was cold going down his throat. "I'm not here to cause trouble, though. Quite the opposite. I'm looking for Hugo Evans."

A thin man with a beard stretching to his waist stumbled across and banged a hand on the steel drum. "Four more, Donna. Need to keep this buzz going."

Donna—the large woman—placed her hands on her hips, then wagged a finger. "You know the rules, Cartwright."

Cartwright laughed, a throaty sound that ended with a brief cough. "*Puh-lease.*"

Donna handed him four beers. "That's better." She returned to a bar stool that Dick hadn't realized she was sitting on. The supporting bar looked as though it might bend beneath her weight and snap at any minute. "You won't have much luck going straight to Hugo," she informed him. "Hugo doesn't bother with the lowlies or the new. You ever been inside a rally gang before?"

"I've flirted on the edges. Never a need to penetrate the middle."

Donna raised an eyebrow. "Don't get dirty with me, filth." A stubby finger dragged across her lower lip. "Look, this whole system is built on layers. If you want the big dog, you've got to work your way inside. Initiates and recruits are tended to by Maurine. You want to find Hugo, you get her say-so, and you can rise to the next level. Get your next badge, as it were."

"Like Scouts?" Dick asked.

Donna laughed, her folds and fat wobbling as she did. "I suppose you could say that."

Dick looked out at the crowd. "Where can I find this Maurine?"

Donna extended a round arm and pointed into the crowd. A collection of cheers arose near the water's edge, and Dick could make out a group of bodies massed around something of interest. "Check fighting pit number three."

"You have them fight for sport? Is that necessary?"

Donna smirked. "Oh, honey. You're in for a real treat." She handed Dick a second beer after noting that he'd cleared half a bottle. "One for the road."

"Thanks."

Cheers and excitement, music and engines filled the air. The onslaught to his senses was dizzying, but Dick followed Donna's advice and made his way toward the crowd.

Bodies were packed so tightly around the pit that it was almost impossible to see what was going on. Dick slid past sweaty bodies, the top halves of many were naked, until he managed to secure a spot on the corner and get a look at the action.

The pit was the size of a boxing ring, a crudely carved thing set into the sand. It sank around six feet deep, and bottles and beer cans littered the surface. Some broken glass posed an extra threat to the two recruits scrapping in the center. A hastily put-together wooden fence rimmed the pit.

A man and a woman were inside, fists raised as they circled each other. The man sported a nasty shiner on one eye and had a cut lip. The woman had bruises forming on her shoulder, chest, and hip. The man wore a pair of shorts and a tank top, while the woman had a grey tank, cropped to show her stomach, the grey so rinsed with sweat that it had almost turned black.

"Get him!"

"Go for the dick!"

"Finish it!"

The frenzied crowd pumped their fists and roared their jeers at the fighters. Dick gleaned that the woman was the favorite to win from the general atmosphere and chants, and he could see why.

Her kicks were well-placed, and she used all her assets in her fight. From his experience, he spotted the defensive stances and offensive strikes of the Muay Thai form. Dick had attended a few sessions and recognized the movements of the "eight limbs" style of combat.

The man, meanwhile, had nothing to him but brute force. The fight was an octopus versus a shark. They had both trained for this, but could speed and accuracy win over muscle and determination?

Someone in the crowd shouted, "Maurine!" Dick turned in all directions but could see no one responding. He looked down and wondered if the woman was Maurine. If perhaps she was the test of the recruit's mettle.

Seems unlikely. Would be a strange way to bring in recruits, tiring out the old ones.

The man charged at the woman, but she slipped out of his way and jabbed his cheek as she ducked under his arm. She followed with three kicks to his back that shoved him into the pit's sand wall.

The man pushed back, avoiding a couple of rogue spectators kicking him in the face. He swung around and came for her, eyes flashing with anger. She threw another jab that he grabbed in his fist. He twisted sharply to the right and sent her off-kilter before hooking an arm around her waist and scooping her upside down into his grip.

He raised her high, preparing to pile-drive her into the hard, wet sand. There were gasps and cheers and claps from the crowd, although Dick was silent. He felt sick watching the fight unfold. All the man had to do was crack her down on her head, and she would die instantly. No one could survive an attack like that on such terrain without sustaining immense injuries.

The man grinned and roared his excitement, the woman remaining still in his grip. He made to drive her down, but as he started moving, she whipped out her hand and jabbed her fingers into his eyes.

The man's grip loosened. He stumbled backward, hands pawing weakly at his eyes. The woman fell to the ground and landed with a heavy thud, just managing to block the worst with her hands. She was winded.

The man shouted in frustration, sand from his hands now working its way into his eyes and blinding him as he stumbled around the pit looking for some kind of help.

But none came. The woman rolled away from his stomping, then rose to her feet. She approached the man cautiously, resuming her stance. The man found a corner and stood still, and it was at that moment that she attacked.

She scaled him like a lizard climbing a tree, using his bent knee for leverage and standing on his shoulders like they were a platform. When she was at her full height, almost in line with the ever more excited spectators, she jumped down but kept her elbow trailing in front of her. The added gravitational force, combined with her strike, caught the man on the dome of his head and elicited a whopping crack. The man's eyes crossed inward as his consciousness vanished. As she landed softly on the sand, breathless and exhausted, the man folded to the ground.

There was a mixed response from the crowd. If Dick was to assume, at least fifty percent of the throng had bets on the big guy winning. Now that the fight was over, a group of gang members dropped and swarmed around the guy, checking his wounds and offering medical help. The woman stumbled to the opposite corner where people reached down and praised her, grabbing her shoulder and shaking her in triumph.

Dick was about to make his way over to her when another woman hopped down into the pit. She was muscular, her leather jacket absent of sleeves. She wore an eyepatch and Dick wondered what the story was there. It wasn't often these days that people sported the badge of pirates.

The woman made her way toward the victor and raised her arm. "Your winner—Lacy Duschain!"

Lacy gave a half-hearted grin, dazed and exhausted from the fight. The woman reached toward a jacket offered by one of the spectators and handed it to the fighter. Her smile broke out across her face as tears rose to her eyes. She hugged the eyepatch woman and wordlessly thanked her as she shrugged her arms into the sleeves.

"Who will be the next to conquer the arena?" the woman asked the crowd. A deafening roar of cheers and cries met her words. "I will remind you all that this is a once-a-year occurrence, only held during our anniversary celebrations. A quickstart boost into the ranks of the Dead Devils. You want to ride with us, here's your chance. Hop on down into the pit and prepare to climb the ranks. Prove your worth in no-holds-barred fisticuffs with whoever's brave enough to take you on."

Dick leaned over the railing, noticing the trail of blood left behind as the medics dragged the beefy man out of the pit. They made no effort to hide the bloodstains in the corner.

A pair of hands shoved Dick from behind. He held onto the bar, but others soon joined that pair of hands. Caught off-guard, Dick found himself shoved over the railing where he somersaulted and landed on his back.

The woman turned to him. "We have our first contender! Who's brave enough to take on this hunky sack of flesh?"

Dick rose to his feet, hand holding his back. "Hold on. I was pushed. I'm not taking part in this—"

"I'll take him on," a deep voice declared as a man slid into the pit. He wasn't huge, but judging by the eight-pack he sported, and the tight, lean muscle, he easily had some kind of training going for him. The man spat on the ground. "What do you say, big guy?"

Dick shook his head solemnly, then turned back to the edge of the pit. The gap had closed, and people leered down at him. There was no going back now, not without some kind of fight.

Besides, I need to get to Hugo. Or at least someone who knows about Petrov.

Dick shrugged off his jacket. He folded it, then neatly placed it in the corner of the ring. He clicked his neck and held up his fists. "Fine. Have it your way, clown."

The woman stood in the center of the pit and gave a smug grin. "Two fighters enter, one fighter leaves with the prize. Over to you, gentlemen." She moved to the side, and the crowd parted obediently to allow her to climb as the cheers rose in excitement once more.

Dick held his stance, studying his opponent's moves. The scraggly man demonstrated his footwork, bouncing lightly on his toes as he zigzagged back and forth on the other side of the pit. He shadow-boxed and tried to psych Dick out, but Dick was having none of it. He knew the mechanics of brawling. He understood that at least eighty percent of a fistfight was the mental game. As long as he remained focused and strong-willed, he'd be okay. *The moment you start doubting yourself is the moment you lose. Psych out the opponent, and you've won half the battle.*

"You going to stand there dancing, or are you going to show us what you got?" Dick asked.

"Pretty boy's got a strong tongue," the man replied. "Let's put your money where your mouth is, shall we?"

He raced toward Dick and closed the gap in seconds. His fists were a flurry of movement as he launched the attack. Dick blocked the first punch but was too slow to stop the second, which found the bottom of his ribs. The man crowded into his personal space and went for body shot after body shot. Dick only had enough time to register the stench of body odor that poured off him before the man backed up and stopped his attack.

The crowd went wild.

The man beamed. "Thought you'd have some better defense than that. You looked tougher. This'll be a cinch."

Dick readied his fists again. "Big talk from such a little guy. I'll give you that first one for free."

"You'll have no choice," the man replied. A moment later, he came back at Dick.

This time, Dick was more prepared. As the man flew toward him, Dick reared back and slammed his boot forward, catching the guy in the chest. It threw him several feet back where he landed on his back in the sand but quickly lifted himself to his feet. "Real men punch."

Dick grinned. "Real men use all they have."

"So that's how you want to play it?" the man asked.

"That's what you've got. Come and get it."

This time, the man approached more slowly as he measured his distance and threw jabs into the empty air. Dick followed his footwork and shuffled around the pit as they circled each other. A bottle flew into the arena from somewhere in the crowd and smashed into brown fragments on the ground as the residual liquid drained into the sand.

What a waste.

The man noticed his momentary distraction and pressed the advantage. Dick blocked most of his punches. The man also threw in a few kicks that caught the sides of his thighs and bruised the flesh. Dick retaliated by striking with an uppercut that melted through the man's attacks and caught him on the chin.

The man's eyes flashed. He doubled down on his attacks.

Dick fought against the onslaught but found himself being pushed back toward the edge of the pit. He felt angry eyes boring into him, and as he neared the wall, a spectator's foot reached out and caught the back of his head.

They're rooting for him. If I get near the edge, I'm toast.

Dick had at least a foot of height on this man, and at least sixty pounds. He pressed this advantage and surprised the man as he blocked a punch and simply charged at him. He brought his knee high and winded the man as it caught him in the chest. The man fell backward. Dick fell on top. His knee hit the sand as a piece of glass sliced through his shin and stuck in the flesh.

The man struggled beneath Dick, although after a swift punch to the cheek, his attempts to escape grew weaker. Another punch and it looked as though Dick had won. The man's eyes rolled into the back of his head as he lay on the sand, arms falling to his side.

A mixture of jeers and cheers met this sight. Dick waited a few seconds, then was about to stand when the man grabbed a handful of sand and threw it at him. Dick had just enough time to turn away and avoid getting blinded, but it threw him off-balance, and the man shoved him roughly aside.

Dick was on his hands and knees, that sharp, stinging sensation in his palms now. He examined his hands and was dismayed to find small cuts and scrapes from the glass mixed in the sand.

"Thought it was over, did you?" The man launched at him, dropping an elbow on Dick's back.

Dick folded onto his front. The man pushed himself up and straddled Dick after turning him over to launch a series of punches at his face. Dick took three before he grabbed the man's fist in one hand. The man threw another punch, which gave Dick the other hand.

The man tried to pull away, but Dick squeezed tightly. He put pressure on the balled-up fists in his grip until the glass embedded in his palms sliced into the man's hands. Something clicked as a bone popped, and the man howled in pain.

Not bothering trying to hold on, the man fell away as Dick struggled to sit up. He held onto those fists until he felt blood running between his fingers then, as the man howled in pain, Dick let go.

The man examined his hands, surprised to find that no bones had broken despite the blood painting them. While he fought to understand what had happened, Dick rose to his feet. "Let's end this. Now."

He kicked the man in the side of the face and knocked him unconscious. A moment of quiet passed among the crowd before the mixture of cheers and jeers resumed.

The medics hopped down into the pit and helped the man up, examining his wounds and attending to his needs. Dick grimaced as he flexed his hands and found the pieces of brown glass in the crevices of his fingers. He drew them out as the woman hopped down and came to his side. She grabbed his wrist and raised one hand in the air as she declared him the victor of the battle.

As the crowd went wild, she muttered out of the side of her mouth, "Thank you."

"For what?"

"My bet was on you. You were the underdog. Better odds, greater reward." She announced Dick's entry into the Dead Devils and handed him his jacket. "What's your name, cowboy?"

"Dick Chambers."

She smirked. "Seriously?"

His stare told her he was.

"Maurine." She offered a hand, then drew it back at the sight of the blood. "Maybe clean yourself up, first."

"Sure."

"Come on, let's get you out of here," Maurine instructed. "Go find Pearl by the surf and I'll join you both in a minute. Congratulations…Dick. Get ready to ride."

She said this last bit with a tone that suggested she had more in mind than simply racing. With her unique look, he would be lying if he said his interest hadn't piqued.

CHAPTER THIRTEEN

Pearl had a tender touch and a soft voice. She soothed Dick as she pinched the tweezers to remove the glass and answered his questions with soberness he hadn't yet fully encountered at this event.

"The Devils were Hugo's creation around a decade or so ago. Probably 2017, I reckon." She leaned closer to get a better look for gleaming brown fragments amidst the blood. "Legend tells that he was at a stoplight in the middle of the night, waiting for it to turn green when a car pulled up beside him and thrummed its engine.

"He raced against the rival, and the competition to see who had the best acceleration quickly turned into laps around the city. The AJS tried to catch them, but they were outside. Money buys good cars, and even in Atlantica the federal budget can only spread so far."

Dick winced as she pulled a large chunk from his palm.

"They eventually found a spot to hide, and it was there that Hugo met Sergei Petrov," she continued as her face soured. "A piece of shit if I've ever met one."

Dick looked up. "You know Sergei Petrov?"

"I know *of* him." Pearl dipped the tweezers into a glass of what Dick hoped was sterilizer. "Petrov and Evans parted ways back in '25, and since then Petrov has formed his own little team, The Ragers."

"The Ragers?" Dick scoffed. "Sounds like a cheap version of the Power Rangers."

"Don't I know it." Pearl's concentration never left her face as she spoke. "We still see them from time to time, out on the streets at night. Hugo and Sergei have something of an agreement. Hugo keeps to the east, Sergei keeps to the west. It doesn't always pan out that way, but that's the way it goes. Those who break the agreed-upon lines get prosecuted."

She turned Dick's hand over and examined her work. "There. I think that's the last of it. How does it feel?"

"Sore," Dick replied.

Pearl nodded sympathetically. "We'll bandage that baby up and get you on your merry way. You must have fought bravely in there. Your opponent hasn't woken up yet." She nodded to the side where a man lay facedown and sleeping on a sheet of fabric. A couple of medics were stationed by his side.

Dick looked at the crowd gathered around the pit, where another fight took off. "What's the purpose of the pit? Seems like a surefire way to get someone killed. You guys want the AJS out here getting you fixed for murder baiting?"

Pearl chuckled softly. "We never let it get that far. So far, our record is eighty-seven to one in mortality. People get beat up, sure. But it's a price they're willing to pay to become fully-fledged members." She scanned Dick curiously. "Ain't that the reason you jumped in?"

"Somebody pushed me," Dick replied flatly.

Pearl shrugged. "All amounts to the same thing." She tightened up the last of the bandage and placed her hand delicately on his. "Welcome to the gang, Dick Chambers. It'll be nice to see your face around here more often. Don't get many guys like you."

Dick raised an eyebrow. "What do you mean?"

"Good guys." Pearl smiled. It was reassuring and measured. "Most of our guys are narcissistic assholes with more money than sense. Coin and cars may buy you a cheap shag with some of these floozies, but integrity and honor will get you further."

Dick nodded. He wanted to say that he didn't plan to be a part of the gang for long, but knew that if he did, he might blow his chance to find out what he'd come here to discover. "You mentioned Sergei Petrov and his gang. Do you know where they meet?"

She gave Dick an assessing look. "You already looking to jump ship?"

"Just curious," Dick replied.

"No one knows," Pearl answered. "At least, no one here. Evans may be your guy there, but if I were you, I'd avoid inquiring about the enemy. It won't make you many friends here. These guys are fiercely loyal. You slip up, and you're hung, drawn, and quartered before you can bat an eyelid."

Dick tapped his nose. "Thanks for the info."

"Anytime." Pearl looked past Dick to where Maurine was breaking free from the crowd. "Ah, here you go, captain. Your charge is all healed and sorted."

Maurine glanced down at the blood-soaked bandages wrapping Dick's hands. "Are you sure?"

"Positive," Pearl replied. "Just go easy on him for tonight, okay?"

Maurine nodded. "You ready to go, sunshine?"

Dick rose to his feet and gently flexed his hands. "I think so."

Maurine threw something at Dick. He awkwardly caught the bottle of Blue Moon and winced in pain. A little bit of beer splashed down his front.

Maurine smirked. "You left one ring-side. I got you a fresh one. Come on, new cadet. Let me show you where the big boys hang."

She walked away before Dick could respond, leaving him to jog after her.

When Dick finally caught up, Maurine waved a hand around her. "What do you think of our little celebration?"

"It's...nice?" Dick replied uncertainly. "Surprised you guys put on such a show. Don't you worry about the AJS showing up and shutting you down?"

"What are you, a cop?" Maurine asked.

"Just curious," Dick replied.

"The AJS has better things to deal with than a bunch of booze-addled car enthusiasts. We keep things as above the law as possible, but mostly we stay out of their way." Maurine waved at a group of people as she passed. They waved excitedly back. "And, for the record, no more of this 'shutting *you* down' business. You're one of us now, Dick. Act like it."

"If you're not worried about the AJS, how come you have measures in place to distract them from where you truly are?" Dick asked. When Maurine gave him a strange look, he added, "I ran into your lot uptown. They pointed me in your direction. Turns out they were impressed by my combat skills, too." He held up his fists and grinned.

Maurine's studying look melted into an impressed smile. "There's something different about you, Dick. You ain't the typical type we get in this gang."

"You say that like it's a bad thing," Dick added.

Maurine grinned. "No. It's refreshing. You're the first guy I've come across tonight who hasn't looked at me like I'm a piece of meat. I admire that in a man."

"In all honesty, I probably haven't had the chance." Dick's eyes scanned her body.

Maurine laughed. "There it is!"

She guided him through the throng of drunks on the beach, such a strange gaggle of individuals. That was the one thing that Dick could get on board with about gangs like this. No matter how much of a misfit you were out in the wider world, in a gang, you were home, united by the common fact that you stick together *because* you're different, with only a single shared interest.

In this case, cars.

The money invested in some of the vehicles they now passed could only be guessed to be in the six-figures. The cars themselves were top of the line supercars but modified to within an inch of their lives. The bodies were low, the lights were bright, the music was loud, and the customized paintwork was to be envied. The further up the beach they went, the more they rifled out the riff-raff as they came upon those who Dick correctly guessed were higher up the pecking order. Maurine led Dick through a roped-off section of the beach where there were fewer people and more conversation.

Dick wondered what it must be like to be surrounded by people like this. As a private investigator, he had made a point of keeping people at arm's reach. The further away people were, the less likely he was to hurt them. Any friendships he'd made over the years had been reduced to fleeting calls and flying visits.

But this seemed nice, too.

He drained the dregs of his Blue Moon as Maurine led him to a makeshift pagoda set up where the sand met the grass. Dick's bunker could only be about a mile away from where he stood, the industrial estate stretching across the coast for a fair few miles on top of that.

A half-dozen men and women sat beneath the pagoda on deck chairs, sipping their drinks and listening to the tinny rumble of 70s rock coming from a cheap boombox. There were two empty chairs, and Maurine took one while she signaled Dick to take the other.

Dick helped himself to a beer from a nearby cooler.

"Recruits," Maurine announced while studying them all one by one. "Congratulations. You're the first batch of boosters to have graced the pit tonight. You should be proud. You did it. You're here."

Dick noticed then the array of bandaged wounds and bruises that decorated all of the other recruits. Everything from black eyes to busted lips to bandaged hands and torn clothes.

"You battled bravely," Maurine continued. "We need people like you, fighters, survivors. People who will pledge their allegiance to the Dead Devils and commit to our cause. We're more than rally racers and car enthusiasts. We're a family. You know what family means, don't you?"

"Loyalty," a woman with defined muscles and a missing tooth replied.

Maurine smiled. "Loyalty. Fealty. Dedication. Honor. All those things that bind us together." She got up from her chair and paced around the pagoda as a group of topless muscleheads walked by, grinning and laughing as they checked out two of the ladies. "Your time with the Dead Devils will be some of the best years of your life. We can promise you that. You will ride with us, and you will die with us. We will adopt you as our own and treat you with the respect you deserve, if you treat us with the respect we deserve also."

Dick's eyes narrowed as he wondered what he was getting himself into.

Maurine continued. "If you fail to adhere to our rules, and you are found to be a traitor, we will expel you from the Dead Devils for life. We offer no second chances. This is a one-time deal so suck it up or get the fuck out. You got it? We don't allow moles, and we purge corruption, we expunge toxins. You want to leave, then fine. On your way you go. Remember, the door locks on your way out. The choice is yours."

Maurine crouched and grew silent. Somewhere nearby, an engine roared as a keen driver showcased the car's capacity to make noise.

"In a few minutes you'll be taken through to the Six

Horsemen of the Apocalypse," Maurine crooned, leveling her voice for apparent effect. "You will cite the pledge, and you will bind yourself to us. If you need a reminder of what an honor this is, you have shortcut more than a year's worth of hazing and initiations. People sweat, bleed, and steal to get to the position that you find yourselves in. Luckily for you, the anniversary celebrations are timed for tonight. You have proven triumphant. We are proud of you for that."

A hand rose. Maurine addressed the bearded man, a thick nest of hair nestled on his chin. "Isn't it the four horsemen of the apocalypse?"

The others warily looked at each other. Maurine offered a gentle chuckle. "Not here, sunshine. We go for better. We have our six prophets. Do not anger them with unnecessary questions. Got it?"

The bearded man nodded eagerly.

Maurine rose to her feet and settled her hands on her hips. Dick wished she hadn't mentioned the hungry eyes that feasted on her, because now those thoughts plagued his mind. She was objectively attractive, but Dick always liked a woman with power and confidence.

Maybe that's *the reason the mercenary gets my engine revving.*

"Before we go in there, I have one more question to ask you all," Maurine declared. "Think long and hard before you answer it. Remember, liars get found, and they get booted."

Dick sat straighter in his chair, finding this whole process fascinating. So this was what truly went on inside a gang recruitment drive. This kind of speech was specifically designed to weed out the weak and create the group bonding glue that kept gangs together. "Them versus us" in language. Clever.

Maurine puffed out her chest. "Does anyone here have a true reason why they shouldn't be initiated into the Dead Devils? Declare all affiliations with current members, past members, or if you are in any way connected with the federal law, speak now or forever hold your peace." She mimed a cross over her body. "So help you God."

Dick chuckled, unable to help himself. Maurine shot him a look. "Does that work?"

"What?" She raised an eyebrow. The others shifted uncomfortably.

Dick continued. "Surely if anyone here is doing something that you disapprove of, or that counts as 'bad' for the Devils, they're hardly going to admit it now, are they?"

Maurine turned on Dick, eyes narrowing as the kindness faded. "We take the care of our flock very seriously. One way or another, the truth prevails. We can smell it on you like a foul stench. Deceive us, and there will be hell to pay."

The other recruits shifted uncomfortably. Dick held steady. There was a moment of pause before Dick rifled through the jacket on his lap and flashed his badge.

The other recruits mumbled to each other, a few of them gasping.

Bit dramatic.

To Dick's surprise, Maurine smiled. "Good. I was wondering how long it would be before you owned up to it. Nice to see that we've at least got someone here who knows the power of telling the truth."

"He's a traitor!" one of the recruits shouted and pointed a judging finger. "5-0!"

A couple of nearby heads turned from the already initiated. Maurine raised a placating hand. "Mr. Chambers, care to explain?"

"I'm a private investigator," Dick confessed. "I'm in no way associated with the AJS, nor am I on their payroll. I'm here of my own volition, and I'm seeking an audience with Hugo Evans. I have no business interrupting anything else that's going on here. I focus on what I'm paid to focus on, and you aren't my targets."

The man sitting next to Dick looked up at Maurine with

curiosity, wondering how she would play this latest revelation. Maurine held her smile as he asked, "How did you know?"

"We lifted his jacket from the pit," Maurine explained. "You've got quite the array of instruments in those pockets. I wanted to see if you intended them for use at our little celebration, or if there were other matters you sought to pursue."

Dick accepted the badge back and placed it in his jacket.

Maurine returned her attention to the group. "You see, this is a good man. Someone who tells the truth in the face of adversity. An honest man is someone we can tie into our ranks." She side-eyed Dick. "If, of course, you still want a place with us?"

Dick considered this. The last thing he wanted was to be tied down in a cult who obsessed over high-end vehicles. On the other hand, what other leads did he have? Sergei was his target, and if he'd learned anything over the years, it was never the straightest path that led to the truth.

Why not ride the wave?

"I wish to speak to Hugo," Dick replied.

Maurine grinned. "Then you've got your work cut out for you."

The recruits were given a tour of the quieter section of the beach and introduced to several veteran members and their vehicles.

Dick followed at the back, happy to bring up the rear since those in front of him couldn't believe their luck. The owners of the vehicles were celebrities to these guys, and Dick wondered how they had gained such a name for themselves.

They came to a neon pink Tesla Roadster with its hood popped to show an immaculate engine with lights flashing and playing around the rims. Maurine introduced the owner of this vehicle as Leanne Simpson, but she hardly needed to mention her name to the other recruits. One woman in particular—the same woman who had dominated the match before Dick's in the pit, Lacy Duschain—clutched her hands together and spoke in rapid bursts, explaining how much she loved Leanne and couldn't believe that she was in her presence.

Leanne smiled and embraced her, leaving Lacy wide-eyed and with a grin that didn't leave her for some time.

"Pleased to meet you all," Leanne declared as she patted the top of the car. "Can't wait to see what you all bring to this group. Remember, it ain't all about the cars you own. It's about what you can bring to this family." She placed a hand to her mouth and leaned forward conspiratorially. "Still, the car definitely helps."

There was a round of laughter before Maurine led them onward.

Dick remained silent for the most part, his fascination at seeing the inside of this group overwhelming him. Eyes tracked their movements as they made their way along the sand, another beer was placed in his hand that took the edge off the painful throb that came from the cuts, and endless, clashing music created the soundtrack of the night.

As Maurine introduced them to more drivers, Dick kept an eye on her and wondered what her story was. She was happy to play hostess to these recruits, but didn't she have more work to do down at the pit? Dick was almost certain there had still been a crowd when he was taken forward to meet the others.

Finally, they came to a series of large tents at the far end of the beach. Dick couldn't count how many from this angle, but the white canvas roofs caught the straggles of moonlight and bounced them back into the sky.

As they approached the pavillion, a small bubble of excitement arose in Dick's chest. There was something about the two guards monitoring the entrance that gave Dick an indication that he might be on the right track to making his mark and finding Hugo.

That feeling was confirmed once Maurine spoke to the guards

and came back to the group. "This is where I leave you, cadets. Once you're inside, you'll be given your proper welcome into the Devils. Stay strong. Don't fear what is to come. You have proven yourself worthy, and in that, you are already one of us. Do not embarrass me. Do not embarrass yourselves. First impressions last a lifetime."

Maurine passed the group and paused only long enough to place a hand on Dick's shoulder and whisper, "I'm taking a chance on you, detective. Don't make me regret my decision."

Dick watched her walk away, her figure swaying as she disappeared in the crowds.

"Oi. Inside," one of the guards declared. Dick turned back to realize the others had gone ahead, and he was outside alone.

Not a good start, Dicky boy.

Dick entered the tent.

CHAPTER FOURTEEN

The man stood in the shadows of an alleyway, his anger and frustration bubbling to the surface as he tried to piece the clues together and bring his work forward.

Dick Chambers was in hiding. He knew that hunting a private investigator would be a challenge, and he had been prepared for it at the start. The problem now was that he had met dead end after dead end, and he was beginning to question his capabilities in delivering his client's instructions.

He rested against the wall and watched unblinkingly as Karine entered the alley. She wore a dirty white tank top and combat trousers, and there was a slight limp with every left step.

"You say you have news?" The man attempted not to sound too desperate.

Karine smiled. She had a narrow face and a strong jaw. Her arms were toned and ready for action. She smirked and gave a small nod. When she spoke, it was with a Russian lilt that the man had grown accustomed to living in Atlantica. "Your man is dangerous. He fights valiantly."

"He's not my man," he replied. "Not yet, at least. Tell me what you know."

Karine informed him of her dealings with Mr. Chambers, detailing his impossible preparedness for their ambush. He was astute, hardly missed a trick, and had tools that prepared him to get out of sticky situations. "He's more than a PI. He's an artist."

The man frowned. "Shame you two didn't get a chance to wrestle naked."

Karine snorted in derision. "He is dangerous. Be careful."

"I don't need to be careful," he retorted. "I need a location." The man was getting annoyed now. He didn't want his capabilities brought into question. It was bad enough that this lowly fish had gotten hold of the hook in a much larger pond, getting lucky enough to stumble across Chambers before him. He didn't have any minions running any errands, but he worked in the right circles.

Unfortunately, this could cost him badly. He would work for Sadie, and he would chase Chambers, but he also knew that Sadie wasn't the end of the daisy-chain. Those goons higher up than Miss Turnberry commanded a big deal of Atlantica's territory, and he found himself in a precarious situation in which he now needed to buy Karine's silence. Although he might have a history with her, that didn't mean she wouldn't run off and snitch to her employer, and set them all into a world of trouble.

"How much is it going to cost?" he asked.

Karine grinned. "To what are you referring?"

"Your silence." The man frowned.

Karine considered this. "One half of whatever you're owed."

"Fine." The man wasn't happy, but he would do whatever it took to get there. "Give me a location.

She listed the address of a pharmacy. She had waited behind the store to ambush Dick in the middle of some deal with the old man that ran the joint. He made a note of the address and thanked Karine.

She stared levelly at him. "I will find you when your deed is done if you do not tell me first—"

Her words dried up as her blood poured out. The man had the information he needed. There was no more use for this traitorous Russian. The knife made a clean entry wound to her heart, and as she looked at him with wide eyes, he shook his head. "I'm sorry."

Although his eyes told another story entirely.

The pharmacy was dark, but he didn't let that deter him. Judging by what Karine had told him, there was likely to be someone pottering around somewhere inside.

He approached the building from the rear and found an innocuous grey door that usually allowed room for deliveries to enter. There was a single camera watching that spot, which he took out with a silenced pistol, knowing that most of the people around here would either be asleep or would hardly notice the slight popping sound that came from the shattering glass.

He rested his hands on the back door and investigated the lock. A few minutes later, the mechanism opened as he finished fiddling with his picks. Even in advanced societies such as Atlantica, he couldn't believe how basic locking mechanisms could be. Lockpicking was a dying art, and he used that to his advantage.

The building was cold and quiet. He peeked through a window in the door that led to the main pharmacy counter. There was no one there. There was another door, however, and he heard the sounds of someone shuffling around and mumbling to themselves from the other side.

This door wasn't locked. He wasn't surprised. Given that the other doors had been, the person downstairs likely felt pretty safe in his own company. The man slipped through the door and removed his shoes, which allowed his feet to pad silently down the stairs toward the sounds.

A light spilled to the bottom of the stairs. He waited a few seconds to listen to how many people were down here and to get a sense of whether it would be dangerous for him to do what came next. Satisfied that there was no real threat, he emerged around the corner, gun trained at the back of the man's head.

The man scurried around a workshop that was in pieces. Boxes were everywhere, and there were big gaps where old machines must once have been. He pulled at his hair and mumbled his problems, unaware of the man behind him.

"Tell me where John Chambers is," the man announced, eliciting a sudden turn from the crazy-haired old man.

The man clutched his chest, and his face turned white as his breath caught. His face fell at the sight of the gun, and so did he.

CHAPTER FIFTEEN

Inside the tent was vastly different from the world outside. The canvas walls and ceiling were fitted with everything someone needed to be comfortable and live as though they weren't outside. Couches, tables, and drink coolers filled the expansive space. The lights were dim, and the half a dozen cars situated around the area provided the music and the lighting ambiance.

There was also a great deal of smoke that obscured the way. If Dick didn't know better, he'd presume he was in some sleazy club downtown. A smattering of people danced and swayed while laughing and kissing, but no one was inside any of the cars. Everyone gave these cars a wide berth, used more as sanctimonious props than the speedsters that they clearly were.

The guard led the procession through the strange alternate reality, and as they neared a far corner, Dick spotted a car with a set of wide, angry devil horns fixed to its roof. He figured he could make a smart guess and presume that he was looking at Hugo Evans' vehicle.

No way I can sneak into that backseat now, is there?

The guard stopped at a velvet rope, which seemed unnecessary considering the few people inside the marquee. He unclipped a loop and walked them the rest of the way to where a group of five men and women awaited on plush couches at the end. These were raised on platforms, cast like imitation thrones, although Dick assumed that these people truly saw themselves as kings and queens.

"Welcome," a large woman with a beaming smile announced and spread her arms wide as she sat up straighter in her chair. "You are new here, yes?"

The guard gave a stern nod, then folded his arms in front of him.

A man with a severe mohawk sat beside the large woman and elbowed her roughly. "Of course they are. Look at how excited they are to see the inside of this place." He thumped a fist against his chest with one hand while the other held a joint to his lips. "Let's get these intros underway so we can go back to merriment. I'm Spikes. You can call me Spikes, and there's no debating that, okay?"

A few of the recruits nodded eagerly.

The large woman rolled her eyes. "Abigail Thornton. My associates over here are Boulder, Ninetails, and Clegg."

She waved toward a man who clearly valued his appearance and hit the gym regularly, a woman with a series of what Dick assumed would be nine ponytails, and a middle-aged man with a rash of stubble and keen eyes that bored into them all.

"Where's Hugo?" Dick called.

Abigail raised an eyebrow. Boulder sat up a little straighter.

Dick continued, undeterred by the array of firearms positioned lazily around the group. "You are the Six Horsemen of the Apocalypse, are you not? Where's your number six?"

"Hugo goes where he likes," Clegg answered in a voice that held an edge of education. "He is not bound to our limits."

Spikes grabbed the neck of a beer bottle and threw it at Dick. "Show your leaders some goddamn respect, boy. You may have boosted up the ranks, but that don't mean we won't tear you down. Remember where you are."

Dick dodged out of the way as the bottle smashed on the floor behind him. The other recruits distanced themselves by stepping away to give Dick some room. "Apologies, oh wise ones," Dick replied in a voice laced with sarcasm. "I figured that this introduction would see us meeting all six of the horses, not merely the five deemed unworthy."

Dick grew satisfied as a smile appeared on Clegg's and Abigail's faces. Spikes and Boulder were less than impressed, while Ninetails simply sat back and acted as though she could barely hear any part of the conversation, pupils dilated from the smoke that poured from her mouth.

"Unworthy?" Spikes bellowed. He grabbed another two bottles of beer and launched them one after the other. Dick dodged one and caught the other. "Deano, get this asshole out of here."

The guard nodded and moved toward Dick, careful to tread over the large pieces of glass. Before he could lay his hands on Dick, Abigail called, "Wait."

Deano looked back at the five.

Spikes lip curled. "What's your problem?"

Abigail shrugged, eyes not leaving Dick's. "This is the most entertainment we've had all evening. Why would you send him out when he's clearly trying to play mind games?"

She rose from the platform and carefully descended the stairs. The whole process was torture to watch since the woman was so large that even if she split into three identical versions of herself, there would be room left over. As she approached Dick, he felt an aura of power around her, but he wasn't intimidated, more intrigued by what was happening.

Her shadow loomed over him. "You're the investigator, correct?"

Dick nodded.

She studied him closely while biting her lip. "Oh, and Maurine was right. You are a treat. Tell me..." She emphasized his name for effect, "Dick. Say we give you an audience with Hugo. What would you do for that honor? How far would you be willing to go to see your mission through?"

Dick tried to work out how Maurine had passed a message so fast. He hadn't seen her dial into anyone or speak to anyone else along the way.

"Depends what's on the table," Dick replied.

Abigail came closer and moved her hands to her chest as she pressed her breasts together. "How about seven minutes in heaven with a pretty ol' thing such as myself?"

Something crashed against the back of Abigail's head. Her hands moved to the sore spot where Spikes' bottle had collided. "You'll sell out the big dawg for a quick shag? What the hell is wrong with you?"

"We're not selling anyone out," Abigail spat back. She took Dick's half-finished bottle and threw it at Spikes. It missed by a foot and thudded against the marquee wall. "Deano, get the other recruits out of here. I want to speak to Mr. Chambers alone."

The other recruits glared at Dick, crestfallen as they were ushered out of the tent. A minute later, Dick was alone with the five, and the dregs of people dancing inside the tent as though they were in a world of their own.

"That's better," Abigail declared. She leaned close to Dick. "Now that they're gone, we can get the party started."

Dick felt hands clawing at his sides and looked down to see Ninetails crawling on all fours, her hands digging into his pants as she attempted to undo his belt.

He took a step back, wondering what the hell he had gotten himself into. Ninetails' eyes were virtually blank, her movements groggy and laborious as she moved in a trance. "Look, I'm not here to fuck around, and I've likely wasted enough time already.

I'm looking to either speak to Hugo or someone to tell me where the hell I can find Sergei Petrov."

At the sound of Sergei's name, Clegg rose from his seat and walked away from the group, disappearing into the folds of the canvas. Spikes growled. "How dare you utter that prick's name in the home of our sacred covenant?" His hands clenched into fists. "You have no idea where you fucking are, do you? How the hell did you make it through the pits?"

"Because he's talented," Abigail crooned, studying Dick like a piece of meat. "Ain't that right, handsome? You know how to handle yourself well. I wonder how well you can handle someone else?"

Ninetails sat on the ground and licked the back of her hand as though she were a dog. Dick eyed her curiously. "Is she okay?"

"The pills pep her up," Abigail explained. "But they take something of her humanity along the way. It's fine. She can still drive well, even when she's high as a kite. It's quite impressive."

Dick shook his head, trying to work through it all. How the hell had this crowd of misfits pulled together and formed what they had? Drink, drugs, sex, cars, was that all that life was to them?

Dick rubbed his forehead. "Please. I need some information on where I find Petrov. That's all. Then I'm out of here. I don't need you to give me anything more. I won't tell anyone about the operation you have going here. I won't ruin your night. Just please, someone, tell me where the hell I can find..."

"Petrov?" The voice came from behind Dick. He turned, and a man walked across the tent toward him. At least, he thought it was a man. Through the disco lights and fog, it was almost impossible to make out.

The man wore a leather jacket, zipped up high around the neck. What Dick could see of his skin was covered in tattoos. He wore a half-mask on his face with great bullish horns stretched on either side of his head, and painted in the devil's colors.

Only his mouth was free, and a set of teeth filed to points completed the gruesome vision emerging from the smoke.

The man continued. "Those who utter the name of Sergei Petrov in this marquee are doomed never to leave. True Devils know the significance that Petrov holds. True Devils know the blasphemy his name posits into our community." The man stopped a short distance from Dick, practically spitting the words. "Who the hell are you?"

Dick expected Abigail to have something to say, but instead, she shrank back and sat on the edge of the platform. Even Spikes remained silent in reverence as he sat on the couch.

The music continued in the background, but the other dancers had stopped. Dick couldn't believe what he was seeing. They were *bowing*.

Dick held his own, not wanting to show any weakness. "My name is Dick Chambers, and I'm a private investigator working on a case that involves me finding Sergei Petrov."

At the mention of his name, the bowing dancers flinched.

Dick continued, "I've been informed that you may be the best source of information to uncover where I can find Petrov, so I ask you now: where is he?"

The man studied him closely. Dick barely made out the narrow eyes beneath the mask. He reached up and removed the cover in one swift movement, then curled his lip at Dick. "An investigator of your caliber doesn't cotton on quickly. You should not have uttered his name again."

The man tossed the mask to the side and sent it clattering onto the floor. He settled into a stance as he curled his fingers into fists and stared at Dick. "We fight now."

Before Dick had a moment to respond, the man raised a leg and kicked him square in the chest. Dick fell backward and hit his head on the sandy floor.

The man lunged at him, flying through the air like a maniac.

Dick rolled sideways to avoid a punch that would have found the center of his face.

He tried to push himself to his feet, but as he rose halfway, the man launched at him, wrapped his arms around his waist, and bowled him backward. Dick's knees hit a drink cooler, and the icy contents spilled as the pair tumbled over them.

Something glinted, catching Dick's attention.

The man had a knife in his hands and raised it high, ready to strike. Dick reacted quickly and grabbed the man's wrist in both hands. His cut fingers throbbed and the bandages blossomed in red once more.

"What the hell is your problem?" Dick managed through gritted teeth.

The man didn't answer. Dick held his hand steady and snatched a glance at the five horsemen, who simply stood watching in stone-cold fascination. No emotions on their faces, no attempts to help either party as they scrapped in the center of the tent.

What the hell have I walked into? Dick wondered. *This isn't Kansas anymore, Toto.*

The man smelled of cologne and booze. His face had contorted into a strange mask that reminded Dick of the one he had removed before he launched his attack.

Really? All of this because I said someone's name? What is this guy's problem?

Dick twisted the man's wrist and bent it at an awkward angle. The knife slipped free, and Dick used that moment to crane his head forward and headbutt the man.

The man groaned, barely audible against the music. Dick pressed the advantage and tried to pin him down, but he was too quick. Dick caught his jacket, but he twisted free and got to the side, where he rose to his feet and ran for the knife.

Dick lay prone on the ground as he reached into his pocket and found his tanglers—the metal balls bound by tough, flexible wire. He threw them at the man, expecting him to become bound and fall like the Russian woman Dick had evaded at Chuck's, but they missed when the flashing lights dizzied Dick and affected his vision.

The man crouched for the knife. Dick pushed to his feet. The man grinned and stood where he was while tossing the knife from hand to hand. "Give up, old man. Accept your fate."

"My fate is to retire to Rio and eat my weight in chicken wings."

As the man broke into a run once more, Dick reached down to the cooler they had knocked over and brought it in front of him like a shield. The knife punctured the center. Dick twisted the cooler and tossed it aside, the knife still buried in the plastic. He ducked as the man threw a punch, then scooped up a bottle by the neck on the downward move. He aimed at the man's head and caught him in the temple. The brown glass shattered in a spray of fragments and sticky beer.

The man toppled sideways and landed against the platform where the other five watched with fascination. Spikes appeared as though he wanted to get involved, but stood still regardless. Abigail had the ghost of a grin on her face. Ninetails lay on the couch on her back and stared at the roof.

Blood trickled down the side of the man's face. He eased himself to his feet and swayed as he raised his fists. "You put up a good fight, shitbag. Let's see if you can finish this."

His eyes widened when he saw that Dick held the knife. In the few seconds it took for the man to get up, Dick had tugged the blade free and now pointed it at the man's face. "End this. Let me leave, or I'll end it myself. I'm not against taking down someone who stands in my way."

The man's face hardened. He took a step toward Dick, then another. Before long, he was within arm's reach of Dick, and the tip of the blade pressed into the flesh of his neck. "Do it, then."

Dick held steady. The man crept forward, the blade piercing

into the skin as continuous droplets of blood pooled around the silver and slowly worked their way down his throat. His eyes were manic, half full of doubt, half full of belief.

Dick wondered how far the man would push this. Did it count as murder if the man forced himself onto the blade? What was his end game here? Did he actually want to kill himself to prove a point?

Another millimeter, and the man howled, a strange sound that Dick hadn't heard before. Any farther and Dick was certain that the blade would puncture the man's throat.

As he was about to withdraw, something sprinted toward them.

CHAPTER SIXTEEN

Dick almost missed it, with his eyes fixed on the man throwing himself onto the knife. A large mass sprinted from somewhere in the tent. The music stopped as heavy footsteps came closer.

A blur of movement appeared and bowled the man backward, the knife now poking air.

"You fucking idiot," a new voice cried.

Dick stared down at the two men wrestling on the floor. The one that Dick had been fighting had the lower hand and received several blows before he eventually stopped fighting back. On top of him was a man in a black tank top with thick gold chains around his neck. His back and shoulder muscles worked away as he neutralized the threat. Eventually, they both stilled, and the man straddling him lowered his head and drew a few deep, steady breaths.

Dick stood where he was and watched with grim fascination. The knife was ready to attack should he need it again. He wondered what kind of madness he'd walked into. Outside the tent had exactly what he expected. Crazed fans, booze, and a party. Inside here was like walking into the Cirque de Freak while hopped up on mushrooms underneath a full moon.

The man glared at the horsemen. "You idiots. Why didn't you stop him?"

Spikes' eyes lowered.

Abigail answered. "You told us not to, remember? The last time he went ape-shit, you beat Spikes' ass nine times to Sunday. You said it was 'family business.' Don't go turning flavor now."

The man rose to his feet. He was in great shape. Dick could tell that from the back. His dark hair was coiffed and styled, a short beard decorated his face, and his skin held a copper tint—although that might have been the lights.

The man snapped his fingers at two people who had been dancing not long before and pointed at the unconscious man on the floor. Clegg flitted in through the canvas at the back of the tent and silently resumed his place on the couch. The two dancers gave a slight nod and wandered over, then unceremoniously took an arm each and dragged the man out of sight.

Boulder cast a fierce stare at Dick, while the others were more fixed on the man in front of him. The man strode a step toward Abigail. "That was when good ol' Spikes got carried away on LSD and thought that he was fighting off a dragon." Spikes' eyes lowered further. "Do I need to tweak my dialogue to allow you to do the right thing? Stay out of family business *unless* he's about to murder himself for the sake of fucking bravado!"

The last words were barked and exploded from the man's mouth. He fixed them each with a stare. The five horsemen knew better than to respond at this point. When he finished, he turned to Dick and finally acknowledged his existence.

"You the troublemaker who started this shit?"

Dick held a steady gaze. "Depends which perspective you're asking from."

The man's eyes narrowed. "I'm asking from the perspective of someone who wants to know what the fuck just happened."

"He started it, if that's what you mean," Dick replied.

The man studied him closely. Abigail called over his shoulder,

"He's telling the truth. Brandon started it. Came from out of nowhere."

"Nowhere?" Spikes scoffed. "Your boy called the forbidden name. Of course, it's going to set Brandon off."

The man's eyebrows raised. "You uttered his name?"

"Who?" Dick asked. "Sergei Petrov?"

Spikes put a hand over his eyes and shook his head.

The man advanced on Dick, who once more held his ground. He knew that this was a power play, and the last thing he would do was back down. Still, he sensed no real threat from this man whose eyes cast down to the blade in his hand.

The man's voice was a low grumble. If the music had been playing, Dick was certain he wouldn't have heard a single sylla-ble. "What's your business with Petrov?"

Dick could smell the man's cologne. There was no booze mixed in with this guy. While the others might live their life high on alcohol and narcotics, it seemed this guy was clean—on the surface, at least. "He has a bounty on my head. I need to track him and end the mark. I've heard that Hugo will know where I can find him."

A flicker of a smile appeared on the man's lips. "It takes a brave man to walk the death-marked road. Most run and hide, but not you. You seek the danger."

"I would hardly say I seek it," Dick replied. "My line of work pisses people off. It's a hazard of the duty."

The man was silent for a moment, and Dick wondered what was going on in his head. Finally, he took a step back and offered a hand.

Dick lowered the knife.

The man held his hand steady. "Any enemy of that STI-riddled fleabag is a friend of mine. It seems your journey hasn't been in vain."

"Hugo?" Dick knew the answer.

Hugo nodded.

"Dick Chambers," Dick offered while accepting Hugo's hand and shaking it.

Hugo raised an eyebrow.

"Yeah, I get that a lot," Dick commented. "Let's move past it."

Hugo let out a soft laugh. "Rad. Okay, Dick. How about me and you have a private conversation, away from the distractions of the party?"

"That's one way to label it," Dick replied.

Hugo turned to the others. "Keep the party going, won't you? That's one thing at least that I know you useless shits won't fuck up." He snapped his fingers, and the music started again. The dancers found their groove, and it was almost as if the party had never stopped.

Abigail's eyes trailed Dick to the back of the tent.

Hugo led Dick to a concealed entrance that led to a smaller attachment off the main canvas. The room was small. There was a double bed stationed in the far corner where three naked women lay strewn in some kind of haze. They hardly registered as Dick and Hugo walked in.

Hugo closed the entrance behind him, which blocked some of the music. "Ignore them," he instructed with a flourish of his hands. "A little late-night entertainment. You know what I'm talking about."

Dick kept his lips tight. Truly, he'd never quite gone as far as a four-way, but kudos to Hugo.

Hugo spun and flopped into a large bean bag in the other corner of the room. He offered Dick a seat in the one beside him, but Dick was reluctant to sit.

Hugo picked up the remains of a joint from a small table and placed it between his lips. "Suit yourself." He took a long drag. "Talk to me, Dick Chambers. Tell me what you want to know."

"The first thing I want to know is what the hell happened back there. Your boy almost killed himself at the end of his blade."

Hugo nodded empathetically. Although Dick had seen his tough side, there was something soothing about his presence. Dick had stood before murderers, rapists, and low-life scum before, and somehow Hugo didn't set off any of those internal alarms.

"Brandon's my brother. Fiercely loyal. Incredibly stupid. Our parents passed away some years ago, and ever since then he's been on a general downward slope."

"He seemed almost...feral." Dick tried to be careful with his word choice. "Is he okay?"

"Not really. I mean, he was on the decline a long time ago, hitting mushrooms, LSD, heroin, anything he could to try to numb the pain of our parents passing. I thought he was a mess way back then, but it wasn't until he started getting involved in the bad sort that things went from bad to worse."

Dick stayed silent, not wanting to disrupt Hugo from his tale. The women on the bed shifted and snored, their skin glistening in the light of a single candle-lit lantern.

"Petrov is a bad man," Hugo declared. "I don't say that lightly. I know that every group has their dark sides, but Petrov sure showed his when we ran together. He was once like another brother to Brandon and me. When we first started racing and forming this shit, we were close. Inseparable. He was my crutch to lean on when things with Brandon got heavy. He put himself out there, grew closer to Brandon too, and for a while it looked as though things were helping. He was the glue to unite us and make us stronger."

Hugo took another drag, and his eyes grew dark. "But then things changed. Petrov got wind of this new trending drug everyone was trying. Figured it could be our biggest money-maker if we jumped on the bandwagon early. We could finance our racing habit and get the latest rims and accessories with cash to spare. The way he saw it, we'd be rich enough to pay off the

Feds. We'd run the town. Atlantica would be our playground, and all we had to do was invest."

"Ink…" Dick muttered.

Hugo nodded. "He pushed it. Hard. A mention of that fucking thing punctuated every conversation. I held back. I didn't want to hop up on drugs. I wanted to race and have a good time. Don't get me wrong, I've dabbled in narcotics, but ink was untested. It was new. I've seen what new shit can do to people, y'know? People injecting unclean doses of horse steroids and eating shit in stupid quantities. It fucks people up."

Hugo's attention drifted away. His eyes unfocused as he stared at the floor, lost in a memory.

"What happened next?" Dick nudged him although he had a pretty good idea. This story wasn't the first of its kind, and the one guarantee he held was that it wouldn't be the last.

"Petrov hooked Brandon in," Hugo replied. "That was the beginnings of the cracks in our foundation. I learned that Petrov was tempting my brother, trying to get him fixed. I don't know if it was a strategy to infiltrate the Devils, or if Brandon was more complicit than I'd like to think, but I found them both injecting that shit and floating on cloud nine. When Sergei sobered, I told him to get the fuck out. Our friendship ended there and then, but he took Brandon with him. Brandon became a mule for his ink scheme, and together they made a fair bit of coin."

Dick's brow furrowed. "But paradise is a fleeting mirage."

"You got that right." Hugo rested his head against the canvas wall. "I found my baby brother a year later, lying flat in the middle of the road. He was unconscious, spread out for anyone to collide with. I still believe to this day that Petrov planned for me to hit him. He knew our routes, knew our timetable. There's no coincidence there.

"I took him to the hospital. We got him cleaned up. He's never quite been the same since. He's better, don't get me wrong. But he flips out at the mention of Petrov's name. That's why we forbid it here. Some things aren't worth bringing up again."

The music played in the other room. The world outside continued partying, but it didn't lift the somber tone inside. Hugo took another drag, then looked up at Dick. "What does Petrov have on you?"

"Nothing. No motive other than I've been digging through something better left unfound, and now he's after me. I don't know whether he's the main dog or a loyal pup, but he's my next stepping stone to getting the answers I want."

Hugo's eyes lowered to Dick's bandaged wrists. "You know how to handle yourself. Anyone else, I might be unwilling to help them, but given your pedigree, you may be able to get what you're after." He rubbed a hand down his face and sighed. "He won't be easy. I'll tell you that. We reached a compromise with our territories, but Petrov is always hungry for more. You want him? You poke a hornet's nest."

"If that's what it takes," Dick stated.

Hugo laughed. He reached into a cooler and tossed Dick a beer. "Here. Sit with me a while, and I'll give you what you need to know. Maybe after we can tag team these gals and make a night of it."

"The beer will do just fine." Dick moved beside Hugo and sat. "Just tell me whatever you can so that I can remove the target from my back."

CHAPTER SEVENTEEN

"You need a ride?" Hugo asked as they finally exited the tent sometime later. All eyes of those along the beach turned to Hugo as people put a hand over their mouths and muttered to each other as if they couldn't believe that the boss of the whole operation had left the tent.

"I'll be okay." Dick held back from adding, "I don't live too far from here."

Dawn was breaking. The sky was lightening, and the festivities were muting somewhat. Although the shoreline still accommodated many, the party was tapering off. Dick was impressed by how little rubbish was strewn along the sand, and spotted a couple of lowly grunts going around and cleaning up after everyone.

"Strange night," Dick stated.

"Strange life," Hugo agreed. "Look, Dick. If you ever need anything from us, just let me know, okay? Petrov is bad blood, but loyalty and honor go a long way. I don't want to see you hurt under his hand, especially in the same way my brother was."

Dick nodded and offered a smile. "Appreciate that."

Dick made his way along the sand and up to the grassy divide between the beach and the city proper. He could make out the abandoned factories where his temporary home resided in the distance. While every part of him wanted to head straight back there, he knew better than to lead anyone following straight to his hiding place.

The detour took him on a three-mile circuit before he eventually snuck back to the entry. He cast a glance over his shoulder and waited until he was satisfied that no one was watching before he unlocked the door and made his way to the bunker.

The silence rang in his ears. He couldn't quite believe the night he'd had. His fists ached, his throat was dry and more than anything he wanted to hop into the shower, scrub down, then sleep.

Which is exactly what he did.

Gillian was having the best night's sleep she'd ever had when a clattering in the apartment disturbed her dreams.

The money Dick had given her stretched her imagination—a wad of cash so large that for a while, she had no idea what to do with it all. She was born into Atlantica and supported by wealthy parents until she was of an age to fend for herself. She had no tuition bills to speak of and no loans or debts, but she knew that her parents' business had affiliations with bad people and she didn't want to be part of that. She emancipated herself completely, then wandered around the city with big dreams of what she could be and the changes she could make.

But money bought power, and she had little to speak of.

She'd worked a dozen part-time jobs in her life, and the clerk position at Chuck's pharmacy was well within her wheelhouse of skills. She accepted the job eagerly, despite the eccentric old bag giving her bad vibes, and took her paychecks as they came.

While working away at the counter, she dreamed of what to

do if she came into money. If her parents offered her a lump sum, she always wondered if she would take it. Would there be strings attached? Was it blood money? How would this affect her down the line?

She had never once imagined that someone like Dick Chambers would hand her a wad of cash. Even when flicking through the crisp notes, it took her a while to fully believe that what she held was hers. After she'd steadied her shaking hands and returned to her apartment, the first thing she did was order a new bed. Her old one was leftover from the previous tenant, and there were some questionable stains she couldn't get out. Springs prodded her back, and her back had begun to hurt.

The new bed was heaven. It was delivered the same day since an extra injection of cash could persuade any company to go above their usual conditions, and she couldn't wait to sleep that night. While Chuck may have fired her ass—with good reason, too—the money would last her while she hunted for her next port of call in life. Where that road would lead, she had no idea.

The clattering came to her at first woven within the fabric of the dream itself. In the Land of Nod, she was riding a horse through the meadows, a far stretch away from the urban city of Atlantica. She had always dreamed of owning a horse, riding out in the open, and in the dream, wind flew through her hair as she encouraged the chestnut mare into a gallop and leaped across streams and creeks. The sun warmed her skin, and the air was fresh, sunlight dappled the…

The ground shook beneath her. It was gentle at first, but enough to knock the horse off-kilter. It tried to rebalance, but another groundswell toppled it sideways. Gillian held on for dear life, but there was nothing she could do. She skittered across the ground as the sky darkened and another tremor caused her to flinch. She gripped her knee in pain, tried to sit up, and…

The man was on top of her.

She snapped open her eyes, aware of the heavy weight

pinning her to her bed. He locked her arms to her sides, the duvet covering up to her neck as he leered down at her. The darkness of the room hid most of his features except that dark glint in his eye.

He held a knife inches from her throat.

"If you so much as try to scream, I'll stain your pretty new bed with red sauce." The man's voice was a low grumble, each word spilling out a slight hint of halitosis. "Do you understand?"

Gillian nodded and bit her lip to keep her silence.

"You know Dick Chambers, don't you?" There was intelligence in the man's voice, but still she lied.

She shook her head.

The man chuckled although there was no humor in it. "Don't lie to me, precious. Your employer sold you out. Strange man to pick to defend your honor. How does that relationship work? Does he diddle you after hours?"

Gillian remained still, eyes wide, all thoughts of the horse and fields gone.

"Where is he?" the man asked.

She whimpered. "I don't know."

He shuffled closer to her, the weight of him constricting her breathing. "Oh, but you do. You drove away with him not that long ago, didn't you? Where did you take him? I've already fingerprinted your car, sweetheart. I know he was there."

She couldn't tell if he was lying or not. How would it be possible to break into her car and fingerprint in such a short amount of time? Then again, how had he broken into her apartment and managed to climb her without waking her up?

"Uptown," she replied.

"Be more specific, darling," the man crooned. "Before my knife finds a way to be more persuasive than me."

Gillian gulped. She liked Dick. She truly did. The man had given her a chance to escape and the means to improve her life. She didn't want to sell him out to this psychopath.

"East and Tenth."

The man sat back a little, which eased the pressure around her waist. "You must think I'm stupid."

She shook her head as a tear rolled down her cheek.

He examined the knife theatrically. "I've been in this business a long time, Gillian. I know when people are lying. I've seen it all. I know the signs. My buddies in the business once called me the human polygraph because I'm accurate. You try lying to me again, and I'll have to start accepting flesh payments."

"You wouldn't," Gillian breathed.

He held her stare, a cold glint in those eyes.

Gillian let out a weak sob. "East and Third."

"That's better," the man declared, returning his weight and leaning closer to her. "Why there?"

She opened her mouth, but he stopped her talking with a wag of the finger. "No lies, remember."

Gillian closed her eyes and told the man what she knew. It wasn't much, but she was almost certain that it would be enough for him. Dick had told her only the briefest of snippets about his location, citing something about some kind of Devils. While the man pressed her for more information, she was thankful that he accepted the rest of her tale as gospel. She hated herself as she told him what she knew, but what choice did she have? In this city, in your home, anything goes. She could be dead for days before anyone in the surrounding apartments began to sniff the decomposition.

The man sat back once more, seemingly satisfied. He pocketed his knife and fished the other hand into his pocket. "Thank you for your cooperation. For the purposes of my escape, you're going to give me a head start before you begin screaming, okay?"

Gillian raised an eyebrow. "What?"

The man laughed, this time with a hint of mirth. He drew a white rag from his pocket and pressed it against her mouth. The smell was strange but not awful. She instantly knew what it was.

She had watched films where chloroform was used to knock someone out almost immediately.

Her head hit the softness of her pillow, the feathery sheets combined with the encroaching darkness and cuddled her, and soon she was back in the land of dreams, riding a chestnut mare...

Only this time she ran from a feral wolf with a dark glint in its black, beady eyes.

CHAPTER EIGHTEEN

Dick helped himself to dry toast and coffee in a little diner a few miles from home.

The one good thing that had come from laying low was that he was exploring a part of the city he had rarely frequented. Before, he had only driven through this part of town, but now he was growing familiar with the vibrant rows of small stores and the selection of family-run diners. It seemed that no matter which city you lived in, there was a certain pride in the local businesses, as well as the conglomerates. Dive in the ocean, and you'll rarely see a shark without the suckerfish eating the scraps off its stomach.

The diner's menu was expansive yet underwhelming, but the toast was good. The black coffee perked him up a little, but it didn't do much to soften the throbbing pain in his hands. The waitress's eyes lingered on the bandages that Dick hadn't yet gotten around to cleaning. A judgmental look came over her. Dick offered his best smile. "You should have seen the other guy."

The waitress took his order on a small tablet without another word and left.

Dick sat in the corner of the diner for some time, his notepad in front of him as he worked to assess all that he knew. As much as he tried to clean up the messes made along the way, the case kept growing messier.

He had recovered the pendant for Santana.

Check.

There was still a mystery surrounding Sadie Turnberry.

Sergei Petrov's prints were all over the note found in his apartment, but he had yet to uncover his motive or how this linked with Sadie Turnberry.

And, if that weren't enough, a name still floated somewhere in the ether. Dexter Lockhart, an identity leaked by a Russian attacker, and signed on a note?

Who the hell was this?

How were they connected?

How far would Dick have to take this before he got his answers?

He sketched some notes on the pad while trying to determine the connection. The only commonality that ran through all of them was a connection with Russians. He had encountered a Russian family when he confronted the Guardian. Sadie used Russians to attack Dick. Sergei was Russian. Even the goddamn pawn shop was filled with Russians.

Somehow, there was something bigger afoot. Dick wished he knew what the hell it was.

"Sergei is the key," he muttered to himself, totally unconvinced.

A soft voice replied, "Men are always the answer. I knew you'd come to our side of the table."

Dick laughed softly and looked up from his pad. Valentina sat across from him, her scarlet hair cropped by her shoulders and matching her lipstick. She wore no hat this time, placing it comfortably on her lap instead. A few heads were turned and staring at her back as she grinned smugly. "Hello, Dick."

"Are you sure you should be out in public?" Dick asked. "Aren't there a dozen people with targets on your back?"

"If there were, they'd already be dead. Besides, I'm not here for the long haul. I'm only here to play the delivery girl." She handed over a clean white envelope.

"You're now a postal worker?" Dick laughed.

Valentina shrugged. "The price was right. Turns out your lady friend and I crossed paths. She wanted to wish you thanks, but rumor has it that you're in hiding and wouldn't appreciate a direct call."

"I am," Dick replied.

"And doing a stellar job of it," Valentina mocked. "Took me less than an hour to find you."

Dick's eyebrow raised. If Valentina had found him so quickly, had he truly been as careful as he believed? What if someone else was on his trail right now, hunting for him? Could he afford to sit around in a diner for hours if it were that easy?

"How *did* you find me?" Dick replied. "Bank statements? Call logs?"

Valentina shook her head and chuckled, the sound of it musical. "Remember that I'm the one who fixed your cell."

"You're tracking me?" Dick wasn't surprised.

"Not for any malicious cause." Valentina leaned across the table. Her perfume wafted toward Dick and brought him back to their nights together. "It behooves me to know where my booty call is if I ever need him."

Dick tore his eyes away and opened the envelope. Inside was a blank piece of paper.

"Code?" he asked.

Valentina smirked. "Nope. Just fun for me. Her message is oral since we couldn't afford to write anything down. She suspects that you have a dog on your tail that you can't shake off, and she didn't want to put you in harm's reach. Sweet girl. Tells me you like her ass."

"I do," Dick replied simply.

Valentina pouted. "I hope she's not my competition. You know what I do to those who get in my way."

Dick did. He didn't need to say it. "What's the message?"

Valentina leaned back in the booth. "You're no fun. She wanted to extend her thanks again for helping her recover the pendant, but she also wanted to warn you. She found signs of someone trying to enter her apartment when she was absent. Some of her traps were triggered—can you believe how paranoid that girl is?"

Dick sipped his coffee. "With good cause, it seems."

"Anyway," Valentina continued, waving away a waitress who looked set to come over and take her order. "She says to be careful. Someone's onto you both. They want that pendant, and they're not happy that it's gone."

"Where is Santana now?" Dick asked.

"I can't tell you that." Valentina grinned. "Lady's promise. All I can say is that she's safe in the place she feels most at home."

"The jungle?" Dick nudged.

Valentina rose from the booth and placed her hat on her head. "See you around, Mr. Chambers. Let me know when you're safe back in your home. It's strange seeing it so empty."

She leaned over the table and grabbed Dick's collar and pulled him in for a passionate kiss. Her lipstick smeared across his lips. When she pulled away, that grin was still on her face. "See you around, Dick."

Dick sat back in his chair, his heart thumping fast. He touched his lip and felt the sticky residue of her lipstick. Using a napkin to wipe, he removed the makeup as several heads stared his way, a mixture of envy and disgust on their faces.

Dick returned his attention to the notepad and circled "Sergei Petrov." Hugo Evans had been instrumental in providing him a location that he was almost certain no one else would know. As much of a risk as it was, Dick felt the excitement coursing through his veins. If he could play this right, he'd have Sergei in his clutches by midnight.

And then wouldn't the game be a little easier to play?

On the way back to his bunker, Dick stopped by a nearby pharmacist and purchased some medical supplies to tend to his wounds. Although the worst of it was over, there were still a few cuts bothering him, so he made a point to stock up on iodine and bandages.

That afternoon, Dick spent his time recovering underground. He sat on the couch and cleaned his hands while wincing slightly at the sting the iodine brought. He wrapped the bandages like combat wraps and ensured that they were tightly bound to finish.

He napped on the sofa while letting his subconscious percolate on his action plan for that night. According to Hugo, Petrov liked to hit the cathouse religiously on Thursday evenings. It was a pastime that he and Hugo used to share weekly, the one time of the week that Petrov put aside any notions of his drug lord schemes as he submitted to his primal desires and watched the ladies dance.

It was a long shot, but it was something.

The Pink Flamingo was located on the other side of Atlantica. There was nothing particularly showy or special about it that Dick could determine from his research, but that didn't put his guard down. As he woke from his nap and prepared to take to the streets, he made a mental map of his journey there and wondered if he could call in a favor to get him across town.

Hugo answered on the third ring, his voice groggy as if Dick had woken him up. "Hugo, can I take you up on that offer last night?"

"You're going *now*?" Hugo replied. "It doesn't open for another few hours."

"Doesn't bother me none. I'm early to the party." Dick grinned.

Hugo grunted. "I hate people like you."

Fifteen minutes later, a car parked curbside and met Dick at the street near the industrial estate. Dick hopped in the supercharged vehicle, surprised to find Maurine in the driver's seat with her hair tied back in a ponytail and a smile on her face.

"Surprised to see me?" Maurine asked.

Dick shook his head. "Nothing surprises me anymore."

"Oh, I'm sure that's not true," Maurine replied. "Even a man of your constitution must find things in their life that make this all new and exciting." She grinned as she pressed hard on the gas and the car sped onto the street. "Heard you caused quite the ruckus with the horsemen last night."

Dick stared out the window, the city blurring by. Although there was a steady stream of traffic on the road, Maurine handled it with the precision of a champion, carving out into small gaps and hitting the lights a moment before they flicked to red.

"I would've thought that would all be under wraps," Dick replied. "I'd imagine that your horsemen wouldn't want the truth of the show to leak to the lowly grunts."

Maurine playfully slapped Dick's thigh. "Do you still know nothing of the Devils? Despite all you went through last night?" She shifted gears as the engine *thrummed*. "You're right, though. Most people are oblivious to it all. Still, I'm high enough in their ranks to earn some respect from people in the borders of the group. I know things. That's all I'll say on the matter."

Dick gave a soft laugh. "That how you managed to communicate to the gang about my profession ahead of me arriving at that tent?"

Maurine laughed, the sound alluring to Dick. She was incredibly pretty, although her features were hardened from a tougher life, there was something attractive about her that he couldn't quite place. Chemistry lingered in the air. He felt as though she were the kind of lady he could sit and share a beer with.

"I can't share my secrets, Dick," she replied. "You know that. Isn't your whole profession secrecy?"

"It is." Dick rested his head back.

"Still," Maurine continued. "I've never seen anyone do what you did back there. Make it through the hoops and come out on the other side in one piece. Moreover, to get the information from the big guy and have him set you free without conditions? That takes something tough. What do you have on him?"

They paused at a set of stoplights. Dick's eyes narrowed on a couple standing on the sidewalk, both parties growing more irate as some argument ensued. The man grabbed the woman's hair, and bystanders ran to her aid. As the first punch was thrown, the car drove away.

"Dick?" Maurine nudged.

Dick drew a deep breath. "Petrov."

Something dark fell over Maurine's face. A cloud hung over her. "You're serious?"

"I am."

They sat awhile in quiet, Maurine navigating the roads with ease. Dick recognized a few of the streets they passed down, but Maurine knew a way that he didn't. He became aware of the lingering silence in the car as a thought struck him.

"No music?" Dick asked. "I thought you guys were all about your sound systems and booming bass?"

"The engine roar is my music," Maurine replied, eyes fixed on the road. After a beat she turned to Dick, eyes laced with concern. "You really going to do this?"

"You doubt me?" Dick asked.

Maurine stoically shook her head. "Not really. No." She sighed. "Petrov is bad news, Dick. Whatever you have planned, you need to be careful. Petrov is the dark stain we can't remove from the Devils. We're not allowed to utter his name at meetings, for God's sake. He may be the very reason we have 'Devil' in our name."

"Maybe you should change it," Dick suggested.

Maurine's face broke into a smile, despite her best efforts to stop it. She slowed the car as she pulled onto a quiet back street. The car stopped, and the engine died.

They sat in the car for a minute in silence, stationed on the very border between the east and west sides of the island. Dick could tell that Maurine wanted to say something, but she couldn't find the words.

"I'll be careful," Dick assured her, surprised by how much he cared about this woman's opinion of him. He had only met her last night, but she was clearly concerned for his safety.

She turned in her seat, the bare flesh of her knees touching his leg. "Petrov is a bold motherfucker. Every month, he tries to push the boundaries of our turf agreement, and every month, one of ours gets hurt. He's never satisfied, and that's a dangerous man who'll do whatever it takes to get more and more until he dominates and has what he wants." She looked down at her hands. "The Devils are about community. Petrov and his guys are about power. You go in there and make one wrong move, and it's all over."

Dick raised an eyebrow. "And yet you have wannabe recruits fist-fighting in pits. I'm fairly sure you're not as morally clean as you think you are."

Maurine laid a hand on his thigh, face solemn. "Take care, Dick. I mean that."

Dick rested a hand on hers, then climbed out of the car. He slid his hands into his pockets and felt the first chill of night as the car sped away, gone before Dick could make it to the next corner.

Dick checked the time on his phone and was pleased to see that he had a couple of hours to spare. Across the road was a large green, bordered by a painted metal fence. The gate was still open, despite the late hour, and Dick decided to take a detour through the neatly curated park as he headed closer to his destination.

In the daylight—what little there was in Atlantica—the park might have been nice. The shrubs and hedges were manicured, the path was free of weeds, and a few koi ponds dotted the green.

In the night time, however, the darkness pressed in on Dick. The lights had extinguished, and Dick wondered why the gates were open if the lights had timed out and no one was welcome inside.

Dick passed a bench and almost didn't see the homeless man lying on it. As he neared, the homeless man sat up and shook a polystyrene cup that rattled with change.

"Please. Any change?" he crooned.

Dick threw a note into the cup and continued walking, hands in his pockets. The pistol lent a satisfying weight to his hip as he made for the gate at the end of the park.

There was no thank you from the old man, just a surprised and overwhelmed gasp as he discovered the note. Dick wasn't sure how much it would have been worth, having not looked at it as he threw it inside, but somehow he knew it would make the man's day—well, either that or become the currency needed to buy the man drugs and booze.

He was almost at the gate to exit when he sensed someone behind him. Dick turned and found the homeless man ten feet away, clutching the note in his hands. He extended it toward Dick. "Please, sir. It's far too much."

Dick didn't know what to say. He had never encountered this situation before. Most vagrants eagerly accepted whatever they were given and that was the end of it.

"It's fine. Honestly. It's yours."

The man's face was kind. He could make out the gentle wrinkles lining his forehead and eyes in the limited light from the streetlights beyond the gate. His beard was thick and wiry, and his face grubby. He wore a low beanie and a thick, tattered jacket. "No. Please. I couldn't." He advanced and pressed the note against Dick's chest.

Dick pushed the hand away. "Keep it. I don't need it."

Something changed in the man's eyes. Without a word, he reached for Dick's pocket and shoved the note roughly inside.

"Stop," Dick warned. "That's enough."

The man shoved his hand deeper into the pocket, and now Dick understood why. His grubby fingers clawed for the rest of the change, struggling to free the other notes from his pocket as a greedy expression washed over his face.

Dick fought against him, but the man was relentless. After a minute or so, Dick drew the pistol and pressed it against his stomach. "Back the fuck up. Take what I gave you, or you'll find yourself with a hole in your belly."

He wasn't serious, of course. The last thing Dick wanted was to kill a man on the streets in cold blood, but he hoped the man would listen.

The man did.

Dick took a step back toward the gate, gun trained on the man. The vagrant held his hands up and lowered his eyes to the ground, apologies slurring from his lips. Dick kept his eyes fixed on him, ready for any sudden movements.

Which was when the others came out of the bushes.

CHAPTER NINETEEN

Their telltale rustle alerted Dick way before they leaped, but there were too many of them to counter all at once.

Reacting quickly, Dick holstered the gun and readied his fists. Two vagrants jumped out, approaching from either side of him, leaving behind their cover in the bushes. Dick realized his mistake in offering even a little charity to this man sitting in the dark who now grinned and beelined once more for his pockets.

Dick threw an elbow to his left and caught a woman in the chin. In the brief flash of a turn, he could make out a series of missing teeth and hair that was pulled back in an untidy nest. The vagrant on his right bowled into him and almost knocked him off-balance, but Dick managed to stumble and remain upright.

"You don't want to do this," Dick warned as he took note of the pond a few feet behind him. It was almost impossible to make out in the dark, but the faintest of lights rippled on its surface as a bird took wing and disturbed the water.

The vagrant who bowled into him wrapped his arms around Dick and tried to fish his hands into his pocket. Dick held his wrists and wrestled him away as best he could, but the first vagrant was on the attack, too.

Before he could stop him, the vagrant ripped his hand away triumphantly, notes spilling into the air and floating like leaves, a few landing on the pond's surface.

The female vagrant rose from her knockdown and came at Dick, falling to her feet as she scrambled to pick up the cash. Dick freed himself from the vagrant holding his arms around his waist and slipped free. Distracted by the sudden swell of money flying around them, the first vagrant didn't see Dick coming as he snatched a handful of notes from his palms and stuffed them into his inside pockets.

"You want what's fallen? You can have it," Dick exclaimed, his hands growing sore from the sudden fray. "But remember, warmth beats money any day of the week."

He flicked the wheel of his lighter and touched the flame to the notes on the ground. There were enough strewn among the dry grass that the money caught alight without problem. The embers flared and grew. Two of the vagrants were too busy snatching up loose notes that they didn't see what was happening until a small fire had broken out. The grass around the notes caught flame, and before long they were stamping their bare feet on the fire, doing their best to stop the spread and save the money.

Dick peeled away from the group and watched from the gate, ensuring that they had at least some control of the flames before he disappeared. He didn't want to be the cause of a park's destruction, but it was worth teaching them a lesson. They could keep the money they had. He had no issue with that. Dick wanted to make it clear that the vagrants should know better than to take more than offered.

It was a lesson that might serve them well down the line.

One of the male vagrants gave a final stamp of the fire while the other splashed pond water on the dying embers, and then it was over. They gathered up the remaining notes while Dick slipped away.

The porterhouse steak was exactly what was needed. Dick dabbed the napkin on his lips, sated from the hearty meal. It was rare that he blew money on extravagance, but given the last week or so, he felt he needed it. The protein would heal his tired muscles. The vegetables would pep him up and help heal his wounds and cuts.

The roasted potatoes were to satisfy his tastebuds.

He nursed a tumbler of whisky as the waiter removed his plate. The restaurant was near empty as it drew near their closing time. Dick managed to catch the kitchen at the right moment and put in his order, the encounter with the vagrants stirring up a hunger he hadn't felt in some time.

All too soon, the restaurant staff politely informed Dick it was time to close. Dick obliged and offered a very generous tip before spilling back into the street.

The Pink Flamingo was around the corner. Dick spied the animated neon sign of the flamingo dipping its head in a pool of cash from three blocks away. Outside of the club were security staff, and a modest line of gentlemen in an array of suits and shirts.

Dick drew a long breath of the cold night and found his spot at the back of the line. The line moved quickly, and before long he faced the security guards.

They eyed him with learned scrutiny. Dick understood why. His appearance was hardly what people would consider "trust-worthy." His high collar hid his neck, and his unkempt stubble and long dark jacket fixed him with all the attributes of someone who had something to hide.

"Identification?" a gruff bald ape of a man ordered.

Dick opened his jacket pocket and showed his ID. The ape's eyes flicked back and forth from the ID to Dick, who waited patiently before the guard confirmed, "Inside. Up the stairs."

Dick thanked him with a nod and passed through the double doors.

The air was thick with the scent of stale booze and perfume. He climbed two sets of stairs before he came to a desk where a male clerk, who looked like he'd be more at home in his parents' basement, requested the $20 entry fee. His eyebrows raised when Dick paid in cash. As Dick continued onward, he scanned the wide-open room ahead, trying to get his bearings.

The place was expansive. Lights flashed through thick reams of fog, disco balls glittered, and silhouetted around many podiums and poles around the room were the forms of dancing women. Dick couldn't see more than fifteen feet ahead with clarity, the whole place designed to mystify, confuse, and allure drunken clients, making them more at ease to throw their dollars at the ladies.

Dick wandered over to a bar at the far corner, the only part of the club that had another bright light pointing to its whereabouts. Three men sat on stools along the front of the counter, sipping from drinks, their eyes fixed on the entertainment.

"House whisky," Dick requested.

The man working behind the bar nodded and came back a moment later with Dick's drink. Dick paid up and leaned over the counter. "You'd have thought that operations like this would have been extinct long ago. Aren't we past the point of objectifying women?"

"I'm not," the nearest man to Dick exclaimed, a throaty laugh following. "I could live in this place."

The barman gave a wry grin. "Whatever your opinion, dude, the ladies choose to work here. Working conditions are greater than they've ever been, and hey, if customers pay, the entertainment continues. Ain't no law that says a person can't choose their profession."

Dick considered this, supposing it was true. He had never been the type to frequent a place like this, but most of the people he chased and investigated had certainly dabbled in throwing their cash at the eager ladies.

Dick took an empty barstool and spun around to face the room, his elbows resting behind him on the bar. He let his eyes roam the faces of the customers in the place, trying to gauge whether or not Petrov was present. It was tricky, having seen only a couple of low-res images of Petrov on the net. The man certainly liked to keep his identity hidden.

The man who had spoken earlier leaned over to Dick. "First time?"

"You could say that," Dick replied. He didn't want to engage the man, but what choice was there?

"I come here every Friday night," the man bragged. "It's a ritual of mine. Some people go to the pub. Others go away for the weekend. Me? I couldn't think of anything better than this."

A woman in a revealing negligee walked by with a tray of drinks. She smiled at the man. "Hey Marvin, good to see you."

"Great to see you, Crystal." As Crystal left, he cast a smug grin at Dick. "See? I'm like family here."

I hope you don't perv on your family the way you're perving on these girls.

Marvin chatted idly to Dick, appreciating having someone with whom to brag about his familiarity with the club and its ladies, while Dick focused on the job at hand. After twenty minutes, Dick finished his drink, then ordered another. He took the glass, then said goodbye to Marvin as he found somewhere a little quieter to sit in the club.

He used his peripheral vision to monitor the clientele as he crossed the room. He didn't want to draw attention to himself by obviously searching for Petrov. He found a small rounded booth at the back of the club and took a seat. The plush leather backing was taller than his eye line and blocked those in the adjacent booths from view.

In front was one of the stages, a half dozen or so gentlemen sitting nearby, eyes unblinking on the dark-haired woman gyrating to the music. She used the pole as though it were more than a prop, making it a part of the wonder as she performed feats of acrobatics that Dick couldn't dream of accomplishing himself.

He was staring at the back of a thin man's bald head when someone sat beside him.

Dick smelled the perfume before he got a full look at the half-naked woman. There was glitter around her eyes, and she leaned in closely to Dick, her voice soft and purring. "Hey handsome, care for a dance?"

Dick sipped his drink, holding his gaze steadily ahead. The thin man was with three other gents, but it was difficult to get a good view of them. There was something about him, though...

"I'll give you the first for $50," the woman continued, undeterred by Dick's lack of interest. "House special. I'll have you coming back for more."

Dick looked her in the eye. She was only a foot away from him, a coy smile on her lips. She was conventionally attractive, and under different circumstances, might have tempted Dick. But knowing what was at stake in this case, and understanding this profession's hypnotic nature, he kept the temptations at bay.

Still, he didn't want to hurt her feelings.

"That's what I'm afraid of," Dick replied smoothly. "You're the gateway drug, right?"

The woman giggled and got comfortable beside him. She nestled up until her skin touched his as she rested hands on his shoulder. "You're cute. Tell you what, I'll do $45."

Dick offered a polite grin. "I'll give you $100 if you can answer a question for me, no dance involved."

The woman pouted. "No fun." However, when Dick presented a $100 bill, her eyes lit up. "What can Honey do for you?"

"I'm looking for someone." Dick's eyes returned to the wider room. The gentlemen in front laughed and punched each other's arms as the woman crawled for the notes they threw.

All except the bald man.

"We're all looking for someone, sweetie," Honey cooed. "Half the reason this place gets full is people are looking for that little bit of company. Someone to make them feel special. It's what we do."

"A name," Dick replied flatly. "I have a name. Does Sergei Petrov ring a bell to you?"

Honey fanned her face with one hand, her lips close to Dick's ear. "Can't say it rings any bells. We get a lot of men passing through here, a lot of women too. You'll have to be more specific."

"Russian," Dick stated.

Honey chuckled. "Narrows it down to thirty percent of our clientele. Atlantica doesn't discriminate, but the Russians certainly are a lot more memorable. Pockets that are never empty and faces that don't crack. I tell you, every dance I give to a Russian, it's like performing for a statue. Hard to forget a Russian, easy to forget the face."

It was Dick's turn to break a smile. "You're bordering on racism."

"Just stating facts." Honey's eyes moved to a man standing against the far wall and tapping his watch. She rested her head on Dick's shoulder and placed a hand on his thigh. Warmth involuntarily spread toward the area she touched. "You sure I can't offer you that dance, sweetie? I've yet to find a man I can't please."

"Try pleasing a Russian." Dick sipped his drink. "Help me out here. How many Russians have you seen in here tonight?"

"A couple of dozen." She waved a hand. "A few regulars and a handful of new faces. Honestly, Atlantica seems to have no end of new people coming in. We have our regulars, sure. But every night it's—"

Dick interrupted her. "Are any of those regulars here?"

She glanced down at Dick's crotch. "You got something for me?"

Dick handed her another $100 bill. "Will that do?"

Honey smiled and pointed as she explained, "Stage four, there is a group of ten. One of theirs is a pretty regular client. Stage six has two regulars. They're old and creepy, but neither are Russian like the man you're looking for. Stage eight has one, and there's one over there, and of course," she pointed at the stage in front of Dick. "There's a party there with one regular. If you gave me a description or something, I could be more useful."

"I've never seen him," Dick answered truthfully.

The woman frowned. "Seems like a strange setup. You ain't here to cause a fuss, are you? These guys bring great income. I don't want to be the one messing that up for nobody."

Dick turned to her, and their eyes met. The perfume was overwhelming as it invaded his senses. Artificially created smoke hazed the air, and his heart thumped double speed. The way she looked at him made him believe that he could reach out and kiss her, that she was genuinely interested in him. The ladies in this room, they were the true actors of the world. Those who could convince a guy to fall in love, raid their wallets, then break their hearts.

"I'm not here to cause problems. Just to find a guy."

The woman laughed as her eyes lowered. "That's not a phrase I hear every night in here." She rose and took her perfume cloud with her. "If you want ladies night, it's on Wednesdays. I can see that you have other things occupying your mind, so goodnight, darling. Let me know if that wallet stretches open enough to earn my attention."

The music reached the end of the song and a moment of silence kicked in as the dancers finished their routine. A few of them led excited gentlemen by the hands to a private doorway at the back. As the music kicked in again, the bald man silently rose to his feet and left his group behind, making a beeline for the men's restroom.

Dick made a quick decision and followed him. He walked casually, trying not to draw attention to himself. The bathroom was dully lit by a single faded strip light lining the ceiling. Apart from one man at the urinal, there was no one in sight. Two of the cubicles were taken.

Dick took a spare urinal and relieved himself, and kept his ears open as the man beside him left, and one of the cubicles emptied.

Neither man washed their hands. Dick's lip curled.

When the other cubicle door opened, Dick continued staring at the wall. A poster hung in front, mounted in a silver frame. He could dimly make out the unclear reflection of the bald man behind him, washing his hands at the sink.

At least someone in this joint gives a shit about hygiene.

The man dried his hands and made for the exit. The door swung open and closed. A lock softly clicked.

Dick's ears pricked up. Had someone else entered or exited a cubicle? He zipped himself up and crossed to the sink. He turned the tap and washed his hands as the bald man stood with his back to the door, staring directly at him.

Dick kept his gaze on his hands, holding his nerve as he waited for the man to make some kind of move. Had Dick been that obvious that he was following him?

After clearing the suds from his hands, Dick made for the hand dryer, and a flurry of noise filled the restroom. Dick kept his wits about him, wondering if the man would use that moment of noise to sneak up and attack. To his surprise, when he turned, the man still stood there.

Dick rubbed his hands. "It's $500 for that kind of action, pal.

You want something cheaper; I'm sure the ladies will help you out."

The man fixed him with a studious gaze, not a single drop of emotion shown. His bald head caught the glow of the strip light. He wore a three-piece suit in a shade of navy. His face was clean-shaven, and there was a wary intelligence in his eyes, which Dick noticed were two different colors—one green, one brown.

Someone tried the door handle. A muffled sound of frustration came from the other side before the person slipped away.

"You're a brave man, Mr. Chambers," the man offered at last. His voice was soft and unthreatening, but his gaze made up for that.

"You don't make it very far in this business without showing a sign of bravery," Dick replied. "Few people can do what I do. Even fewer do it as well."

The man didn't blink, simply stared. "The game you're playing...you don't want to know how it ends. There are many roadblocks along the path you're treading, and there are few places to jump off. I grant you one of those now, Mr. Chambers. A chance to leave this all behind and move on with your life. I know what it is you seek, but Pandora's Box cannot be closed once it has opened."

Dick nodded gently. "Your English is impeccable. Better than your cronies...Petrov."

A trace of a smile pricked the corner of the man's lips. "They are mere ants playing among the lions. I offer you this chance, Chambers. I advise you to take it."

Dick put his hands in his pockets. "And what if I can't?"

Petrov's eyes narrowed. "Then you have already made your decision, and now it cannot be undone."

Petrov's hand moved to his inside jacket pocket. Dick moved his hand to the handle of his pistol. "I wouldn't..."

But Petrov didn't remove a weapon. Instead, he dialed a

number on a cell phone and muttered something incoherent into the receiver.

"What was that?" Dick asked.

"You are surrounded." That smile was there in full now. "My men are ready for you, Chambers. Whatever you choose to do now, it's the endgame for you. Good luck escaping this place without a scratch. You'll need even greater luck to leave with your life." He drew a key from his jacket and unlocked the door while calling over his shoulder, "Good luck breaking out of this one, Houdini."

Dick trained the gun at the back of his head. "Stop. I'm warning you."

Petrov paid no attention. Instead, he laughed and left the room.

Dick was left alone in the quiet restroom, the club's music muted by the door. A moment later a man walked in, tottering on his toes as he dashed for a cubicle, stopping only long enough to cast Dick a strange look.

Dick tried to process what the hell had happened. Had Petrov surrounded the place with his men, or was he bluffing? Did the Russian hold that much sway in these areas? Hugo had said this was a private ritual. If so, who the hell had Petrov been hanging around with?

He stood by the restroom door and drew a steadying breath. With his hand on the butt of his pistol, he eased the door open and stepped back into the club.

CHAPTER TWENTY

The smoky atmosphere that had once been a cloak now loomed more threatening than before.

Dick emerged from the restroom and scanned around the club. Not a single thing had changed since Petrov's threat of him being surrounded. Why would it? This was a public place, and it would be foolish for Petrov to cause a scene, disrupt business, and draw attention to himself.

Yet the threat still weighed on Dick.

Dick steadily made his way across the room, acting inconspicuous, although he felt the eyes of others watching him. The ladies continued their gyrations, waitresses served drinks, and gentlemen marveled at the sights, but that all felt like a much larger cover-up to a grander scheme now designed to trap Dick and bring him into the dark side.

Dick took a seat by the bar, eyes open and mind alert. He weighed his options, knowing that he needed to take any threat seriously. If the building was surrounded as Petrov had informed him, how the hell was Dick going to escape?

The front door was out of the equation, for reasons that would be obvious to any man. If Petrov frequented this club often, he would know the building's layout and would be able to guard any other exits.

So what was he to do?

Dick ordered a whiskey and allowed his cogs to turn. If the building *were* surrounded, then there would be no rush. That would only cloud the waters. If you wanted to see clearly in the lake, you didn't thrash around and disturb the lake bed. You calmly paddled until you reached the water's edge.

A couple exited the room to the private dance booths. Dick traced Honey's movements as she smiled her goodbyes to her latest client and adjusted her outfit. At the same time, three men entered through the front door, looking more like '80s body-guards than potential clients to the establishment. They each wore dark shades and scanned the room, fixing their gaze on Dick before taking a seat as close to the main doorway as possible.

Shit. So Petrov wasn't bluffing. There was no way that these guys didn't work for him.

Three more suited and shaded thugs entered shortly after, then made their way deeper into the club and at least had the decency to act a little more inconspicuously. Although they wore the same outfit, and when they identified Dick, their body language gave their intent away.

Dick spotted the weapons holstered on all of their waists.

Dick sipped his bourbon with a grin. If there was one thing he could say about Atlantica, it was that at least the laws allowed for an exciting cat-and-mouse chase when you encountered bad guys who were clued up on how the system worked. Petrov understood the game and knew that his options were to take Dick quietly when he was alone and bring him to private prop-erty to interrogate or neutralize his threat, or cause a scene and risk the AJS getting involved.

While other enemies had underestimated Dick, Petrov had clearly done his homework and knew what he was up against.

There was also a relatively small chance that Petrov would want to risk destroying the property of an establishment he frequented regularly.

How are you going to play this, Dick?

Another couple entered the club, outfitted the same as the others, and took their position toward the back. How long would it be until the only customers at The Pink Flamingo were Petrov's cronies?

Dick drained his bourbon as Honey finished a lap around the room. He caught her attention, and she flashed him a smile.

"Finally changed your mind, gorgeous?" she cooed. "Seen the smile's on my clients' faces and want your turn?"

Dick placed a few bills in her palm. "Sure. Show me a good time."

A surprised look came over her face as she counted the cash in her hand, way more than she would usually charge. "You want the platinum package?"

"I want privacy." Dick's eyes darted to the others who made no attempts to hide that they were staring at him.

Honey nodded. "Oh, I know what that means." She took his hand and guided him toward the back rooms.

The heat of the cronies' stares followed Dick the entire way through the club. A number of them touched a finger to their ear and spoke to someone on the receiving end, no doubt updating them on Dick's movements.

Dick walked through the unidentified door, the smell of perfume overwhelming as the music quieted and a sense of isolation came over him. They passed a hulking figure of a man who watched a series of monitors of women performing in the private rooms, ready to jump in and help them out if the clients got too handsy. Honey whispered something into his ear, and the man gave a stern nod before leering at Dick.

Their room was four doors up on the right. A feeling of

discomfort settled in Dick's stomach. Was this what Petrov wanted? How tied in with the staff was he?

If he had the staff under his thumb, he wouldn't have sent the extra bodies up the stairs.

The room was like entering a fantasy world built inside the Taj Mahal. Decorative pillows and throws surrounded a plush booth. Incense burned, and the fog was gentle but blurred the edges of his vision. Private dances were a sensory experience, and this put his senses on overload.

"Are you ready to get started?" Honey turned to a sound system, where she bent over provocatively and pressed a button to start some slow, pulsating music.

She stood before Dick and threaded her hands through her hair, hips swaying back and forth as Dick lifted a hand and told her to stop.

A look of confusion came over her face.

That's a genuine reaction. She's not in on the bigger picture here.

Dick fixed his gaze on the dancer. "Honey, I'm going to tell you something that may come as something of a shock, and I need you to act normal, okay?"

Honey raised an eyebrow. "Sure thing, sweetie. It's probably worth noting that I'll need to dance for you if you're hoping not to arouse suspicion. Otherwise, Boris is going to come in and see what's going on."

Dick nodded for her to continue.

It was a strange experience, detailing the imminent threat he was under as Honey performed her sultry routine. He outlined the current clientele waiting in the club for him while giving Honey a brief overview of his encounter with Petrov. She sat on his lap and worked her body in a way that would entertain a drunken man into a frenzy, all while Dick doggedly fixed his mind on the situation at hand.

"Is there a way I can get out of here without being spotted?" Dick asked.

Honey considered this. She'd lost almost all of her clothing to the floor. "It would be incredibly difficult. If your friend has this building surrounded, then it's going to be tough. Only four exits lead to the ground floor, and they all come out around the side of the building. If we were connected to the adjacent buildings, perhaps. But we're not, so I don't know how much help I'd be."

Dick listened and nodded along, and snuck a glance at his cell phone as he tapped some commands on the screen and pocketed it once more.

Honey chuckled, "You know, I'm not sure whether to take offense to this or not. Most clients can't peel their eyes away from me."

"Most clients aren't figuring out a way to escape a Russian gang." Dick grinned.

The music ended. Honey climbed off. "Well, that's usually where you and I end. Unless you've got something for me?"

Dick's eyes flickered to the security camera in the corner. He fished out some more notes and handed them to Honey. "You know I'm vastly overpaying you, right?"

Honey smiled.

Dick chewed his lip as the music resumed. "Tell me, what happens when a client gets too handsy? Where do you go?"

Honey moved with the music. "We signal for Boris to get involved and he guides us to a private exit, ensuring that the client is sufficiently manhandled and thrown from the club."

"Where does this exit lead?"

Honey grinned. "To the same exits I mentioned before." She shook her head. "I'm afraid there's no way out without being seen."

Dick glanced at his cell and tapped the screen a few more times. "Fair enough. Looks like I may have to do this the hard way."

"What's the hard way?"

Dick nodded at the camera. "Give him the signal. Tell him you're in distress."

Honey raised an eyebrow and paused her dancing. "Are you crazy? The last guy they threw out of here, he damn near broke his arm."

Dick stared at her.

"Fine." Honey sounded resigned. "Your funeral."

She turned and sat on Dick's lap, then subtly waved her hands to gain Boris' attention. Not two seconds later, the door burst open and the hulking figure entered. He grabbed Dick by the scruff of his collar and easily lifted him to his feet.

"Enough of that, fella. Time to go," he commanded.

He shoved Dick crudely in the back. Dick stood his ground, refusing to move. He caught Honey's confused expression as Boris pushed again, getting rougher with each move until he grabbed Dick's arm and pinned it behind his back.

He marched Dick out of the booth and toward the main room. However, as he neared the door, he took Dick to a side door that he kicked open, which triggered a blinding flash of emergency lighting over a metal staircase.

As he guided Dick through the door, Dick caught one of Petrov's cronies being led into the back room for a private dance. Their eyes met, and Dick grinned. Another security guard quickly attended Boris' booth.

Boris was strong, and Dick had no choice but to follow where he led. At the bottom of the staircase, the man led Dick out a fire door and into an alley off the main street. Boris gave him one last shove, then stood in the doorway, arms folded.

Dick tried to walk back in.

"Get lost, pal," Boris barked. "What's your problem?"

"I need a witness." Dick's reply elicited an eyebrow raise from the backlit Boris.

Dick gestured into the darkened alley where a dozen figures stood waiting in the darkness. They were easy to miss unless you knew to look for them, which was evident when Boris shook his head. "You're crazy. Get out of here."

Dick shoved his foot in the way of the door closing and grimaced against the pain of it. He took a business card from his pocket and quickly scribbled a note on the back. "If I'm missing, search for Sergei Petrov."

He handed it to Boris.

Boris accepted the card doubtfully. Dick was almost certain that the security guard would throw it away the instant the doors closed, but it was worth the risk. If something did go down here, he wanted someone to at least have a lead. If he died, he wouldn't be yet another mystery for another PI to solve.

Boris exhaled through his nose, then shook his head. "PI, huh? You're still a low-life perverted scumbag."

With that, he closed the door.

For a moment, Dick stood in silence. The air was refreshing, and it quickly worked to erase the fog that had come over him in the club. Although now that he was away from the public eye, his heart raced.

He turned toward the people waiting in the alley and held out his arms. "You're going to have to do your worst, I'm afraid. I won't make this easy for you."

He couldn't see the grins on their faces. He could only make out the glint in their eyes. They wasted no time rushing at him. They were organized, their attack planned. A handful of figures streamed toward him while the others waited by the alley entrance to cut off all escape.

Dick readied himself and took his stance. His fingers still hurt, and his hip ached, but the adrenaline countered a lot of his ailments. The first figure to reach him swung something that gave a soft whistle as it arced through the air. Dick ducked out of its path and returned with an uppercut to the figure's gut as the failed hit caught them off-balance. Something hard clattered to the ground as the blow forced the air from the target's lungs.

An arm hooked around Dick's neck from behind. A kick caught the side of his leg. Dick growled in pain as the hold constricted his breathing, but judging by the girth of his attacker's arm, he was stronger than them. He gritted his teeth and folded over, sending the attacker over the top of his back.

While he expected his attacker to release their grip on his throat, that didn't happen. Dick followed with them and somersaulted onto the hard ground with his attacker beside him. The foul stink of their breath found his nostrils as he drove his elbow between their ribs.

Something cracked. The attacker cried out in pain—a man's cry. The constriction around his throat eased.

There was no time to celebrate. He could make out four figures around him now. Each of them launched a fusillade of kicks into his sides. Dick reached out and caught the sole of one of their shoes. He twisted sharply to the side and sent one of them to the ground.

A sharp kick to the top of his skull caused white lights to bloom in his vision. Dick had to get to his feet, or he knew it would be done. They would capture him, take him somewhere they could dispose of him properly, and it would all be over.

Another kick, this time to his hip. Dick grunted in pain.

He reached out, and his fingers brushed against something hard and cold. He gripped the length of wood, guessed it to be some kind of bat or table leg, and swung it in a wide circle around him. The bat juddered as it hit several targets, which granted Dick a brief relief from the attacks.

He rolled to his front and pushed himself to his feet. A kick came at his face, narrowly avoiding its full impact as it grazed his nose. Warm liquid spilled down to his lip, but Dick wasn't done yet.

Dick stood and wobbled a little as he held out a hand to placate his attackers, the length of wood ready in his other. "Hold!"

Somewhere in the distance, AJS sirens blared. This wasn't lost on his attackers as they mumbled among each other.

"I'll come quietly," Dick declared and dropped the wood so that it clattered to the ground. "You win, okay? You win."

An engine roared nearby.

Hands roughly grabbed him from behind and pressed his wrists against his back. They closed on him, and one attacker covered his head with a hessian sack. All went dark. Noises became muffled. They forcefully led Dick somewhere he couldn't make out.

The AJS sirens grew louder. Dick's captors increased their speed and moved with more urgency. A voice remarked, "This better not be your doing, Chambers."

"You know my name," Dick replied, sickly sweet as if complimented by a stranger. "You've done your research. How cute."

A gut-punch knocked his breath out.

Somewhere in the darkness, a car door opened. Dick didn't like the sound of it. The moment he was inside the car, he knew there would be no escape. There were too many of them. He was only one man.

Car tires screeched around the corner.

Urgency flared among his captors as they mumbled, and a few hands left Dick's body. He grinned beneath the sack, knowing what was to come. He was glad that his message had been received although they were cutting things very fine.

The mumbles turned to shouts as lights bloomed somewhere ahead. Dick could make out a powerful light source even beneath the head covering. An engine revved as a vehicle sped toward them. Dick could hear people leap out of the way, draw weapons, and threatening shouts.

The hands left Dick as the vehicle rumbled toward him. A shot was fired and ricocheted around the alley. The shouts grew feverish. Another shot. Then another. Hands grabbed Dick and forced him forward, then pushed his head down and out of harm's reach. Bullets pinged off metal. The hands shoved Dick into the back of a vehicle. The leather was cold on his face as he lay on the back seat. The vehicle reversed as people shouted and AJS sirens blared. The car turned sharply, then sped away.

Dick lay in silence and listened for the people around him, unsure whether his plan had worked or not.

CHAPTER TWENTY-ONE

A minute later, there was movement from the front of the car.

"I thought you said you had things handled," a familiar voice snarked.

Dick eased the sack off his head and breathed a sigh of relief. He was lying in the back of Maurine's car as they sped along the streets of Atlantica, streetlights passing by like blinking flashes of light as she cranked the gears higher and navigated the turns and corners like a pro racer.

Dick sat up and winced as his aching body protested each movement. The inside of the sack sported a splash of the blood that still poured from his nostrils, and he was certain that his body would resemble a Rorschach test come morning. "This is how I handle things."

Maurine looked in the rearview and grinned. "You're one crazy son of a bitch."

"In fairness," Dick replied, "I've never had things take the turn that they did. I found Petrov."

Maurine's eyebrows raised.

"Rather," Dick clarified, "he found me."

Maurine shook her head. "Whatever game you're part of, I don't think I want to play it."

"I didn't mean to drag you into it."

Maurine downshifted, slammed on the brakes, and skidded around a corner. Dick turned to the rear window and, to his dismay, spotted a convoy of vehicles following them. Three sleek black supercars and AJS cruisers a short way behind them.

"Fuck." Dick rested his head against the backseat. "You got this?"

Maurine laughed. "You have no idea. Strap in, Chambers. Things are about to get wild."

Dick clipped on his safety belt and watched the road ahead. Traffic was minimal at this time of night, but it wasn't barren. Cars dotted the roadways and paused at stop signs while others cruised around the city. The modern age dictated that there were always some wheels of the world turning. Dick had never seen the roads empty.

One of the black supercars sped up and bumped into the back of Maurine's vehicle. She shook her head and yanked the steering wheel to the left, drifting around a sharp corner as two of the supercars failed to anticipate the change and continued in a straight line. The AJS cruisers followed swiftly behind, their sirens blaring as their lights painted the rearview mirror with blues and reds.

"The law and the bad guys?" Maurine asked. "What the hell did you do?"

"I got out of there."

They came to a T-junction, and Maurine picked up speed as they careened toward a building that was easily thirty stories high. At night, it was lit with a strange array of lights and advertising boards that hurt the eyes. Maurine muttered, "Hold on," as she turned the wheel sharply to the left and sent the tail out as rubber burned on the tarmac. A millisecond later, she turned in the opposite direction, hoping to throw off the two black cars behind her into turning the wrong direction.

Her maneuver failed as they followed and fell into her slipstream. She at least gained some distance from the AJS vehicles.

"Surely the law should have faster cars," she commented.

"Give them more public funding. Also, do you really want them to catch up with you right now?"

"We've done nothing wrong," Maurine protested.

Dick pointed ahead to where the AJS had set up a roadblock. They'd barred the way forward, blocked the way to the left, and were in the middle of setting up the right-hand turn.

"Oh, shit," Maurine remarked, right as one of the following supercars pulled alongside her by accelerating sharply in the opposite lane. She turned her head and gasped as the passenger pointed a gun straight at her. She ducked and hit the brakes hard enough that the shot missed by a good margin. The car behind hit the rear end and dented the trunk.

Maurine's eyes narrowed, her pride wounded. "Oh, no you didn't."

Her grip adjusted on the wheel and her knuckles turned white. She pressed harder on the gas and caught up with the vehicle in front, which had now covered her passage forward. Red taillights declared the vehicle braking as the two attempted to box her in front and behind.

They neared the roadblock. Dick identified a number of officers waiting with their guns ready and pointed at the speeding vehicles.

"Hold on tight," Maurine announced as she slammed the brakes and whipped the wheel to the left as far as it would go. The tires screamed as the car spun in a half-circle. When the vehicle moved to the desired direction, she adjusted the steering wheel and floored the gas.

The two black supercars were slow to respond although they tried to duplicate the maneuver. Shots fired, and bullets hit the car nearest to the roadblock. The tires popped and shredded as the driver attempted to escape, only to find that sparks now flew from the metallic rims, which had no rubber to protect them from the road.

Dick held on tightly inside the car as Maurine careened toward the AJS vehicles, which blared their horns when it looked like Maurine would collide head-on with one of them. She swerved to avoid the collision although they did exchange paint on the pass. The black vehicle was less lucky and hit the corner of one of the cruisers, which sent it swerving into a nearby parking meter where it abruptly came to a stop.

"Press the advantage," Maurine muttered to herself as her eyes flicked to the rearview. "Keep moving."

She turned right, then made a series of turns designed to evade anyone who might be pursuing them. AJS sirens blared behind them, but slowly faded as they pulled away and gained distance. Maurine didn't slow down until five minutes later. Their journey took them to the far reaches of the eastern side of town, a place Dick hadn't spent all that much time since he had last been put on the case of a missing child several years ago.

Maurine stuck to the quiet streets and slowed to the legal limit. She pulled into a darkened parking lot behind a newspaper office and cut the engine. The vehicle lights died and plunged them into darkness.

A moment of silence passed between them.

Dick drew a long breath. "Thank you—"

Before he could say anything else, Maurine reached behind her seat and slapped his leg. She assaulted him with several hits before he secured her wrists and stopped her. "What. The. Hell. Was. That?"

Their faces were inches apart as he pinned her wrists to the side of her seat, her body bent at a strange angle. "I'm sorry," Dick declared. "I didn't mean to drag you into that, but I had no choice. I found Petrov, and he surrounded the building with his cronies in a matter of minutes. I needed an out, and I knew you would still be around. Without you, I'd likely be dead already."

Maurine growled. "You nearly got us both killed."

Dick looked at her earnestly. "I didn't doubt you for a second."

Maurine held his stare for a few seconds before finally softening. "I love adrenaline as much as the next girl, but if you ever want to get your rocks off again, leave me out of it." She freed herself from Dick's grasp and stroked the dashboard. "This is going to take some capital to repair."

Dick fished out the remaining wad of notes from his pocket and handed them to Maurine. "This should be a start."

Her eyes lit up. "Why do you carry so much cash?"

"Long story."

Maurine counted the notes one by one, then put them in the glove compartment. "Are you going to tell me exactly what happened?"

"Are you going to take me home?" Dick rebuked.

Maurine smiled softly. "We'll wait for the heat to die down a little first, shall we? I want a story."

Dick told her everything. From the moment he had followed the suspect into the bathroom, to Petrov's threat, to his lap dance when he had messaged both Maurine and the AJS to announce the situation and ask for help.

Maurine held her head in her hands. "Hold on. The AJS...that was your fault?"

"I needed a way to knock them off-kilter. If the AJS sirens blared, it would speed them up. Make them more prone to mistakes."

"So the roadblock, me scraping my car, the goddamn speed chase afterward, you planned that?" Maurine turned in her seat.

Dick nodded, his expression passive. "I'm not proud of it. Needs must. I would have been dead if they had taken me."

"Couldn't you have stayed in the club?" Maurine asked. "Used their security? Hidden away?"

Dick shook his head. "Like every organization in this place, The Flamingo only cares about itself and its cash. What do they care if some detective gets his ass kicked outside their premises? As long as it doesn't hurt their ladies, their clients, or affect their cash flow, they won't give a shit." He eyed Maurine curiously. "I would have thought someone like you would understand Atlantica a little better than that."

"Call me an optimist."

"Anyway, thanks again. I do appreciate you getting me out of there."

Maurine cast her eyes down. "It was kind of fun."

They looked into each other's eyes. The tension was palpable. Dick's heart thumped as his eyes moved to her lips. Hers moved to his, and for a moment they froze. After a beat, Maurine turned away. "I'll get you back."

Dick offered a smile and sat back in his seat. "Thanks."

"You can stop saying that."

Dick chuckled as Maurine shifted the car into reverse and slowly eased out of the parking lot.

They made it halfway across the city without incident. Maurine was right. The music of the car's engine was enough entertainment to keep Dick occupied. He was thankful for the quiet inside the car as the city blurred by.

They barely spoke a word. Maurine focused on driving, and Dick's brain whirred with the events at the club. The city took on a familiar feel as they neared the area where Maurine had picked him up earlier that night. When she finally pulled curbside and cut the engine, the pair sat in silence for some time.

Maurine was the first to break the quiet. "Have you ever heard the tale of the invincible armadillo?"

Dick raised an eyebrow. "No."

"There was once an armadillo, a proud creature who roamed the forest in search of food," Maurine explained, eyes fixed ahead and one elbow resting on the car door. "Along the way, he found predators, other animals eager to kill him and eat him from the inside out.

"With each attack, the armadillo curled into a ball and used his shell for protection. His shell was as tough as nails, and every time, the predators broke their teeth and claws and were left empty-handed and with an empty stomach."

Dick chuckled. "Gotta love a good parable."

Maurine continued. "One day, the armadillo was walking along beneath a cliff and stumbled across one of its brethren. He hadn't seen his brother in years but recognized the face since that was the only part of the armadillo left intact. Its body was destroyed, and bones picked clean as flies buzzed around its corpse. Only the shell and its head remained.

"The armadillo couldn't understand it. How could this have happened to its brother? What possible creature could pierce an armadillo's armor? It seemed preposterous. Yet it was true, lying there before him.

"Years passed, and the armadillo never solved the mystery of his brother's passing. Predator after predator failed in its attacks. The armadillo's shell grew more scratched and worn but held fast. Each time, the armadillo grew cockier.

"Until, one day, years later, the armadillo's eyesight started to fail. The world grew blurry, and food was harder to find. Predators attacked and the shell still held, but the armadillo grew careless. Until, one fateful day, the armadillo was walking along the beaten track, and the road disappeared beneath him."

Dick stared intently at Maurine as a group of stragglers filed out of a nearby club.

Maurine turned to Dick. "The armadillo walked straight off the cliff where he lost his brother. The fall shattered him from the inside out. The predators that hunted him for years finally got their taste of the armadillo, and the meat was sweet."

"That's a pretty story," Dick replied. "Although I've yet to see the point."

"The point is simple. You can't rely on the old ways forever. The world will find a new enemy to defeat you if you're not careful. You went after Petrov, and now he has your number. Don't let him be the cliff you don't see coming."

Dick smirked.

"What?" Maurine asked.

Dick shrugged. "I guess I've always imagined gang members to be heartless layabouts with no more emotion than a stone. I didn't realize you'd grown so affectionate of me since we met."

Maurine shoved him playfully. "I know a good guy when I see one, Dick. Petrov is not, and you've angered him. You've gone out of your way to cause trouble, and you have nothing to show for it. I don't want him to be the reason I see your name in tomorrow's paper."

"What do you mean I have nothing to show for it?"

Maurine's face creased. "You got a lap dance, and you bailed. What part of that was a success?"

Dick raised his eyebrows.

"You're disgusting," Maurine replied.

Dick laughed. "Well, that...and this." He reached into his pocket and pulled out a crumpled flyer.

"What's that?"

"I snagged it while wrestling with those assholes in that alley. Caught it while trying to get free." He examined the artwork. "Looks like our boys have a little affinity for gambling. This should be right up my alley."

"You're not serious. You can't go in there alone. They'll destroy you. It'll be The Pink Flamingo all over again."

"Oh, I won't go alone."

"What are you planning?"

Dick examined the flyer, an image of a dealer fanning out a deck of cards, and the date set for two days later. "I'm not sure yet. I have an idea, but I may need to run it by some friends of mine."

Dick reached for the car door and felt a hand pull him back. Maurine looked at him earnestly. "Dick…"

Dick placed a hand on Maurine's and felt that spark of electricity pass between them. He offered a smile, then opened the door and emerged into the cold night.

Maurine only waited a moment or two before she pulled away and left Dick behind as she sped into the night. Dick waited until she was out of sight, then lit a cigarette and exhaled a plume of smoke.

An engine rumbled from somewhere nearby, the opposite direction from where Maurine had left him. Dick crossed the road, hands in his pocket, and walked along the path toward his safe house. He only made it off the main track and into the shadows when a vehicle roared nearby.

Dick turned to investigate the source of the noise when the headlights flashed and blinded him. Something screeched to a stop mere feet away. A dark figure ran at him and caught him with a strong blow to his head.

CHAPTER TWENTY-TWO

Dick raised his arms to shield his head. The attacker landed another three blows on his forearm before he worked out what was going on.

He stepped back and followed with a sidestep, then pushed his attacker back and got the lights away from his direct line of sight. Terra Kris came into view, illuminated harshly by the high beams as she attacked Dick once more.

"Terra, calm down! What the hell are you doing?"

Terra distracted Dick with a punch, then swung a roundhouse at his hip. The force was blinding and brought Dick involuntarily to one knee. Her movements were quick and precise, and as Dick tried to push back to his feet, another blow caught the side of his head.

"What are you doing?" Dick exclaimed.

Terra ceased her attack and stood before him as her chest rose and fell rapidly. "What are *you* doing?" Her motorcycle's lights lit her features harshly, and her dark hair turned white in its glow. "You're supposed to be laying low and hiding out. I put my neck out for you, and this is how you repay me?"

She shoved him again, and Dick fell on his back. His body

ached, and he groaned as he fought to sit up. "Terra, I can explain."

"Please do," Terra commanded. She nodded at her gun. "You're lucky I don't drag you somewhere private and explode your head like a goddamn cantaloupe."

Dick sat up and used his arms to prop him upright. "Look, I owe you an explanation, I do. I get that. But shouldn't we go somewhere more private to discuss this?"

Terra considered this, Then her eyes softened a touch as she spotted the bloodstain around Dick's nose and lips. "Fine. This better be good."

Dick led the way as Terra cut the bike's engine and pushed it alongside her. She parked it around the corner of a nearby building, tucked away in the shadows, and followed Dick in silence. The heat of her anger bored into the back of his head as he unlocked the door and led Terra into the very safe house she had procured for him in a tight pinch.

Dick flicked on the lights in the underground bunker and held the door for Terra. She followed inside and stood by the counter.

"Drink?" Dick offered and motioned to the coffee maker.

Terra's nostrils flared.

"No? Okay then." Dick milled around the kitchen and started the coffee maker. Once the dark liquid started dripping into a mug, he turned and rested against the counter. "You wanted an explanation?"

Terra nodded. "Please." There was little patience in her tone. "You look like shit."

"I feel like shit." He sought the right words while gauging how much to tell Terra without dragging her into his crap. He sighed. "I'm on a hell of a case, Terra. That's about all I can say right now. It began with Santana, and the damn thing is only growing bigger the further I delve."

"What's the case?" Terra asked, arms folded.

"I wish I could tell you. The truth is that I don't know yet. There's a cover-up, something that's spurring a large group of high-powered motherfuckers to do whatever they can to hide its tracks. Every time I chip away at the rock and find a piece of gold, someone swoops from nowhere to cover it up again. It's torturous."

Terra drew a long breath and unfolded her arms. She leaned against the wall and kicked one foot up behind her. Her muddy boot left a track on its surface. "You'll have to give me more than that, Dick. You're playing games with the AJS, and I'm complicit to it. What the hell were you thinking tonight? Sending me an alert to funnel AJS resources to a club because of a bomb threat, then proceeding to race through the city and escape the law?"

Dick lowered his gaze. "In my defense, it was that or die."

Terra's eyes narrowed as she studied him for a long moment. "You're serious?"

"I am."

The coffee maker finished. Before Dick could collect his cup, Terra swooped in and took it for herself. She sipped the scalding hot drink without complaint as the scent of coffee filled the room and made Dick salivate.

"I guess I'll make two."

Terra lowered her cup and spoke as Dick busied himself setting up another drink. "Dick, I hate to say this, but you'll have to give me more information on this case. Whatever you're looking into, it sounds big. Big enough to warrant awareness from the AJS. If you go on like this, you're going to get yourself killed."

Dick scoffed as a smile crept onto his face. "Like the armadillo."

"What?"

"Nothing." Then, under Terra's withering gaze, he added, "I get it. I do. And, truth is, I may need your help. I'm willing to tell you my piece, but I need your complete cooperation and promise that you won't call this in until it's time. Can you do that?"

She looked out from under the shelf of her eyebrows. "Are you kidding me?"

Dick held her gaze. "As it stands, a lot of this is out of AJS jurisdiction. A lot of the case exists in private residency, so there's little your guys could do at this point, anyway. At least, not until I get the information I'm after."

Terra contemplated this. Eventually, she gave in. "Fine."

Dick motioned to the sofa. "Take a seat. There's a hell of a story to all of this. Do you mind if I clean myself up a little while I tell it?"

Terra shook her head. "Be my guest."

"I may also omit certain facts that may affect me negatively and cast any liability on my reputation," Dick informed her. "I hope you'll understand."

Terra took a seat. "I'd expect nothing less."

They sat on the sofa for over an hour as Dick outlined the case and his journey since he had encountered Santana Sokolov in a quiet little tavern a couple of weeks ago. He removed his jacket, t-shirt, and pants as he tended to his wounds.

She watched in silence as he explained the steps he'd worked through, and didn't volunteer to help as Dick cleaned his wounds with warm water and a cloth until there was no blood remaining on his person. His torso looked like a Jackson Pollock of yellows and blacks, and the lacerations on his knuckles flared an angry red. He had no idea how his back looked, but when he asked Terra, she merely replied, "You'll live."

She was attentive to his story and occasionally interjected a question to clarify specific steps along the way. Dick removed any incriminating parts of his tale. While Terra was one of the good ones, she was also an AJS officer, and he didn't want to put her in a more difficult situation than she was already in.

He worked away with iodine and antiseptic. His brain fogged

from tiredness as the adrenaline of the evening wore off and the morning began to crow. When he finally finished his story, he sat back in the plushy arms of the couch and closed his eyes.

Terra absorbed the information that Dick had given her while mulling over the right questions. "So, let me get this straight. All of that, and you still have no idea who Petrov is and what he's hiding?"

"Nope."

"And Sadie Turnberry… You stole back this pendant, and you've heard nothing more from her since?"

"Nope," Dick repeated. "I'm certain you're to thank for that. This safe house seems to be enough to keep me off the grid."

"Not that you're not already doing everything you can to ruin that." Terra's eyes narrowed. "When I brought you here, I figured you'd lay low for a few days. Maybe a week or two. Not gallivant around the city and find new enemies."

"In fairness, I think these are the same enemies."

Terra shot him a look. "And now you have information about a card game that you're planning to attend? How do you know Petrov won't be there? How do you know that he's not going to surround you again and put you in a new predicament? One that you can't get out of this time?"

Dick grinned. "Because I don't plan to go alone, this time. I'm going to request someone's help. Someone to go undercover and give me some assistance."

Terra scoffed. "Are you kidding, Dick? You're trying to enlist an AJS officer to go undercover to help *you* solve a case? I never thought I'd see the day you'd give even an ounce of respect to the AJS. Isn't that like Superman choosing to work with Lex Luther?"

Dick tilted his head. "I suppose."

Terra shook her head. "You'll have to find someone else." She rose from the couch. "I've already spent long enough on duty sitting down here and listening to the incredible ramblings of Mr. Chambers. Why would I get involved in the rest of the story when I know that the path you're treading will get you killed?"

"Because we're not so different, you and I."

"How do you figure?"

"We both have an innate sense of justice," Dick explained. "We both want what's right for the city, and we both know how to sniff when something foul is going on." He stood and grimaced as he put weight on his leg. His hip throbbed with pain. "Look, I've thought about this in a hundred different ways. We need both sides of the law to come together on this. You can hold them to account from an AJS standpoint, and I can cross the lines you can't. It's the only way that I can see us getting to Petrov and clamping down on this shit."

Terra's lips thinned. "I'm sorry, Dick. You're on your own here."

"Come on," Dick encouraged. He held up the flyer. "You have nothing going on that night. It's your night off, remember?"

Terra frowned. "How did you know?"

Dick grinned. "I didn't until now."

Terra let out a soft laugh. "I'll think about it. How's that?"

"That's all I ask." He followed her to the door. "Look, I'm sorry for all the mess that has come out of this because of me. I get it—you're stuck between a rock and a hard place. I appreciate all that you've done for me so far."

Terra nodded with a serious expression. "Don't ask me why. I'm still trying to work out how I'm going to get any reward from all this."

"Justice is its own reward, isn't it? Cleaner streets for an incredible city."

Terra sighed, then tapped her HUD. "The precinct is calling me back. I'm going to have a whale of a time explaining where I've been for the past hour."

"Tell them it was a booty call." Dick smirked.

"You wish. All they know is that I went on the tail of an

escaped suspect. Now I'll be coming back empty-handed." She turned and started up the stairs.

"Tell me you'll consider it," Dick called after her.

Terra shut the door behind her. The lock clicked loudly into place.

"She'll think about it," Dick muttered to himself.

He crossed to the couch, switched on the TV, and was asleep within minutes.

CHAPTER TWENTY-THREE

The man hated the sound of Sadie Turnberry's shrill voice. She was a stone-cold bitch through and through. He had learned that the moment he had accepted the job from her.

Sadie barked down the phone, calling for the man to continue his investigation and hurry the fuck up. She complained about the money she was spending on him, threatening to withhold his final paycheck if he didn't make progress soon. She was frustrating, not listening to his counterarguments that progress took time, and to hunt a private investigator was a different skillset to tracking a regular civilian.

He pinched his forehead and gritted his teeth. If the bitch weren't paying him so much money, he would cast the job aside. No job was worth this.

But the adrenaline rush he got from the excitement of chasing down Chambers was a thrill in itself. He was getting closer. Could smell his scent on the trail. There were only a few pieces of the puzzle missing.

The redhead chick's information was useful, leading him to East and Third and into the territory of a rally gang, a sprinkling of their members propped around the streets to act as a decoy for the AJS. They were cooperative, more so with a gun barrel between their lips, and their description of Chambers matched to a "T."

From there, they directed him to the south coast of the island, toward a congregation on the beach where a party was underway. That was the most frustrating part. He knew that Chambers had been there and was certain that the PI was somewhere among all the partying bodies, but with alcohol coursing through their systems and their hackles raised at his brash demeanor, no one gave him any real info other than, "I saw him earlier."

"Where did he go?" the man asked, only to be met with a shrug and the offer of one pill or another.

After the crowd yielded no further information, he stuck to the shadows and trailed in loops around the outside of the congregation. It was nigh-on fruitless, with too many bodies to properly search. That was the most frustrating part, feeling that he was so damn close but having no way to zero in on the target. Once he reached another area of the beach, there were fewer people here, but he knew better than to ask them questions. They weren't as inebriated and had their senses. One wrong word and the lights would turn on him, and he'd risk losing his element of surprise on the PI.

Deciding there was nothing left for it than for Chambers to slip up somewhere, the man found his place in a nearby twenty-four-hour diner and bided his time. The glass front gave a view of the beach, but it didn't offer a full perspective. His only hope was that Chambers would reveal himself unintentionally, or the man would have time to process and find something that he was missing.

"What the hell are you searching for, Chambers?" he grumbled through a mouthful of scrambled egg. "You've turned your search from Turnberry to something else. Why?"

The man couldn't help but feel that Turnberry was withholding vital information that could be useful. All he had received was instructions to find Chambers, but the bitch had no idea what kind of investigatory work that took. Since Chambers hadn't visited his abode in days, he could only assume he had a temporary safe house. But what cause would Chambers have to hide out unless he knew that people were after him? And, if that was the case, who slipped up to cause Chambers to flee?

All of these questions he pushed on Turnberry. Her brief visit to the hospital had done little to slow her down, and she was already back running her mini financial empire. When he asked questions about who else might be involved, she protected her allies' identity, which made this job that much fucking harder. The man understood, in one sense. In Atlantica, almost everyone had a dual identity. Life in the shadows was the norm, and if you tattled, you broke the unspoken covenant. People paid good money to remain hidden.

But that information was key. He could smell it.

"Who else have you hired?" the man asked once more but expected the same answer.

"You know I cannot discuss that information," Turnberry barked. "And if you're as good as they say you are, you should be able to work that shit out. Quit stalling and bring me Chambers. My time is running out."

"What time?" The man knew the answer although she wouldn't admit it. Someone was putting the heat on Turnberry. Someone slipped up somewhere, and pressure was being applied from higher up to ensure that Sadie played her part and cleaned up her mess.

The man growled. "You want results? You give me the information. It's your money you're wasting by withholding. Every penny that goes into my pocket is from you neglecting to provide the whole damn picture. Tell me who else is involved."

Turnberry must have been desperate because she let out a frustrated growl before caving. "Fine. But if this comes back to bite me in the ass, I'm dragging you down with me."

Good luck with that one.

The man waited patiently.

"Sergei Petrov," she said at last.

The man's eyebrow raised. "Petrov? That's Lockhart's dog."

Silence came from the other side of the line.

"Oh, you're in some deep shit, aren't you Miss Turnberry?" Although he knew the stakes, there was a hint of pleasure in the man's voice. "That's why you've been keeping this shit on the DL."

The initials were purposeful. DL and Dexter Lockhart went hand-in-hand.

"Fuck you." Turnberry's response was sharp, followed by a deep inhale as she steadied herself. "Are you going to complete this shit or not?"

"I can now that you've given me something to go on." He smirked. "And when Petrov hears you've sold him out…"

"I've done nothing!" Sadie exclaimed. "I haven't put him in shit, and I haven't turned him in to the Feds. I've done nothing. He did me a favor, and that's all it is. Nothing more."

The man knew that couldn't be entirely true. Everyone had dirt on everybody else in this city. If one domino was knocked, they all fell.

"You have yourself a pleasant evening, Miss Turnberry."

His farewell met the tone of a dead line.

The man finished his breakfast and thanked the waiter with a twenty-dollar bill. He sat and looked up his old friend, Petrov, and wondered what he was up to. The name ran in circles he moved in, but you were never sure what was and wasn't true these days. All he knew was that Petrov was a low-life, and he had to get hold of him, find out what he had on Chambers, and if he knew where the guy was.

If only he knew that Dick Chambers had been walking not two hundred meters away, making his way back to his safe house after an exciting evening with Hugo and the Dead Devils.

The man opened his phone, ran a brief online search on Petrov, and found articles written under his name for some showboat magazine. He wondered how Petrov had found his way into the public eye but still kept his true persona hidden. He wasn't surprised that Chambers worked his way into the rally scene after the man put two and two together. Whatever he sought, it couldn't be a coincidence that both parties dealt in supercars, with Petrov's gang and these Dead Devils as famous rivals.

"What breadcrumbs are you sniffing, Chambers?" the man muttered. He shut down his phone and exited into the night, wondering if Petrov still frequented the same places he had taken the man so long ago.

Old habits die hard, or so they say. But let's see if these old habits can help a man die harder.

The next afternoon, the man hailed a cab and drove to the west side of town. He stopped outside a block of premium apartments and thanked the automated system. The car sped away.

A year or so ago, the man had engaged in one of the wildest nights of his life in these apartments. The party in an apartment that took almost the entire level on the nineteenth floor had lasted three days. Drink poured from every room, powder, blow, and ink was in never-ending supply, and women of all different shapes and sizes were eager and willing to entertain you until you were complete—regardless of who was watching.

The parties in Atlantica were wild. What happened behind closed doors stayed behind closed doors. The man once engaged in a game of Russian roulette in which forty percent of the players lost their lives, and not a single tear was shed. He'd had the pleasure to torture suspects inside their houses, because what could the law do other than watch through the window? The system was fucked up. Even he had to admit that. But it did have its advantages.

That party left the man exhausted and broke. Petrov kept the party riding the wave as he switched DJs, ignored noise complaints, and constantly brought in a fresh stream of wide-eyed partygoers. As the man knocked on the door, he pictured himself, younger and less wise from that long year ago. He wondered if Petrov would be partying right now.

Not that he could hear any music.

On the fifth knock, a woman answered. She was buxom and clad in a thin robe and panties. She appeared let down by the man's presence and called back, "Not pizza. Some guy!" She eyed him up and down. "You'll do. Care to join?"

Petrov appeared behind her, clad in a business suit as he adjusted his tie. The fluorescents shone off his bald dome. "Long time no see."

"Indeed," the man replied. "May I speak with you?"

Petrov checked his watch with a look of frustration on his face. "Be quick. I have places to go."

"Titty bars ain't real places," the woman exclaimed. She cackled. "Honey, they open all night. I don't know what the rush is. Just stay with me, sugar. We can make this an all-nighter."

Petrov indelicately shoved the woman from the room and ushered the man inside. He closed the door before she could get back. Fists hammered against the wood as he crossed to his island bar and poured himself a drink. He offered one to the man.

The man smirked. "I thought you were in a hurry."

"I am. I always have time for a drink," Petrov replied.

He didn't look that intimidating on the surface. He was average height with an average build, and nothing on his person screamed that he was the savage the man knew him to be. The only inkling might come from the cold hard stare he cast when his patience ran dry.

Like now, for example.

"What do you know about John Chambers?" The man narrowed his eyes, heart thumping.

Petrov raised an eyebrow. "Why do you ask?"

"You know that's not how this works," the man replied.

Petrov nodded as his eyes lowered to the floor. When he looked at the man again, his hand was in his pocket. He pressed something, and a bullet ripped through his trousers pocket, narrowly missing the man.

"This is how it works," Petrov informed him. "You're in my house. You ask me a question, and I give you answers if you answer mine. All around this room are a series of sensors and triggers designed to take down anyone who dares to threaten me or flex their masculinity in my home. No warning. Boom. Dead, and I'll have no trouble cleaning your viscera off my floor. Why do you think every inch of this place is tiled, wooden, or wipeable?"

The man smirked. "You know I can't tell you."

"Why not? I thought we were friends?" While his smile suggested they were, his eyes told another story.

"Chambers is sniffing around the Devils." The man played the cards he was dealt. "It may be nothing, but it seems an awful long way from his home to jump in with the crowd you used to associate with, don't you think?"

Petrov touched his chin. "Chambers? Chambers... Ah, the PI?" He smiled. "I wondered when that little shit would be knocking around here. I hear he's rather exceptional at his job. Goes to show, really. I was meticulous at his place. Didn't leave a scrap of evidence."

"Well, I guess that's hardly true," the man replied. "If that were the case, how would he have come this far?"

Petrov narrowed his eyes. "You're sure that his muzzle is pointed in my direction?"

"No," the man admitted. "In truth, I've yet to work out his intention. The problem is that it all looks a little too circumstantial, don't you agree? I hoped you'd be able to give me a little more information. What's your connection with him? Why have I found my way here?"

Petrov drank his drink and set the glass down. "Chambers is...something of a pest. He stole something from a friend of mine. Something that didn't belong to him. My friend wishes to have that item back, but it's proving rather difficult considering the person now in possession is off gallivanting in the goddamn jungle." He grabbed the glass and threw it across the room. The glass shattered into small fragments across the floor that glittered under the lights.

"Is there anyone who knows where you play or where you might be found?" the man asked. "Any regular fixtures that someone might be familiar with and know where to find you?

Petrov shook his head, although his eyes told a different story. "This game has gone on long enough. If Chambers has found my scent, he'll soon wish he'd never sniffed around our affairs. When I find him, I will erase every possible mention of the name John Chambers from this world."

The man raised a finger. "I believe he prefers going by Dick."

Petrov shot him a look.

"And besides, you'll have to find him first," the man added coolly. He took his leave without another word, pausing only to place a small device on the doorjamb as he exited to the crying eyes of a dismayed concubine.

CHAPTER TWENTY-FOUR

Dick took it easy the next day. He woke a little before noon and ran another shower. No matter how hard he scrubbed, it seemed he couldn't shake the aches and the feeling of dirt that plagued his skin after his encounter in The Pink Flamingo.

When he was clean, he secured new bandages on his body's worst-hit areas, then dressed in fresh clothes and headed outside. He paused to light a cigarette in the sun's glow. It burned bright in the sky, almost painful to look at, and nearly powerful enough to break the fog.

But in all Dick's years in Atlantica, that phenomenon had never happened.

He strolled in the crisp air and found his way to the nearest diner. It was painful to walk, and many parts of his body throbbed. The lacerations on his hand were some of the worst, but he knew they would heal soon. Another day or so, and all that would be left were tiny cuts.

He ate a breakfast of sausages, bacon, chicken, and vegetables, foregoing his usual toast for something that would build his strength back up. The protein would go a long way to his recovery, although the coffee was simply a temporary pick-me-up, something to stave off the coming headache.

Dick studied the outside world as he dined, as always amazed by how normal the city could seem in the light of day. Dick had seen most of the corners of the industrialized, inhabited parts of Atlantica, and he knew the reality of what lay beneath the tough exterior. The true Atlantica couldn't be found on the pretty surface of a postcard, only in the minds and beating hearts of its corrupt citizens.

Well, most of them, anyway.

His breakfast hit the spot, and soon he was out of the diner and onto the streets. He walked along the coastline, tracing it parallel to the site of the Dead Devils' celebratory evening, surprised to find very little evidence of their activity on the beach. No trash remained, they'd filled in the pits, and all that was left was a stretch of coast that accommodated some of Atlantica's citizens lying on towels as they soaked in as much sun as possible.

Walking always helped to clear Dick's head, and it felt nice not to have anywhere specific to go. He mulled over the case in his mind but allowed his thoughts to go blank after a short time. Sometimes it was nice to simply be—even if there was still a price tag on his head.

A mile along the coast, Dick sat on a bench and stared at the rolling waves. He was disappointed with the evening before and annoyed that he'd raised Petrov's suspicions, but he couldn't shake the feeling that Petrov had been prepared for him. He had no idea how. Unless Sadie had given him some indication, or Hugo Evans and his crew were in cahoots with the Russian rally driver, then there was no plausible reason for him to have his goons ready for Dick or to expect him at The Pink Flamingo.

Everything seemed a little too coincidental, a little *too* planned.

"What the hell have you gotten yourself into, Dick?" He drew from his cigarette and watched a young jogger running along the sand. Their eyes met. She turned away abashedly as her cheeks flushed red.

Still got it.

What would Petrov's plan be now? Now that his back was up, would Dick be walking into the lion's den by attending this game listed on a flyer? Terra might be his only shot at finding out the truth, but that only mattered as long as they remained in public. The minute they stepped over the threshold of a private residence, they could be screwed.

Terra's tougher than that. She can hold her own.

But we don't know who we're dealing with.

Dick stamped out his cigarette and reached for his cell. He dialed Santana's number and waited. The line went to voicemail. "What the hell is that girl up to?" he wondered aloud.

He thought for a moment, then dialed another number, a smile on his face as Gillian picked up the line. "Hey, Gilly. It's Dick."

"Oh, hey Dick." She sounded chirpy although Dick detected something amiss in her voice.

"Everything okay?"

"Fine." She replied too hastily for his liking. "Hey, I don't suppose you fancy meeting up somewhere, do you? Somewhere private?"

Dick scoffed. "Now you're speaking my language. I was about to ask you the same thing."

They arranged a meeting place a few blocks away, under the shadow of a new high-rise in mid-construction. According to the media, the old building that occupied the site once belonged to an incredibly wealthy woman who formed some powerful enemies as the CEO of a business that dealt in the blood diamond trade. Evett Romaine passed away two months previously under suspicious circumstances, made more so when the new building's contractors that demolished her work within days of her death were revealed to have been competing business owners, Shay & Shay.

Dick could connect the dots with no trouble, although no convictions could be made with a lack of evidence.

"It's like peeing on your enemy's gravesite the day they're buried," Dick muttered.

Gilly sat in the little green area that centered the block's square. Dick checked for vagrants before sitting beside a pond, its surface covered in a layer of algae. "I guess."

Gilly looked all around them as if expecting someone to join. Eventually, she glanced at her feet.

"What is it?" Dick asked. "You're not your usual cheery self."

"You don't know me, Dick."

"I know you well enough to have given you a huge stack of cash," he countered. "I saw you smile then. Don't tell me you've blown it already." His smile was playful, and his tone friendly.

Gilly shook her head. "Is that what the money was for? To buy my emotions?"

Dick frowned and shifted closer. "Gilly? Talk to me."

Gilly looked earnestly into his eyes with conflict written in hers. "What kind of shit are you in?"

Dick was taken aback by the question. "I'm always in shit. As my old ma would say, 'I'm paddling in the pigs' puddles until the plows come home.'"

He waited for Gilly's reaction, but she held his stare.

Dick's smile faded. "Why are you asking?"

Gilly ran a hand through her hair. "Someone was in my apartment. They broke in during the middle of the night. I thought it was a dream, that maybe it was something I concocted in my mind that felt real, but..." She drew a steadying breath. "There was a footprint by my door—dirt tracked in by a heavy boot—when I went to leave the house the next day."

"Someone was in your house?" Dick repeated. "Who? Tell me what happened."

Gilly told Dick all that she remembered, although in her fugue state there were pieces she admitted that she didn't entirely recollect. The man had been too close for her to see properly. All she knew was that his hair was dark and his face was unkind. There was a smell about him too, but she couldn't identify what it was, only that it was unpleasant.

"He was looking for you, Dick," Gilly finished. "He wanted to know where I'd taken you."

"What did you tell him?"

Gilly's lip wobbled. "I told him where I dropped you off. East and Third. I didn't know what else to do. He had me cornered. Trapped. In my *bed*. I didn't know what he was capable of. I've seen movies where people lie, and they get found out. I couldn't do that, Dick. I'm so sorry."

Dick put an arm over Gilly's shoulder and held her for a long moment as she cried into his chest. Dick wasn't mad—of course he wasn't. He knew the game and how it could be played, and to have lied to a potential psychopath would have been dangerous. When she surfaced and wiped her eyes, he asked, "Better?"

"Not really." Gilly drew a breath and looked at the sky. "I hope I haven't made things worse for you."

"Why didn't you call me?"

Gilly scoffed. "I tried! Your number kept bouncing back. You're impossible to reach."

Dick nodded. "That's intentional."

Gilly's face turned shadowed. "I only wish the best for you. I hope you realize that."

"Of course. It's not your fault that you're caught up in all of this. If anything, I'm thankful you're only playing a minor role."

"What does he want with you?"

"That depends on who 'he' is. Could be any number of things. The life of a private investigator isn't one of comforts and normality. You have to constantly watch behind your back and measure your enemies—and your friends."

"Sounds exhausting." Gilly smiled.

"Yeah. Yeah, it can be. I wouldn't trade it for the world, though."

Gilly raised an eyebrow. "Why? Why couldn't you seek something more stable? Less dangerous?"

"That would involve moving to a different country," Dick quipped. "Besides, someone has to do the dirty work. God knows I've earned my position on this God-forsaken island. If I can do my part to help rid the scum and make this place somewhat bearable, I'll die happy."

Gilly leaned back in her seat after removing Dick's arm. "I hope that's not too soon. Even if it means more of your hunters will likely find me."

Dick smiled although there was no humor in it. He had been thinking the same but hoped that would be the extent of Gilly's involvement in this scenario. It only confirmed Dick's assumption that anyone he pulled into his life was marred and affected by his past. In his line of work, friends and family were liabilities, people who could get damaged or hurt while the bad guys came for him. It was like being a superhero, only with none of the cool powers or the brightly colored capes.

They sat for some time in the sunshine while Dick asked a few more questions. After a short while, Gilly hopped to a nearby café to grab them both takeout coffees. They watched the fish swimming in the pond while Dick kept an eye out on the civilian foot traffic, once again feeling as though eyes were always on him. Gilly's mood cheered up considerably after she told Dick about her encounter with the man, although Dick was more distracted than ever. Initially, he thought it might have been Petrov, but Gilly's vague description didn't match that, particularly the part about his bushy head of hair.

After an hour or so, Dick walked Gilly halfway back to her block. He refused to get closer, afraid that someone would be monitoring her place. He also wasn't sure they weren't watching him.

"You should find somewhere else to live. For a short time, at least," Dick told Gilly. "You want somewhere safer. That money I gave you should fix you up for a few weeks at least."

Gilly nodded. "Thanks, Dick. Once again, I'm sorry. I don't know what any of this is truly about, but if you ever need someone there to help you, I'm available."

She looked up at Dick with glassy eyes, and he wondered what the intent was there. She was pretty, and he'd seen that look before, late at night in the bedrooms of strangers, but was he jumping to conclusions?

Dick said his goodbyes and was surprised when Gilly's arms wrapped about his waist. He awkwardly patted her back, then turned and left her to her day, his mind whirring from the information he hadn't expected to receive.

CHAPTER TWENTY-FIVE

Dick returned to his safe house and got to work.

The news from Gilly had alarmed him and set him on edge. Earlier that morning he'd felt spritely if a little battered and bruised, but now his hackles were raised. He drew out his notepad and listed all his encounters over the last few days, then tried to work out exactly what he was dealing with here. Someone had tracked him. Someone knew where he had been. Someone knew where Gilly lived.

He started from Gilly and worked backward, which drew a straight line to Chuck's pharmacy. If this psychopath had found Gilly, there was no way he hadn't spoken to Chuck.

Dick sighed. That was the last person he wanted to revisit. The pharmacist-slash-black market evidence tech had more screws loose than anyone he had met, although the chances were that he wouldn't expect to see Dick anytime soon. Especially not after their last encounter.

Who else had Dick interacted with since he vacated his apartment?

There was Jessica, of course. Dick had made use of her talents to investigate his house and retrieve the note. There was also Louie, who ran the flower shop and looked out for Jessica.

Whatever creepy dynamic that setup has. It occurred to Dick on more than one occasion that Jessica could easily pay for her accommodation with her body. He only hoped that she wouldn't.

Dick shuddered.

Who else? Who else?

There were the obvious few from the last couple of days. Since Gillian sent this man to East and Third, then it was more than likely he'd encountered the Dead Devils. Whether or not he could glean more information from their outpost guards was debatable, but the trail would immediately lead to the coast where the Dead Devils held their celebratory events.

Less than a mile from my goddamn safe house.

Would that mean that Maurine and Hugo were somehow compromised? Dick hoped that whoever this intruder was, he wouldn't be able to get much further past the Dead Devils. The gang could be his barricade.

But what if they're not?

Dick's brow creased as he sketched links to each name and made additional notes. Not only was he now in a position where Petrov clearly knew who he was and was somehow ready for him, but there was another man out there seeking him, too. They were flanking him and leaving Dick few places to run.

Dick set the notepad down and paced the underground house. He poured himself a bourbon and sipped, then leaned against the kitchen counter. The more he tried to work out the truth, the more he dug himself a pit from which he could no longer find an escape. Like a Chinese finger trap, he was getting to the point where the harder he pulled, the more secure it would grip. Sooner or later, they'd find him.

What to do? What to do?

Dick closed his eyes and imagined his targets. First, there was Sadie Turnberry. He believed that she was still the instigator in all of this. She had a motive. She had due cause for wanting to see Dick suffer, particularly after all that he'd done to her in claiming back the pendant.

Then there was Petrov, the slimy Russian creep who knew to expect Dick and had him surrounded. Petrov would be tricky to get to, but Dick had to find a way. How else would he topple this goddamn Jenga tower of corruption?

Third, there was the mysterious marksman. A ghost in the system who was trailing Dick and not being too careful about the tracks he left. If he cared one iota about being discovered, he was doing a lousy job of remaining hidden. Usually, the pricks in this town silenced their witnesses with a bullet or strangulation. Why leave anything to chance?

So, a stalker with a conscience?

Finally, there was the mysterious Dexter Lockhart. Dick couldn't shake that name or his confusion about where it fit in the equation. It was written in black and white on his pad and circled many times. Dick knew better than to let a strand of investigation drop until it made sense. The ones that seemed innocent or pointless usually held the strongest path to discovering the secret behind everything.

Dick stretched and examined his wounds, not wanting to head back outside until he'd had a chance to recover fully, but knowing that he had to do something. He couldn't sit around while some psychopath drew ever closer.

Dick tramped up the stairs and out into the abandoned warehouse's lobby. He thumbed Jessica's phone number and waited for an answer. None came.

Shit. Maybe I spoke too soon. Maybe he did kill her. Fuck. I hope not.

Dick tried the number three more times, but it went to voicemail each time. He sighed, adjusted his jacket, then headed back into the city.

Dick kept his wits about him as he hailed a driverless cab and climbed inside. Although he was leery about leaving tracks, he knew he had to get there fast. Time was of the essence, and as long as he was strategic about where the cab picked him up and dropped him off, he decided that he should be fine.

He hoped. It was worth the risk.

Louie's Florists was closed. All the lights were off.

Dick checked his watch. It was mid-afternoon. The shop should still be open, according to the sign pinned to the window.

He cupped his hands against the glass and peered through. There was no sign of activity. No flower displays outside. Nothing.

Dick got a bad feeling.

He stepped back and looked up at the apartment windows. The curtains were drawn. He rang Jessica a fourth time and once again got her voicemail.

"What the fuck have you done?" Dick grumbled while imagining himself talking to this mysterious pursuer. He didn't want to jump to conclusions, although he had to admit that things looked bad.

Dick circled to the rear of the building where the deliveries of fresh flowers came once a week. There was a steel door fastened shut with no handle to access from the outside. Dick scratched his head and looked up, wondering if there was another way to enter.

There's always another way.

Several cameras and fitted alarm systems protruded from the wall, although their lights weren't blinking. Dick knew better than to presume they weren't active, so he thumbed his blocker device and hoped for the best.

A nearby pile of wooden pallets became his first step in climbing toward a window fifteen feet above him that was slightly ajar. The makeshift route to it looked rather precarious but could do the job. It involved heaving himself up to a small overhang that created a cover for the delivery folks on rainy days. From there, he'd have to sidle across the ledge that created the awning's foundation and ease himself up into the window.

Dick began his climb.

He wasn't as dextrous as he'd hoped, and his body protested the exertion. He pulled himself up onto the initial ledge with great effort, using the camera and device fittings as handholds, then sucked in his gut to stick close to the wall.

One slip and Dick would tumble onto solid concrete. One mistake, and he might be dealing with more than a simple concussion.

Dick steadied his breath and worked his way along the ledge. The progress was painful, each step measured and delicate. Behind him, the back of another building cast him in shadow, although there were windows where people might spot him. Despite this, he continued with purpose and eventually found his way to his target.

The window was on a metal latch and levered from a hinge at the top. While this was good in one regard—Dick could pry the window open relatively wide—it also meant that it would press against his back and try to close while he climbed through.

Dick brushed aside some vanity products from the window ledge, now able to see that he was entering a bathroom. He heaved himself onto his stomach and pulled himself in while disregarding the noise he made. There was no way to avoid it. He clambered through as toothbrushes and bottles clattered to the floor.

On the final push, Dick slid to the floor with a crash.

"Son of a bitch," he muttered while hoisting himself upright. He scolded himself internally, knowing that he could have completed that maneuver with more grace on a normal day. He stood and brushed himself down before listening for any sign of disturbance from other rooms.

The place was silent.

Dick opened the bathroom door and entered a quiet hall. The stairs Louie had once guided him up were nearby, so he knew something of the layout. Dick trod carefully toward Jessica's room and paused at the door.

The room was quiet, but something was amiss. Tiny plumes of smoke filtered through the gap beneath the door.

Dick nudged the door open and walked into a world of smoke.

He scanned the room and barely made out the back of Jessica's chair. He took a step inside, then froze and put his hands up as a figure whirled on him, the barrel of a pistol pointed directly at his face.

"No!" Jessica shouted as her hands trembled. Her eyes were wide, and Dick could see their whites despite the thick wall of smoke.

Dick held his hands high. "Jess. It's me. Put the gun down."

Jessica ran toward him in a flurry of limbs. She pressed him back against the wall and beat at his head with her fist and the gun butt. The metal cracked into his skull and caused his head to throb. "Jess! Please."

Dick grabbed her wrists and restrained her although she countered with kicks to his shins. "What are you doing?"

"What. Have. You. Done!" Jessica shouted, her eyes glassy with tears. Dick had never seen her look so distraught. Amid the smoke, she looked more like some crazed nautical wench washed up on the deck of a ship than the woman she had been. Her eyes were dark with smudged makeup, and her face was gaunt and pale. She wore a black gown that flew behind her as she shoved away from Dick and returned to her chair. She gripped it with one hand and looked as though if she didn't hold onto something she'd fall over.

Dick composed himself and kept his hands where she could see them. He was acutely aware of the gun still in her hand, and knew that accidents could happen if he didn't play this right.

"Jess? Tell me what happened."

Jessica's lips thinned. She turned and found her cigarette, before forcefully bringing it to her lips and taking rapid drags. "Louie's dead, Dick. Louie's fucking dead."

Dick's surprise was apparent on his face.

"Yeah, weren't expecting that were you, Mr. Knows-Everything?" Jessica ran a hand through her hair and streaked the white with ash.

"How?"

Jessica narrowed her eyes. "You have no idea, do you?"

Dick held her stare.

Jessica chewed her lip. "Some crazed psychopath came here looking for you. He pinned me down and demanded answers on your whereabouts. That innocent errand I ran for you? He followed me. Made it clear as fucking day that it was easy for him."

"Did you tell him where I was?"

Jessica shook her head in disbelief. "Always about you, isn't it? Of course, I didn't. I had no idea where you were. You watch your back more than you watch your front." She lowered her eyes. "That's always been one of the things that drew me to you."

"So what happened to Louie?"

Jessica threw her arms in the air. She waved the gun as if to draw Dick closer to the conclusion. "What do you think happened? He got in the way, so that bastard shot him. Left me to pick up the pieces. I've been on the phone non-stop, trying to piece together funeral arrangements and work out what's going to happen with this goddamn business."

Dick cautiously eased closer and motioned for Jessica to sit. Initially, she resisted, then regained some of her former composure. "I'm sorry to hear that happened to you. To him. Louie was a good guy."

Jessica blew out a mouthful of air. "Please. He was an obedient dog. Gave me a place to live, though. Away from the public eye and out of my enemies' sight." Her face soured. "Not enough to protect me from yours though, was it? And now I have to sort out the paperwork, sell this space, and find somewhere else to hide."

"Can't you take over?" Dick suggested but knew the answer.

"Please." Jessica rolled her eyes. "What do I know about floristry? Fuck all, that's what. My line of work is to know things and people and sell my knowledge to the highest bidder. What do I want to be the face of a shop for?"

"Could do you good. Take off the heat. You could go on the straight and narrow. Life doesn't have to be this hard."

Jessica looked down her nose at Dick. "Then where would you get your knowledge? I wouldn't be able to do shit for you anymore."

Dick looked down at the floor.

Jessica sighed and finally set the gun on the side table. "He was a great man, really. Honest, loyal, kind. A little too touchy-feely at times, but they all are at that age, I suppose."

Dick looked up at Jessica. "Can you tell me a little about the man who came here? What did he look like? What do you remember?"

"In trouble are we, Dick?"

Dick narrowed his eyes. "What do you think?"

Jessica leaned back in her chair and dabbed her eyes with fresh tissues. "He wasn't all that dissimilar to you. Same build, same height, I'd say. Dark stubble and a glint in his eye that spoke of sex and danger. He wore a dark brown jacket and carried a Colt .45—that's what he hit Louie with." She made the sign of the cross on her chest.

"Anything else? Any distinguishing characteristics?"

Jessica shook her head, then her expression changed. "Wait,

there was something. He had a silver tooth—one of his canines, I think. When he smiled, it glimmered in the light. I don't know if that's any help."

Dick shrugged. "It might be something. Tell me, where did he go after he left here? Did he say anything at all?"

"I had nothing to feed him," Jessica answered honestly. "There was nothing I could say. Once he shot Louie, I couldn't think of you. He tried to push me into confessing, but there was nothing to give, so he left. But not before…"

Dick shook his head. "He didn't?"

"No." Jessica waved a hand. "Nothing like that. He kissed my forehead and called me sweetheart. I'm not sure why. It was creepy as hell. The next thing I knew, a rag covered my mouth, and I was fast asleep."

"Chloroform," Dick stated. "Again, Jess, I'm so sorry this happened to you. If there's anything I can do for you to make up for all this, let me know. I didn't foresee anything like this when this case opened."

Jessica leaned forward with a determined expression on her face. "You want to do something for me, Dick? You catch that sonofabitch, put a slug between his eyes, and tell him, 'That one is for Louie.' Okay?"

Dick held Jessica's stare and nodded.

CHAPTER TWENTY-SIX

Dick gleaned little additional information from Chuck.

His visit was brief, with Chuck visibly trembling from the moment Dick walked into the store. It was the first time in years that he'd seen Chuck stationed at the counter, which provided a perfect place to ask his questions and get out quickly.

There were no customers, and Dick's pistol pointed from his hip to Chuck's stomach, out of camera sight. Chuck answered his questions quickly, and Dick couldn't detect any lie in his eyes. Chuck knew what Dick was capable of, and he wouldn't risk offending him yet again.

When Dick exited the pharmacy three minutes later, the only possible lead he could think of was the Russian woman who had joined forces with Chuck and ambushed Dick. However, Chuck could give little information on the woman when pressed, and Dick's suspicions rose. It didn't seem to be a coincidence that Petrov was Russian, and a Russian minion had somehow gotten involved.

Which means there may be a link from the unnamed psychopath to Petrov. That's not a good connection.

Dick quickly left the pharmacy's immediate vicinity and

headed back toward his safe house. He tried Santana again, but couldn't get through. He was starting to grow worried. She was tied up in this since she possessed the object that had triggered all this madness into fruition.

He hoped that she was okay.

When Dick arrived back at the safe house, he took a nap and woke up as night fell. He emerged into the darkness a little more refreshed than earlier, but by no means any less confused. He found the nearest bar and bought himself a scotch, then nursed it as he sat at the counter and watched the slowly building crowd.

Young men and women in their twenties milled around as they laughed, danced, and conversed. Dick wondered what it was like to have a group of people you could let go with. He imagined it wasn't ever that easy—at least, it hadn't been for him. Even your best friends could let you down and hide secrets you never dreamed could stay hidden. Dick had solid friends in the past, but they all faded away for one reason or another.

Solitude bred peace.

At least, that's what he convinced himself.

The drink didn't last long, and when Dick finished it, he stepped back onto the streets and made for the one person remaining who he imagined he might get any sense from. He was tired of second-hand information. This time, he needed to go straight to the source.

The city blurred by in the driverless cab, and Dick once again ensured that it picked him up and dropped him off in locations that might mystify anyone hacking his bank account or GPS locations. He strode along the quiet streets of the suburbs, with their large mansions and villas stationed on either side of the road behind large, protected walls.

Dick laughed. No matter how much money you had, you could never buy total protection. Even the most prolific and wealthy celebrities were vulnerable to a well-placed bullet fired from a distance.

Dick's heart beat harder as the manor came into view. He knew that his next move was high-risk, yet he also knew that he now had an advantage.

Dick took the next side alley and cut down into the shadows.

Sadie Turnberry lay in her bed as Sabrina the ocelot purred at her feet. She couldn't switch her mind off, and couldn't get to sleep no matter how hard she tried.

The last few days had been a shitstorm as the oppressive hand of revenge pressed down on her. She had been a day away from handing off the pendant to her benefactor to do what he wanted with it, but things hadn't gone to plan.

Dick Chambers was a pain in her ass—literally. Her body was still sore following her visit to the hospital nights ago. She never in a million years would have imagined that someone could break through her security measures and infiltrate her manor while she was gone.

But there it was. There was no one hundred percent success rate in protection. Just ask JFK.

She stared at the ceiling. Sabrina's snoring purrs soothed her but not enough to let her drift. She glanced at her cell. All she needed was one good phone call. One piece of good news to tell her that Chambers was dead, or they'd found the bitch. That way she could rest easy, hand off the jewelry, and get on with her life. Their demands made her call in her favors, and she was fast running out of options.

Not even her PI could find him.

Sadie slipped a hand under her pillow. Her knuckles found the solid metal barrel of her shotgun. It had once lived beneath her bed, but that seemed too far away now. Maybe one day her manor would feel safe again, but it wasn't today. She had replaced her security detail and pumped in more cash, but she still didn't feel secure.

Something bumped at the end of her bedroom. Sadie raised her head, but couldn't see anything. Sabrina growled when it disturbed her slumber, but her eyes remained closed. Sadie stared into the room's shadows but saw nothing of note. Still, the irritation lingered, the feeling that something was amiss.

She reached over and turned on her lamp. It provided soft illumination, but the farthest corners were too distant to gain much from the light. She narrowed her eyes and sat upright as her hand grasped her shotgun.

"I'd put that down if I were you," a voice crooned from above.

Sadie cast her eyes up toward the top posts of her four-poster bed. A man lay across the creaking beams with a pistol aimed between her eyes.

Dick Chambers stared levelly down at her. "Totally your call. This could go either way."

Sabrina grumbled, adjusted her position, and slept on.

Dick lowered himself as the posts threatened to break beneath his weight. He landed with a soft *thud*. The ocelot opened one beady eye before closing it again.

"How the hell did you get in here?" Sadie added after a pause, "Again."

Dick shrugged. "Piece of advice. Maybe don't replace the entire security detail after a massive break-in. It only creates more vulnerabilities as they learn the layout of your building and get their bearings. Besides, I know the layout of this place now— well, the key bits. Once you've broken into somewhere once, it's easier the second time."

Sadie glared at him. "What do you want?"

Dick narrowed his eyes. "I want it to stop. Whoever you have coming after me, I want it to end. Now. I want information on your buyer, and I want to exit this house without trouble. Think you can do all those things?"

Sadie grinned. "Choose one."

"Information." Dick held the gun steady.

Sadie adjusted in the bed. Dick pressed the gun closer. She held up her arms. "All right, I'm only getting comfortable, okay?"

Dick was silent.

"You know I can't give you information," she muttered. "It's suicide. Have you never heard of honor among thieves?"

"Have you never heard of, 'Speak, bitch, before I turn your face into an Impressionist painting?'" Dick's finger flexed on the trigger and caught Sadie's gaze. "A name. Now."

Sadie shrugged. "You think a man of the caliber you're hunting will give me a real name? I have a number. That's it. I pay my money, and he does my bidding."

"And you needed two men to hunt me down, did you?" Dick grinned. "I'll take that as a compliment."

"I hired one," Sadie snapped, annoyed by Dick's bravado. "The other one was provided for me."

"By who?" Dick asked.

Sadie's lips thinned.

"Dexter Lockhart?" Dick questioned.

A little color drained from Sadie's face. "How do you—"

Bingo.

Dick cut her off. "Not important. The important part here is to tell me what links you have with Dexter. What does he want? What's the pendant's importance? Why is he so adamant about removing me from the picture?"

"Oh, it's not just him. We all want you out of the picture. I don't think you realize the impact you have on our line of work in the city. You really think a private investigator can just go about his business? Especially one who stirs up as much trouble as you?" She nodded at a bottle of prescription pills on the side table. "I've hardly been able to walk straight since our encounter the other night. Dexter... Well, I can't say much—and I won't. And my investigator... Let me say that he was all too eager to have the opportunity to hunt you down. It seems your name is known on the circuit, Dick. That's not a great place to be for a man who operates in anonymity, is it?"

Dick's face hardened. He moved closer and leaned on the bed with the barrel of the gun inches from Sadie's face. "You haven't answered a single question."

"And if you think I'm going to—"

Dick jammed the gun into Sadie's mouth, which cut off whatever was going to come next. A look of genuine panic flooded her as Sabrina opened a beady eye and lifted her head in curiosity.

Dick lowered his voice to a growl as his spare hand fished beneath the pillow for the shotgun. He drew the secondary weapon and pointed them both at Sadie. "Last chance. Remember, I found a way in. I can find a way out again."

Sadie's shoulders softened. She mumbled something incoherent around the metal of the gun. Dick removed it from her mouth. "Fine. Fine, I'll tell you, but it won't be what you want to hear."

"I'm listening," Dick informed her as he distanced himself slightly.

"I can't tell you what you want to know about the pendant," Sadie explained. "I don't know what the point of it is. All I know is that the thing's value is immense. The price on that piece of jewelry was enough to drag my sorry ass into the equation. I went through torture while trying to find a way to collect it and cover my tracks, but it was all bullshit in the end. Now it's God-knows-where, and the pressure is on me to reclaim it."

"From who?" Dick asked.

Sadie gave Dick an intense stare. "Who do you think?"

"Dexter Lockhart?"

Sadie nodded. Explaining all this was torture for her.

"How does Petrov fit into this equation?" Dick lowered the shotgun but held the pistol steady. When Sadie gave him another strange look, he added, "What? Surprised that I've figured out the other goon who's after me? There's a reason I've lasted in this industry as long as I have. Who is Petrov? Why has he put a price on my head?"

Sadie smirked. "You know, for a man who brags about how great he is at his job, I find it laughable that you still haven't put the pieces altogether." She shook her head. "The best puzzles are the ones you solve yourself."

Dick sighed and raised the shotgun.

"Fine!" Sadie protested. "Fine." She glanced at Sabrina and gave her a look as if to say, "What's the point of having a pet that doesn't protect me?" Her hand moved to the side of the bed, but before it could go too far, Dick brought the gun back to her mouth.

Dick's face soured. "I'm not playing around, Sadie. Keep your finger away from the emergency panic button. Last warning. My patience is wearing thin."

Sadie growled. "Petrov is one of Dexter's lapdogs. Lockhart turned the heat up on me, but he also has his other dogs working to clean up the mess you've made and reclaim what's theirs. I don't know Petrov personally. Only know the name. But if that guy has your number, it's only a matter of time before you kiss the dirt and find yourself buried six feet under—if enough of your body parts remain."

"Where does he live? How do I get to him?" Dick gritted his teeth.

"Hell if I know!"

Dick curtly nodded, then fixed Sadie with a dark look. "Call off your dog. I'm not fucking around, Miss Turnberry. I don't want to be responsible for more dead bodies in this shit-heap city, but I'll take down anyone who threatens my life. Got that?"

Sadie didn't answer. Instead, she flung herself to the side of the bed and violently pressed a secret button nestled into the bed frame.

She beamed at Dick, then looked around the room in confusion. "Where's the alarm?"

Dick smiled back as he stepped onto the top of the bed frame and made his escape through the rafters. It was trickier than anticipated having to carry both weapons as he climbed. "You think I'd drop in without disabling the alarms? I'm disappointed in you."

Sadie let out an enraged scream, but by the time security arrived, Dick was gone.

CHAPTER TWENTY-SEVEN

Dick walked the streets far from Sadie's house, alone, frustrated and confused.

There had to be something he'd missed—a link to get to the guys that were coming for him. The only good result of his conversation with Sadie was that he'd now fixed Dexter Lockhart as the instigator. He finally had the head honcho under the spotlight, and that gave him a direction of sorts.

But how to track Petrov?

The card game was fast approaching. Dick was proficient in that arena, but there was no way he could enter that room by himself. If Petrov's goons were there, they would surely know Dick.

Or would they?

Of course, they would. It might have been dark in that alley, but Petrov would have shown them something so they could keep a lookout. As far as Petrov and Lockhart were concerned, he was their most dangerous enemy at the moment.

Then there was the case of Sadie's marksman. Dick knew she wouldn't call off the hunt, but at least he'd tried. A small part of him wanted to believe that he could continue on the Lockhart-

Petrov path without interference, but Sadie was an old breed of scum. You couldn't teach an old dog new tricks. Or, as Dick preferred to think of it, "You can't teach an ancient bitch to jump rope."

Dick wandered through the quiet streets while keeping an eye out for anyone who might be tracking him. When he was a reasonable distance from Sadie's manor, he hopped into a cab and requested to be dropped off six blocks from the safe house.

Along the ride, he checked his cell. There was still no report from Santana. Nothing was logged in his messages or missed calls. A strange feeling settled in his stomach that something might be amiss. He only hoped that he could zero in on the bad guys before they finally caught up with the modern-day Lara Croft.

Dick exited the cab. It drove off into the distance. He walked the final few blocks and stopped only to pick up a greasy burger from a takeout diner. He ate as he walked, his stomach thankful for a meal. With everything going on, his sleeping and eating patterns had gone off track from his usual schedule.

Hazards of the job.

Dick was thankful when he entered the shadow of the old industrial buildings. He snaked his way through the old roads and made his way to the safe house. The lobby was silent. He unlocked the secure door and descended the stairs, mind full of mystery, and stomach full of meat and grease.

He kicked off his shoes and grabbed a beer from the fridge, then unscrewed the top before he shrugged off his jacket and launched it across the room. He flopped onto the couch and drew a long breath.

"You look like shit." Valentina's voice came from nowhere.

Dick kept his eyes closed. "I feel like shit."

When Valentina chuckled, he opened his eyes and found her looming over him, her face upside down from his perspective. "Tell me. Do you ever ask for help, Dick Chambers? You look like you could use some. No man should look as bruised and beaten as you."

Dick sipped his drink. "Flesh wounds. Nothing serious."

"This time." Valentina vaulted over the couch and sat beside him. Dick had to force his eyes away from staring at her lean figure, clad in the bright red color that gave her the name, The Red Countess. She kicked her boots onto the coffee table and crossed one leg over the other. "I bet there's a hell of a story to accompany those war wounds."

Dick nodded. "There is. But I'm not ready to tell it."

Valentina pouted. "Oh, Dick. Holding out on me again? I wouldn't expect anything less." She trailed two fingers up his arm and toward his neck. "Although, you know that I have ways of making you talk."

"I'm a bank safe. No sense in trying to crack this vault."

Valentina laughed. "Please. Every man has a trigger. And it's usually the tent pole peeking out from your pants." She looked down. "Right on cue."

Dick shuffled to adjust himself. He rubbed his eyes. "With the greatest of respect—because I know you could kill me in the time it takes for a butterfly's wings to beat—what the hell are you doing here? This is supposed to be a protected safe house. Best of the best. This place is something the AJS is proud of."

Valentina scoffed. "Should it be? Please, Dick. It's not difficult to track you. And when you can pick locks and hack alarm systems as I do, there's little anyone can do to stop me. I do like the fact you're trying, though. It's cute. Gives me a little challenge."

Dick rose and adjusted his pants. He set his empty bottle on the counter, then offered Valentina a drink.

She shook her head. "You know you don't have to get me drunk to have fun, don't you?"

There was a sparkle in her eye that made Dick smile. He still couldn't understand her motivations, life story, or anything else other than the fact she was hot and seemed to like him. He wasn't going to complain, but he'd be lying if he didn't admit that the whole setup confused him.

He grabbed another beer and tipped it her way. "Cheers."

When he sat, he put a little room between himself and Valentina. She closed the gap almost instantly and stared at him intently. "Tell me your woes."

Dick cast his tired gaze at his hands, unsure what to tell her. "First, you need to tell me why you're here. What are you after? Is this a routine check-in that I'm supposed to expect now?"

Valentina smirked. "Expect the unexpected. That's my motto." She twisted toward him, brought her knees onto the couch, and rested her head on her hand. "I guess I was intrigued to find out that you weren't at home. That you had this little safe place to yourself and never told me."

"It's a safe house. I'm supposed to keep it quiet."

"But imagine the fun we could have. No one to know you're here. No one to know I'm here. I haven't stayed in one place for over a decade now. The idea of a place that's hidden and protected is... Well, it's a dream."

She smiled, although Dick detected a pained element of truth in her words. "Sounds like a rough life."

"It can be," Valentina agreed. "I wouldn't have it any other way. Now, keep me entertained. What's your latest problem? Something is clearly troubling you."

Dick chewed his lip, then decided to give Valentina the over-view. He avoided the specifics of names and locations, mainly focusing on the people that were after him and the dilemma of missing the key information he needed to get shit done. Not that he believed it mattered. If Valentina wanted to find out where he'd been and who he'd spoken to, he was certain she could. Although she was a mercenary, her skills and contacts always impressed him. If he weren't such a proud man, he might offer to team up with her. Although he was sure she wouldn't go for it. She'd lose out on a lot of money.

Valentina fell quiet for a moment as she considered Dick's response. She sauntered over to the kitchen area and poured herself a glass of water after navigating the cupboards as if she'd lived there her whole life. Dick studied her hips as she walked and admired every inch of her body.

She leaned against the counter with a thoughtful look on her face. "You want me to take them out?"

Dick laughed. The force of it hurt his tired muscles. "No. I couldn't afford it."

"Friends and family discount," Valentina offered.

Dick shook his head. "I don't think I qualify as either. Do you have friends?"

Valentina dodged the question. "This card game. You're contemplating it, aren't you? You wouldn't turn down a game of poker, even if it meant cutting your dick off to play."

Dick grinned. "Is that always on your mind?"

"You need a better tactic," Valentina informed him. "Someone who can penetrate that game and go undercover. You need to stay away from it but guide the action. What about your cop friend? What's she doing tomorrow night?"

Dick's smile grew. "She's involved. She'll accompany me."

"No," Valentina replied. "Send her in with a bug. You'll be her eyes and ears. She's going to do what you can't."

"What can't I do?" Dick asked.

Valentina raised an eyebrow. "Walk into the lion's den."

Dick thought about it and quickly realized that Valentina was right. While Petrov's men couldn't do anything in the presence of an AJS officer in public, it would play to his and Terra's advantage to have a mole inside with no distraction there from Dick.

"Fine." Dick nodded. "I need equipment. Terra's not going to like this."

"Who cares?" Valentina rolled her eyes. "If you managed to

lure her in the first time, she's not going to argue a second time. Those who hunt justice don't care what it takes to make it happen."

"Do you hunt for justice?" Dick asked.

Valentina walked back over to the couch. "I hunt for coin." She extended a hand toward Dick. "Are you coming?"

"Where?" Dick knew the answer. He took Valentina's hand, left his beer behind, and they both entered the bedroom.

To give her credit, Valentina was gentle with him. After his initial complaint about the soreness in particular parts of his body, she took over and guided Dick on a whistle-stop tour of pleasure town.

They fell asleep quickly afterward, and when Dick woke up, he was unsurprised to discover that Valentina was nowhere in sight.

"Sometimes I wonder whether she's a figment of my imagination." A flurry of memories from the previous night hit him at once, and her perfume still lingered on the pillow. "Don't complain, Dick. Just keep dreaming."

Dick showered, shaved, then was ready for the day. He cleaned up his clothes that were scattered around the room and emerged into the morning air. It was a little before eleven, and the city was awake. Dick inhaled a deep lungful of air and dug his hands into his pockets.

Tonight was the big game. The one that would determine whether or not he could nail Petrov and figure out what was going on. Dick's burning curiosity was driving him insane. It took over his thoughts at all hours, cut into his sleep, and caused him to make reckless decisions. He knew now that he played The Pink Flamingo wrong, but he couldn't go back in time, so it was his job to look ahead.

As he sat in the diner, he thumbed in Ringo's number and dropped him a message. Ringo was reliable. That was one of the things that Dick loved most about him. With any luck, Dick would be sorted for tonight's mission.

Dick sat back and sipped his drink. He was back on dry toast, although his beefy meals the day before had stirred up something inside him once again. He sat in the quiet of the diner, the lunchtime rush due to begin within the next hour. His phone buzzed with a response from Ringo, and Dick took that as his cue to leave. There were better places to meet an eccentric tech-head about covert equipment for a plot to infiltrate a Russian gang.

Ringo waited for Dick at the bottom of a long set of stairs that led into the subway. The tunnels were brighter than the world outside, and the underground space boasted designer and upmarket shops and stores lining many of the long walls. Civilians walked to and fro as they navigated through the labyrinth and hunted for their subway rides. Security guards kept a visible presence, and the smell of bleach overwhelmed the nostrils.

Dick walked with Ringo to an area with available seating. There wasn't a seat to spare during rush hour, but now, in the middle of the day, only a third of them were taken.

Dick sat beside Ringo. "You got what I asked for?"

Ringo scoffed. "Dick. You insult me." He unzipped his rucksack, took out several small cardboard boxes, and handed them to Dick.

Dick opened the first one.

"The latest and greatest in microtechnology." Excitement laced Ringo's voice. "You have no idea the lengths I went to secure this baby. They're still prototypes at AC University."

Dick looked inside the box at a single speck of…something. It looked like a grain of rice, only black. He raised his eyebrows. "You're kidding me?"

Ringo's smile lit up his face. "Not one iota." He tapped the grain of rice, and it clung to the tip of his finger. "This is an earpiece, the smallest one available anywhere in the world. Even the Russians haven't acquired this level of technology yet."

Dick kept his face neutral but wondered if Ringo knew more about Dick than he let on. Perhaps he knew about his plight with the Russians. If someone had made technology this size, it wouldn't be impossible for Ringo to have bugged Dick a long time ago, to trace his every move.

Yet, somehow, Ringo was one of the few people Dick fully trusted. He had to. Otherwise, it would be hard to get anything done.

Ringo continued, "Inside this baby is microtechnology that amazes even me. The heat emitted through the pores in your skin powers the cell, and… Well, I shouldn't give away all its secrets. Here, give it a go."

He reached his finger toward Dick, and Dick recoiled.

Ringo laughed. "Calm down, Chambers. You're getting neurotic in your old age."

Dick steadied and accepted the finger inside his ear. Ringo scraped it against the inside hollow, then sat back.

"Ready?" Ringo asked with excitement.

Dick shrugged. "Sure."

Ringo tapped a few times on his cell phone, and an over-whelmingly loud and devastating sound broke into Dick's ear. It was as though he was at a concert, standing next to one of the large, towering speakers as some crazed guitarist rocked his solo. He clamped a hand to his ear, which only made it worse, vaguely aware of Ringo scrambling on the other side of the table as he shouted in pain.

The sound was everything until it wasn't. A moment later, the volume reduced until it was as though the band was playing in the diner. He removed his hands and looked around for the source of the music, his mind momentarily dazed. He met the strange, questioning stares of the other patrons and turned away.

A waitress approached and asked Dick if he was okay.

"Fine, thanks!" Dick roared, trying to be heard above the music. On the other side of the table, Ringo tapped a few more times, and the sound diminished to a whisper.

Dick caught the waitress grumbling as she disappeared. "No need to shout. Jesus…"

Dick came back to his senses. The music played with perfect clarity in his head, but at a level where he could hear the rumbling chatter in the diner. He frowned at Ringo.

"Sorry," Ringo apologized. "I should have checked the volume settings before beginning."

Dick's lips thinned as the pain of the headache lingered. It felt as though he'd been waterboarded with sound. "I guess so."

"Not bad though, eh?" Ringo continued cheerily. "Crystal-clear clarity. All you have to do is speak through a receiver and whoever is wearing the piece can speak and listen to you as though they're standing beside you."

"That's great." Dick picked roughly at his ear, trying to remove the damn thing.

Ringo jumped to his aid. "Careful! Let me. Hold on." He delicately removed the earpiece with a small set of tweezers. "There. Wow, I mean, do you have any idea how much this could fetch on the market?"

"You said it's not for sale." Dick massaged his ear. "It's still being worked on at ACU. Are you certain it's safe?"

Ringo laughed. "Nothing in tech is safe, Dick. You of all people should know that. I imagine there are still a few bugs and kinks to work out, but otherwise, it should be fit for the function you want to use it for."

Dick narrowed his eyes at the piece of tech. Ringo held it to the light between the tweezers and examined it with wonder. "Is there anything we can't make in this town?"

"What else have you got?"

Ringo snapped from his reverie. "Oh, yes. Of course. Hearing would be useless without sight, wouldn't it?" He pointed at one of the other boxes in front of Dick. "That should be what you're looking for."

Dick opened the box and found a tiny black contact lens, carefully resting on a soft bed of clear liquid. Ringo leaned forward but kept his hands back. "I can't touch that one, I'm afraid. It's all over to you, Dicky Bird."

Dick shot him a look.

Ringo shrank back. "Right. Sorry."

Dick looked down at the lens with mild disgust. He hated touching his eyes and refused to go to the lengths of ever wearing contacts if he had the chance. Something about the foreign body that sat on the most valuable part of his face made him uncomfortable. The majority of his business depended on eyesight. He didn't want to compromise it.

He handed the box to Ringo. "You show me. You demonstrate."

Ringo raised his hands defensively. "You know I'd love to, but these lenses are fit and ready for a single use. If I put one in, I'm wasting it."

"So will I," Dick replied. "I won't be wearing one on the mission. I can promise you that." He held Ringo's stare.

Ringo sighed. "Fine. It's going to cost you extra, though. I only have three of these puppies, and they don't come cheap."

"I'm guessing they shouldn't be in your hands at all," Dick added as Ringo removed his glasses and touched his finger to the lens. He pinched open his eyelids with one hand and tapped the lens into his eye. Dick marveled at how relaxed and calm he kept during the procedure, and how easily the lens took to his eyeball.

Ringo removed his fingers and blinked three times. When he was satisfied, he handed his cell phone to Dick. "There's an app that connects with the lens. The moment it touches the eye, it activates. Here, take a look."

Dick held the camera in landscape mode. The screen filled

with a perfect live video feed from Ringo's point of view. As he looked around the room, the camera tracked every movement in crystal clarity. Dick scoffed as Ringo lingered on the nearby waitress's ass.

"Shame it can't read thoughts," Dick announced with a slight smirk on his face.

"Not bad though, eh? Combine this with your grain of rice earpiece, and you'll be loaded and ready for whatever mission comes your way."

"Look at me for a moment," Dick instructed.

Ringo obeyed. Dick examined Ringo's eye, looking for any obvious signs of obtrusion or tampering. He wanted to be diligent. He didn't need the other people attending the game to identify that Terra was wearing an eyepiece.

There was no color to the lens. No obvious signs on Ringo's face that it existed. Whoever had manufactured these had done an amazing job.

Dick paid Ringo and provided him with food as Ringo packaged the items back together and removed the lens. As they ate and spoke of banal things, Dick's thoughts kept moving back to the tech, wondering what the hell was coming on the horizon if this kind of surveillance went to mass-market. It seemed so strange that the world was creating items like this, which could spy on people when there were still global conflicts and problems that needed attention.

Eventually, Dick waved Ringo goodbye and emerged back into the subway proper. He tucked his hands in his pockets, held the boxes close to his person, and aimed for the stairs, his thoughts filled with the mission ahead.

CHAPTER TWENTY-EIGHT

The day passed without much incident, which allowed Dick plenty of time to prepare. He called Gilly to check in on her and see how she was doing, and was pleased to discover that she had found a new apartment and was in the process of moving as they spoke.

Gilly sounded surprisingly chirpy, given all that had happened. As they spoke, Dick's mind strayed to the mysterious man who was tracking him, hoping that he had somehow shaken him off the scent, but almost certain that he hadn't. Gilly asked how things were with Dick. He remained tight-lipped for the most part. She laughed and told him that he should loosen up sometime. Dick gave his standard response, "When I can, I will. But I can't."

After Gilly, Dick phoned Santana. Once again, the phone went to voicemail. The hairs on Dick's neck bristled as he wondered what was keeping her from answering. Hopefully, she was okay. With people coming for him, he only hoped they weren't coming for her, too. She held the pendant, and for some reason, it was important to them. Would it mean killing the jungle girl to retrieve it?

They killed Eric. Who else wouldn't they kill?

As night fell, Dick made his way back to his safe house where he was due to meet Terra. He unlocked the warehouse door and headed down the stairs. As he opened the door to the main house, he sighed.

"Doesn't anyone knock anymore?" Dick grumbled.

Terra raised an eyebrow. "Anyone? I hope you haven't been inviting guests into your *safe* house, Dick. This property is one of our AJS secret spots. If you're down here having parties and inviting your whores, then that throws a bit of a spanner in the works, doesn't it?"

Dick smirked. "None of that, I'm afraid. You're early."

Terra gave a curt nod. She was out of her AJS fatigues and had adopted a dark pair of pants, boots, and a white, comfortable top. Dick gave her the once-over.

Terra didn't miss it. "Eat me with your eyes all you like. It's never going to happen."

"I wouldn't dream of it," Dick replied.

"You haven't?" Terra stirred her coffee and brought it to her lips, eyes locked on Dick's.

Dick shrugged. "Well…"

"I'll take that as a compliment." Terra motioned to another cup on the counter. "I've made one for you, too. Thought you best have your wits about you while we get stuck into this card game."

"About that…" Dick took his cup and explained his plan to Terra.

Terra was silent the entire time. That was one thing Dick loved about her. She knew when to listen and when to ask questions. It was a skill that the AJS beat into their staff, knowing that if you let a criminal talk for long enough, they're bound to slip up. Her face was impassive the entire time. Dick couldn't read any emotion or insight. When he finished, silence hung in the air.

Terra lowered her cup to the counter. She cracked her knuckles, then punched Dick in the chest. "Are you fucking kidding me?"

Dick protected himself and turned away. "Look, it's the only way we can do this. I've thought it through, and it's not safe enough for me to be in there. They'll recognize me instantly and then we've got another chase on our hands."

"I'm not some puppet for you to pull strings," Terra declared. "You want that? You pay some escort the cash upfront to do your dirty work. I'm a woman of integrity. A woman of the law."

"A woman who was kicked out of her precinct for taking the law into her own hands," Dick reminded her, unsure how to read the expression that fell on Terra's face. He continued, nonetheless. "Justice is bred deep within you, Terra. You love to help, and this is a real chance to do so. All I need is Petrov's location, so I can bring him into some custody and get my questions answered. Then we'll take out a large part of Atlantica's scum. Tell me, what can the AJS do in this situation?"

Terra's lips thinned. "Nothing until they slip up in public."

"Exactly. And these guys are smart enough to do everything behind closed doors. They're untouchable because of the stupid rules on this island."

Terra chewed this over as her eyes bored into Dick's. "That precinct shit was low."

"I'm sorry," Dick replied. "It's true though. There's something in you that wants more. The AJS shackles restrain you."

"The AJS keeps justice," Terra declared, although there was a crack in her conviction. She shook her head and paced the safe house. Dick remained silent and allowed her time to think while he sipped his coffee, thankful for the black nectar.

"Okay," Terra announced at last. "You know what? Let's do this. I've always been curious to see life through your eyes. Maybe this will be my chance. I'll drown myself in bourbon, smoke more than a fucking dragon, and kick the shit out of some criminals during a game of cards."

Dick scoffed. "If you want to walk a mile in my shoes, it's going to take a lot more than that."

Terra raised an eyebrow. "I mean, that's a pretty low bar already."

Dick laughed. "Ready to get fitted?" He produced the boxes from his pocket and tossed them to Terra. She caught them without hesitation. "Careful, they're expensive."

Terra narrowed her eyes as she opened the package. "Then why throw them?"

"I knew you'd catch them." Dick started the coffee maker.

"You really think you know me that well?" Terra chuckled.

Dick shrugged. "You caught them, didn't you?"

Terra shook her head and laughed. "Shut up and make me another, won't you? I want to be wide awake and ready for this shitshow when it gets going."

Terra had parked an unmarked Escalade a few blocks away from the safe house. The vehicle was black and was only noticeable at the right angles when the streetlights hit the silver grill and edging. The windows were tinted.

Dick approached the driver's side and opened the handle. Terra admonished him with a simple, "Excuse me?"

"What?" Dick asked.

Terra wagged a finger. "I think I'll be the one driving the $50,000 vehicle; thank you very much."

Dick rolled his eyes and skirted the car to the passenger side. "You're going to have to learn to trust other people to play, you know."

"Same goes to you." Terra climbed inside.

"Besides," Dick continued, clipping in his seatbelt. "Who's going to be solo in the vehicle when you go in for the game? This guy. That means I'm the getaway driver if things go south."

"Things aren't going to go south, though. Are they, Dick?" She raised her eyebrows, reminding Dick of how his mother used to tell him off for kicking the soccer ball into his neighbor's garden. *You're not going to do that again, are you, John?*

They set off into the night. The music was on low, some generic radio station playing out the beats that the kids danced to in the night clubs. Dick laughed, and Terra asked why.

"Didn't have you down as a raver," Dick commented.

Terra signaled left and took the turn at a quaint pace. It was a far cry from the speeding supercar he had ridden in a couple of nights previous. "You don't know me."

"You say that, but I think we have far more in common than you think." Dick held up a hand and started counting off his fingers. "You and I both wish for justice in this city. We're both single loners. We both like taking things into our own hands and getting things done."

Terra's lips thinned. Dick took a strange pleasure in knowing that he was getting beneath her skin.

"The only thing we don't have in common is that I know how to shoot," Dick announced and looked away from her for dramatic effect. He knew that one would turn her head, and he felt her eyes burning into him now.

"That was an isolated incident," Terra replied, knuckles going white on the steering wheel.

"Isolated incident…" Dick scoffed. "It sure seemed like it at the time, but there was no way you didn't know what you were doing."

"Let it go, Dick." Terra slowed at a red light, eyes darting to the rearview.

"Let it go?" Dick grinned. "You shot me in the ass, Terra. Uncalled for. Totally unnecessary. Do you know what it was like to have to go into the hospital to get a bullet pulled out of my ass cheek? And, even once it was gone, it's never fully healed." He rubbed the side of his ass and smiled. "I wake up some nights, ass still in agony. The cold weather activates muscle memory."

Terra met Dick's eyes, then turned back to the road. "If my aim is so bad, why are you convinced that it was on purpose? Following your logic would mean that my aim is true and I meant to hit you."

"So you admit it?" Dick nudged.

Terra closed her eyes and drew a deep breath as the lights turned green. She pressed the gas. "You make it easy to remember why I don't like hanging out with you."

"Just admit it," Dick pressed. "We're two peas from the same pod."

Terra yanked the steering wheel left and pulled curbside, executing a perfect parallel park. She cranked the handbrake and turned to Dick, brandishing a finger. "If you can't learn to keep your mouth shut, I'm pulling out of this mission. It's bad enough I'm strapped in to be your side bitch, but if this is how you're going to play this tonight, you can find someone else. Surely you have a thousand bimbos in this city ready to clip themselves in and demean themselves so that you can get your version of justice. Stop pressing the fucking issue."

Dick stared at Terra levelly. "That may seem like a better solution, but no one can do what you do, Terra. You're the best of the best. I need that."

Sure, caress her ego, Dick. That'll win her around. Can't keep your mouth shut, can you?

To his surprise, Terra softened almost instantly. She sat back in her seat and rested her head on the headrest. Dick knew that he had her. Nothing could fuel Terra Kris like a few well-placed compliments and a reminder that she was serving the greater good. Even if she wouldn't admit it, they were cut from the same cloth.

"Don't think this gets you off the hook." Terra checked her side mirror and slowly eased out of the parking spot. As the

SUV's nose entered the street, the sound of roaring engines appeared somewhere in the city. By the time they were in their lane, three cars had sped around the corner behind them. They stretched the capacity of their engines and streamed past Terra and Dick. The force of their speed made the Escalade shake.

Terra narrowed her eyes and reached for a button that wasn't there. It took her a moment before she glanced at Dick, her cheeks colored. "Force of habit."

"You wanted to chase them, didn't you?" Dick asked. "Hit the cherry, blare the sirens, and get after those motherfuckers."

Terra nodded.

"Sorry, you're off duty tonight." Dick turned the music up a few notches.

"Then what the hell am I doing here?" Terra asked, hitting the gas and continuing to their destination.

Dick gave a playful grin. "You're playing side bitch, remember?"

Terra's eyes narrowed on the road.

CHAPTER TWENTY-NINE

They drew up to the location listed on the flyer and parked the car. Terra took her hands off the wheel and prepared herself for the game ahead.

She was nervous, but none of that stole the excitement she carried at the mission. It was rare that she ever got to play covert ops, although that was part of why she first got into the game of justice. She spent her childhood watching cop films and crooning over the figures on TV and in film who had the chance to take down the bad guys. The ones who stuck with her were the folks who did whatever it took to make sure the baddies came to justice. Despite the restraints the AJS often placed on her, the thrill of being able to play outside of her jurisdiction always made her smile.

Despite the fact she was partnering with Dick for this one, she struggled to hide her excitement. As much as she hated to admit it, she was often jealous of him. His position as a PI allowed him to be the maverick the city needed. Terra did her duty, of course. But stepping outside the lines of her bounds often got her hands slapped hard by those in charge. Although she knew she was taking a risk in getting involved in this operation tonight, she couldn't help herself.

Let the cards fall as they may, or so the saying went.

Dick fitted Terra with the covert tech while they were still in the car. The night closed in around them, darkness falling ever deeper. Terra bristled as Dick touched her ear and fitted the piece. Terra took it upon herself to insert the lens. Dick didn't seem too eager to help her, anyway.

It irritated a little at first, but a few blinks sorted her out. She wondered where Dick had secured this tech but thought better than to ask. The less she knew about his practices, the less she'd have to say on it if she ever got pulled in and asked to testify. She always wondered what would happen at that moment—if her loyalties would lie with the state, or with justice.

Sometimes the two weren't in alignment.

"Ready to go?" Dick asked, innocently enough. However, Terra yelped in surprise as his voice screamed in her ear at a volume that made no sense. She clapped a hand to the side of her head and groaned until the voice faded away. In its absence was a high-pitched whine.

"What the hell?" Terra yelled. Her voice exploded in her ear as Dick fumbled with his cell phone.

A moment later, the sound reduced, and Terra wriggled a finger in her ear, certain that her eardrum must have blown up. "Sorry," Dick replied. "Must be a bug in the system. That happened to me when I first put it in."

Terra glared at Dick. "This has been in your ear already? Gross."

"Relax, it's not like I'm bathing in wax," Dick shot back. "Besides, now that we know about the faults, we can adapt next time. All I have to do is shoot the volume down."

"If you could, that'd be amazing," Terra replied sarcastically. There was a part of her that was impressed by how clear Dick's voice sounded. There was no delay or echo. The earpiece was doing its job. "Not that there'll be a next time."

Dick grinned. "You said that last time."

Dick examined his cell phone and ensured that the video feed was working. Satisfied, he turned to Terra. "Now, I'm going to guide you through this. Don't question my methods, just do. Poker is one thing that I excel at in this world, and it'd behoove you to obey without question. No gut calls, no off-the-cuff decisions. You're entering my arena, and I'm your guide, got that?"

Terra opened the door and climbed out of the SUV. She didn't want to give Dick the satisfaction of knowing that he had the power, although it was obvious what was going on here.

Terra Kris stood outside her Escalade and dusted herself down. She drew a steadying breath and patted the pistol concealed at her waist. It was her personal firearm, her thinking ahead to ensure that nothing she did tonight would in any way link her to the AJS.

Except for the badge in her pocket. That was always going to be her safety card. Flash that shit in public, and you were near enough invincible, baby.

Terra started down the block, hands in her pockets. It was a chilly night, but the excitement kept her warm. She rounded the block and almost jumped out of her skin when Dick's voice appeared in her ear.

"You should stop those dirty thoughts, Terra," Dick crooned. "I'm not going to sleep with you. You know this."

Terra whispered, "Well, now I'm certain you can't read my thoughts, asshole. That's the last thing I'd have on my mind."

"I wouldn't be so sure," Dick teased. "How's the volume? All in check?"

Terra told him it was. "I'd avoid asking me questions if I were you. You want to give the game away before we get inside?"

"No one's telling you to answer back."

Terra looked at the ground and sighed. "Dickhead."

"No, thanks." Dick accompanied this with a burst of laughter.

Terra ignored Dick and found the address for the game. She was on a residential street with sets of stairs leading to brightly-colored doors. It was almost as though whoever had designed this block had lifted the inspiration straight from the suburbs of Manhattan. Walking through this street made Terra dream of once again visiting New York. Although their tech and their policing structures were primitive compared to Atlantica, it was nice to leave once in a while and remind yourself of how far the island had come compared to the rest of the world.

Even if she hadn't had a chance to take a vacation in years.

The address took Terra to a set of steps leading down into what would otherwise have been a basement of a block of apartments. Faded and cracked signs on the window reassured her that this might once have been a laundromat. She held the rails as she descended and knocked on the door, hoping that this place still held its commercial license.

"Okay," Dick soothed, "keep your cool. First impressions are key. You're here to play cards, and that's all."

Terra bit her tongue, wanting to reply to the patronizing tone, but knowing she couldn't. A letterbox slit in the door opened. A sharp voice announced, "Yes?"

Terra held up the snippet of the flyer. "I'm here for the game."

Although it was dark through the hole, Terra was certain she was being scrutinized by whoever was hiding in the darkness. There was a muttering of voices before someone asked, "Where's your chaperone?"

"Chaperone?" Dick muttered in her ear.

Terra gave her best smile. "I'll be honest. I found this flyer and wanted to find out what was going on. I have plenty of cash to play with. I'm just looking for some people to have some fun."

"No chaperone, no entry," the voice answered.

Terra batted her eyelashes and held up a wad of cash. There was more muttering on the other side of the door.

"Hold steady," Dick encouraged.

No shit.

The door clicked a moment later, and a woman with a severe bob and gaunt cheeks opened it. She had a glass eye and wore black lipstick that made her look more like a servant of the damned than a door guard. "That'll be your entry fee," the woman announced and reached for the cash. Terra drew back sharply. "No fee, no entry."

They stared at each other for a long moment.

Dick instructed, "Give her the cash. I'll pay back whatever it takes."

Just how much money do you have, Chambers?

Terra reluctantly handed over the bills. The woman rifled through the notes, her face showing no indication of pleasure or displeasure. Terra looked past her for the other bodies who had spoken but could find no evidence of anyone else.

The woman took a step back and ushered Terra inside. As Terra passed, she snapped, "Wipe your feet!"

Terra bit her tongue, not enjoying the way these people treated her. As she moved deeper into the darkness, she passed a series of old, forgotten washing machines and dryers, each draped in clothes thick with dust. At the end of the room was a small green light that illuminated the emergency route for the previous occupants. For a short while, Dick was quiet, leaving Terra alone with her thoughts. When she passed through the light, she turned a corner and met a corridor lit with the flickering flames of torches.

Oh, shit. What kind of cult shit has this guy got me into now?

The man was running out of patience.

Everywhere he turned it was one dead end after another. He had never had a case like this. Most of his high-profile cases were figured out within the week, with most targets stupid enough to leave obvious tracks to trace. High-profile executives who paid for escorts and hookers with their personal accounts. Media moguls so obsessed with social media that their GPS was simpler to identify and break than a paper mâché skull. Thugs and mobsters who paid in cash but made a big display of their power to their friends and left a long trail of hearsay that led straight to their hideouts.

A PI chasing a PI. That was another story.

Turnberry was on his ass. Chambers had broken into her mansion and put the scare on her again, asked her to call off the whole damn sting. Of course, Turnberry went in the other direction and turned up the pressure to close this once and for all. She raised her price, reluctantly, but that was what the man insisted. You want better results; you fund better, you encourage better...

You don't hide key fucking information.

The man needed a night off. Often it was rest that solved the case. The unconscious brain could do amazing things in fits of sleep, solving the puzzles that were the hardest to crack. The man had slept most of the day away and decided to cut loose that evening, using some of Turnberry's hard-earned cash to gamble away the evening in her underground casino.

That would hurt the bitch.

He knew she wouldn't be there, of course. She was too busy popping pain pills and getting over her fight with Chambers. Her proxies would run the operation tonight, and they had no idea what he looked like. He made sure of that. He operated in privacy and kept his cards close to the chest.

Not as close as Chambers.

The man peeled the edges of his cards up to remind him of what he had. An eight and a two. A great hand in blackjack. The odds were in his favor of hitting the twenty, and pacing out the dealer and the other two players sat at the table. "Hit me." The dealer flipped the card—a seven.

Fuck.

That fueled the man's incentive to find Chambers. The longer it took, the more pressure there would be on his client, and the less chance he had of getting his full pay. If Turnberry died, a clause in the contract allowed him to claim the money from her estate, but when lawyers got involved, things became messy. He didn't want it to come to that. He'd experienced that on far too many occasions, and the bureaucracy grew tiresome.

Would Lockhart pop one in Turnberry's skull, all for the sake of a piece of jewelry?

Without a goddamn doubt.

The man weighed up his options as his eyes flicked to his opponents. The dealer had a perfect poker face and waited with his hand atop the deck. The man knew he couldn't stick with a seventeen total, so he risked the hit. A queen was placed on his pile, the dealer announcing, "Bust," as the other two players looked on with smug grins.

Not that they did much better on their turn. As they played their cards, the man sipped his whiskey. His mind was half on the game of cards, half on the game of Chambers. As he studied the dealer and awaited his next turn, a woman walked into the room at the far end. She was cute in her white top and dark pants, with boots up to her knees.

The man smirked. If he weren't so damn tired, he might be tempted to play his luck with her tonight. Women were easier than cards, more predictable.

Maybe he'd consider it after a few more rounds and a half-bottle of the brown sauce. For now, he turned back to his game and threw his chips in the center of the table.

Dick watched through Terra's eyes on the small phone screen, struggling to see anything in the darkness. There was a bad feeling in his gut as she stalked toward a green light. That feeling grew when the torches came into view.

"Okay, remain calm," Dick muttered. "You can always back out now if you want to."

He knew she wouldn't take him up on the offer. In the years he had known Terra, she was the last person to back out of a sticky situation. Her tough constitution thrived in situations like this, and that's what he was counting on.

Terra passed by the torches. A hand wiped her warm brow and momentarily blocked the view on the screen. Outside the Escalade, the streets were almost empty. Only a few stragglers walked to wherever their evening entertainments resided. Dick relaxed in the car seat and hoped the tinted windows would provide the cover he needed. He had scooched over to the driver's seat and found it was a lot more comfortable.

"Last time I saw torch sconces like that was in an Indiana Jones flick," Dick commented as Terra continued. At the end of the corridor was a door that read "Staff Only." She glanced behind her to where the haunting crone waved a hand and encouraged her onward.

Terra drew a breath, then opened the door.

The light was overwhelming. Compared to the flickering torches, the overhead fluorescents and white walls lit the room like fireworks on the Fourth of July. The phone screen was overwhelmed for a moment until the sensors in the lens adjusted and he could finally see what was in front of him.

There were several tables set up in a vast, expansive room. To Dick, it reminded him of Sadie's underground casino ring. It was only when he saw a smattering of familiar faces that he realized that was exactly what it was.

"Okay, not to cause any kind of worry," Dick started, "but I've encountered some of these people before. Take a steadying breath and get yourself over to the table on the far left. You'll know it's the right one thanks to the Prince Charming sitting with his back to the wall."

Terra's eyes scanned toward the man sitting at the table in a pristine suit, his dark hair slicked back, and a jaw so chiseled it could have been used to shape Mount Rushmore. She strode through the crowd, avoiding the investigative gaze of the other underground casino-goers, and stood by an empty seat. She motioned to the dealer and asked, "Anyone sitting here?"

The dealer motioned for her to join. Prince Charming checked her out and leaned closer, a slight hint of something exotic in his voice. "We're knee-deep in this, honey. You'll have to wait until the cards reset."

"I'm in no rush," Terra replied in a tone that surprised Dick. He wasn't aware she could be so soft and alluring. All of his encounters had been sharp and laced with daggers on her tongue. "I'm a happy observer."

"Why don't you play something else until the grown-ups are finished?" Another player suggested, following with a haughty laugh. He was large and balding, and his display of wealth was grotesque. Gold chains as thick as bicycle tires hung around his neck, and rings with stones the size of chestnuts decorated his fingers. "Not that I mind having a pretty young thing to stare at while I play, although I do find it distracting."

"You best stay then," a third player added. The woman was easily in her seventies, with a blue rinse and a mouth filled with gold teeth. She looked like the grandmother of the rappers that were always taking the spotlight on MTV.

The others laughed.

Terra sat back and crossed her legs. She glanced down at her knees for a moment and Dick got a look down her top.

"Now, now, Dick. Focus on the mission," he uttered aloud before realizing it. Although he couldn't see inside her mind, he was pretty sure that Terra was scorning him and would have some words to say when it was over. This was confirmed by how quickly she looked up from her chest.

Dick sat back in the car and waited, knowing how long these games could last, excited at the prospect of playing proxy and guiding Terra to a winning streak.

Although, of course, the target was the sullen man across the table with a crop of hair pulled into messy spikes and a suit with no tie. This was all but confirmed when he opened his mouth and spoke in a tone laced with Russian, "Get on with the game, bitches. I have places to be. Rounds to win."

His pile of chips was the highest among the group. Dick couldn't wait to topple him from his tower and find a way to bring him into their custody.

CHAPTER THIRTY

Terra glanced at her cards and laid them back on the table. Dick watched through his mini monitor, feeling as though he was playing some perverse video game. Occasionally he would instruct Terra to look at the other players so he could get a read of their faces, but from what he could tell, none of them could hold poker faces to rival his.

Although it wasn't his face he had to hide. He only hoped Terra could keep hers straight and not give anything away.

They were six rounds into the game. Terra had taken a good stack of chips, and so had the Russian. Prince Charming had spoken directly to the Russian and announced his name as Michail, much to Michail's displeasure. It didn't suit him to get called out, and Dick wondered what his connection was with the handsome man.

"Okay, keep it steady. Turn to Michail and hold his stare," Dick commanded.

Terra obeyed. Michail looked back, eyes occasionally shifting to his cards. The game was no longer a game of four, but a game of two. The others knew this deep down, but they hadn't given up yet.

Terra held a two and a six of diamonds. The center of the table housed a four-card layout of a jack of spades, a three of diamonds, the king of hearts, and a five of diamonds. That would only give Terra two possible options, each one of them favorable, but rare. If the four of diamonds were pulled from the deck, she would have her straight flush, a set of cards all in the same suit and in consecutive order. If any diamond were pulled other than the four, she would have a flush—not as powerful, but also difficult to beat if you based it on the majority of hands people collected.

The odds, however, were against them. The dealer stared at Terra and awaited her call. Prince Charming had raised two blue chips, and now it was her turn.

Dick chewed his lip, wondering what to do. Was the risk worth the reward? He wasn't too sure. Michail was proving to be a worthy opponent.

"Okay," he offered at last, "go for broke. Match the pot and smirk a fraction. A twitch at most. Put it in their heads that they should be frightened."

Terra obeyed with her movements, but Dick couldn't see her face. He only hoped her acting skills were as good as her combat skills. He had been on the receiving end of a couple of her kicks and punches over the years.

Yet, somehow, we remain civil. The enemy of my enemy is my friend, I guess?

The round continued, and the final card played. Dick grinned when the ten of diamonds was placed neatly on the table.

"Okay, we've got them." Dick performed some calculations in his head. "Raise double what Charming places and keep your eyes on Michail. Make him sweat. We want this."

Terra did as instructed. The chips stacked in the center. The large, balding man grinned and matched the bid. When it came to Michail, he raised it higher, doubling what Terra had doubled. He showed no sign of grievance, and why would he? His pile was as high as hers.

Baldy's and Charming's faces dropped, but only for a moment, enough for Dick to capture it.

"We've got the other two," he informed her. "We just need to watch Michail. Match on your next round."

Terra did as instructed and matched the top bid in the pot. Baldy breathed a sigh of relief until Michail upped the pledge another ten percent. Terra matched again, and when the rounds swept the circle, they sat back and Michail matched.

The dealer drew the match to a conclusion. They each waited for someone to announce their hands. Charming broke the quiet and revealed a pair of kings. Baldy threw his cards into the center.

Michail stared at Terra. She held his gaze.

Good girl.

"Wait for him to break," Dick told her.

The dealer waited a few more seconds before encouraging them to press on. "Any higher than a pair of kings?"

"Now," Dick stated, as Michail showed the first signs of conceding.

Terra butted in front. "Flush." She fanned her cards on the table.

Michail grinned and fanned his cards. "Also a flush."

Dick couldn't believe it. It was rare that you saw two flushes of the same suit in the game. It came down to the highest card on that flush, and after a glance at each other's cards, the dealer announced the round to Terra.

"Ten high." The dealer collected the cards and went through the rigmarole of shuffling. "Game to the lady."

Terra raked in her chips and stacked them in her pile.

"Tell him you're sorry to take his money. Close game. Get under his skin," Dick commanded.

Terra did as instructed, pulling it off with sarcasm and wit.

Dick enjoyed being on this side of things, being the puppet master, but he also wished he could be deep in the game itself. He loved the smell of the cards, the feeling of being around the other players. If he were in there, he'd have a bourbon in his hands instead of sitting in a car and wishing he had a drink.

Why hadn't he brought a drink with him?

The next round of play went to Michail, but Dick had his sights on the long game. All they needed to do was outlast and stall the other players, and that's what they did. Four rounds later, Baldy was out. He rose in a temper and threw his cards on the table, then exited with an angry flourish. Prince Charming was more controlled and watched the rest of the game with lazy fascination as if he might learn something from the pair through osmosis.

"You're giving me quite a run for my money." Michail grinned. "I've not seen you on the circuit before. Where are you from?"

"Don't give him anything…" Dick began, but Terra cut over him.

"A woman never reveals her secrets." Terra glanced at her cards.

"Nice play." Dick was impressed.

Terra continued, "In the game of poker, the win isn't in studying the knowns—the numbers, the suits, the likelihood of pulling particular cards and reading the signs found in every minute detail of your opponent's face and body language. No. It's about understanding how the unknowns can impact the game."

She looked back at Michail, who had an interested gleam in his eye. "If you knew, for example, the places I frequent, you might be inclined to deduce my playing style. You might know the others on that block and understand a particular way of playing. If I told you where I lived or what my education was, I'm providing you more pieces of the puzzle. The less you know, the better. The more enigma there is, the greater the chance of the win." She glanced at the dealer. "Isn't that right?"

The dealer met her eyes, then looked back at the cards and chose not to answer.

"I like a woman of mystery." Michail sipped his drink and ignored the two new cards dealt before him. "A woman of mystery is a woman of chance and game. An enigmatic woman will lay all her cards on the table and take the risks that others wouldn't." He examined his cards, his face passive. "A true woman of mystery would be open to an all-in round. Everything to play for. All-in from the start."

"Careful," Dick crooned.

Terra examined her cards. Dick wished he could see her face. In her hand were an ace and a king. A great and promising start, indeed, but only if the rest of the cards were to support them.

Dick exhaled. "Play it cool. Turn him down."

Dick expected Terra to obey. He expected the next words to leave her lips to be, "Thanks, but no thanks." Instead, she replied, "You're on."

Michail's smile broadened. He chewed his lip, then eased his towers of chips into the center of the table. They clattered noisily on top of one another and were soon lost and mingled with Terra's chips.

"What are you doing?" Dick held the phone closer to his face. He was preparing for Terra to go ahead with the game, but she needed to play it right, first. Michail had proven to be a formidable opponent, and it was fifty-fifty as to whether he was drawing her into a trap or not.

Terra didn't answer—how could she, without giving the game away?

The dealer proceeded to turn the cards, taking his time to add to the theatrics. Prince Charming watched, a curious smile etched on his face. Dick's heart stopped in his chest. He wasn't sure what the outcome would be, and that wasn't a great position to find himself in. If he had been in Terra's situation, he would have played with the debate a little more. He would have tried to suss Michail's intentions through his answers, gleaned a little more information so that he had a solid indication of whether this would be a good or bad idea to play.

Now it was all in Terra's hands. His money was on the line.

Even if he wasn't playing directly, Dick hated the idea of losing his money in a game poorly played.

The final hand was dealt. Terra looked at the cards, and Dick's heart lightened. The hand was okay—a king and an ace. Another king and ace showed on the table for two pair, the highest available in the game.

Dick breathed a sigh of relief and sat back in the chair. "You lucky son-of-a-bitch," he announced, happy that Terra couldn't snap back at him about his use of language.

Terra turned her cards and revealed the hand. Michail's smile faltered, but only momentarily. It returned in force when he revealed his and showed a full house: two aces, and a seven to match the other two sevens on the table.

Michail chuckled and leaned over the table to scoop back his chips. "Close one. Close one...I thought you had me for a moment. Great game. Well played, particularly for a woman."

Dick's eyebrows raised. "Terra, keep your cool."

Dick had experienced Terra's rage firsthand and knew she didn't take kindly to the misogyny still rife in the world. She kept her cool and returned, "I'm sure there are other ways to sort payment. Means to make us both feel better about this particular game."

Although Dick couldn't see her face, her tone was clear. Terra was on the flirt path. The three ways to a man's heart were money, food, and sex, and she was more than aware of this.

Michail narrowed his eyes and examined Terra with excruciating detail. Although Dick was on the other side of a screen, for the first time he experienced what it must be like to be objectified by a man. He didn't like it one bit. The primal desire etched in Michail's eyes made his face ugly, and its contours harsher than before. He wondered if that was how he looked when observing the women he passed. Was that how men looked during sex? When they were on top of the woman and lost in the moment? Why would women ever touch them?

"Can I buy you a drink?" Michail offered as he rose from the table and the dealer started tidying the cards and chips. "It's the least I can do."

"Yes!" Dick almost shouted, excited at the progress she was making. Perhaps it was for the best that they lost.

Terra considered this. "I suppose. You'll be buying with my dollar, so it'll be like I'm buying myself a drink. Talk about a cheap date."

Michail laughed and joined her. They walked together to a makeshift bar where a man in a pristine white shirt was in the midst of tossing cocktails around and mixing drinks. His bar flair skills were impressive and drew Terra's eye.

However, the barman wasn't who drew Dick's eyes. His attention was captured by the person sitting at the bar a few stools over. A man with dark hair, a rash of a beard, and a bourbon in his hand. Someone that Dick hadn't seen in years, but who connected all his dots and drew them together.

A man Dick thought he had lost in the past.

CHAPTER THIRTY-ONE

It all came back to Dick in a moment of hot intensity. While Terra flirted and played the game with Michail, Dick's mind filled with the horrors of the past.

Explosions sounded all around them. Desert sand kicked in the air and formed thick clouds that barred everything from view. People were shouting, crying out in pain and anger. Gunshots fired. It was impossible to tell who was a friend and who was foe as the US Armed Forces called the retreat and pushed back from the attackers.

Vehicles roared into life. Dick ran and fired in the direction of opposing bullets. Three dozen of them went out on the tactical mission, intending to gather intel to feed back to camp and push their agenda. They would make the town safe and free its citizens from the dictator's regime. All they had to do was bide their time.

But the enemy was ready for them. The enemy laced the sand with mines and hid over the hills. The first they heard was the bullets ricocheting off the ground as they sprayed toward their unit and started the conflict.

Doug Neville had been Dick's comrade. One of the first friends he had made when he joined the military. They passed through training camp together and were paired in the same bunkers. They played cards in the evening and smoked cigars while talking late into the night about their pasts and dreams. Dick spoke of his early years in England. Doug was fascinated and spoke of his time growing up in Georgia. They drank together on their time off, met ladies, swapped stories, and held each other up when times got hard.

Doug was like Dick in many ways, if maybe a little rougher around the edges. While Dick exercised diplomacy and played the long game, Doug had a habit of rubbing the seniors the wrong way. He pushed boundaries and tested the limits. He never went far enough to lose his position, but his favor wasn't the same as Dick's. Dick's purpose was clear. He wanted to help people. Over his years in the ranks, he worked his way into the intelligence side of operations and pushed forward in low-level detective work. Doug was directionless, and after a few years simply followed Dick.

When the conflict grew once more in the Middle East, the two deployed overseas to get involved in the action. They had nothing to leave behind in the US, so they obeyed without question, excited to make a real impact in the world. Their optimism was dashed on the day that the enemy fired.

They had been positioned three bodies away from each other. Dick still remembered the cocky grin that Doug threw his way as he lined up his M4 carbine and provided cover. There was no indication that the enemy was ready, but that didn't mean they didn't prepare, anyway.

When the bombs struck, Dick turned his head and discovered Doug was missing from his sight. That wasn't unusual, given that everyone was lost in the desert clouds. After a long few minutes of scrabbling around and regrouping in the vehicles, only seventy percent of their unit was recovered. Some sported severe wounds and lost limbs. Others miraculously got away with sand in their eyes and scrapes on their knees.

Doug never returned.

Dick yelled at the officer in charge to hold on. His knuckles gripped the open door of their light utility vehicle. Emotion raced through him, surging with every passing second that came where Doug couldn't be seen. He knew they had to get out of there, but every fiber of his being told him to jump out and find him. Doug had become more than a friend over the years. He'd become a brother.

At one point, he was poised to jump. A hand grabbed his collar and dragged him back into the vehicle. Dick didn't remember what he shouted. He only remembered the way the dust clouds scratched his throat and stung his eyes. He remembered the piercing sound of bullets crashing against the body of the vehicle. He remembered the radios calling retreat and the wheels' desperate attempt to find friction in the sand and start their journey to a safer place.

Doug was gone. For weeks, Dick prayed that Doug would find a way back. That somehow he would return to them. One day he might wake up and find Doug recovered by fellow operatives.

That day never came.

All of this and more passed through Dick's mind as he struggled to come to terms with what he was seeing. It was Doug, of that there was no doubt. A little older, maybe. Who knew if he was wiser? But it was Doug, nonetheless. He'd recognize that ugly mug any place.

Terra chatted away and waved her hands at Michail. The phone screen showed the rows of liquor bottles on a shelf behind the bar. Occasionally, Michail's hungry eyes slipped into view. The barman strode up and down the bar.

But all Dick could think of was what he had seen. The ghost of a man he had long assumed was dead.

It was only when Terra rose to her feet, an unknown time later, that Dick was pulled back to the present. Terra glanced around the casino. Doug's seat was now empty. Dick had hoped he would still be there, that he would get a chance to confirm what he had seen.

But that chance never came. Doug was gone again.

If he had been there in the first place.

CHAPTER THIRTY-TWO

Terra was surprised at how charming this supposed Russian mobster was.

He kept her entertained and told stories of his motherland and his journey to Atlantica. Of course, the whole time he talked she knew it was bullshit, but that didn't stop the pleasure of hearing it all. She always found it endlessly fascinating how criminals and convicts could live a double life and convince themselves that a part of their fabric was good. Even the most prolific murderers, thieves, and con artists compelled themselves to believe that what they did was right. There was always a justification for wrongdoing.

But he was convincing. Terra nodded and accepted the drinks the barman poured. Michail unknowingly paid with Dick's cash, although Terra deliberately drank slowly to keep her bearings. She wasn't in Dick's camp of drowning your sorrows and stumbling through life. She was a professional, and a professional knew how to use liquor to their advantage. There wasn't a compulsive liar around who could barricade the truth from eventually spilling between their lips once they were sufficiently inebriated.

Alcohol, the universal truth serum.

The strange thing among all this chatter was how quiet Dick had become. Terra never knew Dick to be silent on any issue, and she had some trepidation about how he might react to her flirting technique. Terra knew how to play guys like a fiddle. She knew she was objectively attractive, maybe not to everyone's taste, but she had worked her way into a guy's mind on more than one occasion in a bid to get intel. The only difference in this situation was that Dick could see everything, and he could talk without Terra being able to respond.

After ten minutes of talking to Michail, Terra excused herself to go to the bathroom. She strode across the makeshift casino floor and found a shabby facility along the far wall. Inside there was only one woman, as far as she could tell. She entered the cubicle and was about to undo her pants when she remembered that Dick could see what she saw.

Terra sat on top of the toilet lid and bided her time. The woman in the cubicle beside her eventually finished and left her alone.

When the door closed, Terra touched a finger to her ear. "Dick, you there?"

Dick was silent.

"Dick?"

Even from afar, she could tell that Dick was distracted. Her words brought him out of his reverie. "I wouldn't request that in the bathroom if I were you."

"Where the hell have you been?" Terra spoke in a low tone, cautious of anyone entering the bathroom. "I've never known you to be so quiet."

"Sorry. Something came up."

Dick didn't say more, although Terra could tell that something wasn't right. "As much as I hate to say this, I need you to help navigate this next part."

"I don't know," Dick commented, "you seem to be doing rather well. What's the next step? Back to his place?"

Terra couldn't tell if Dick was being sarcastic or not, but either way, he was on the money. "Yes. If that's what this takes."

"Good. Get him to a safe place. Get him *alone*. Once we have that, we can zero in on Petrov, no problem."

"Sounds like a plan." Terra paused as the door shifted in its frame. No one entered. She relaxed. "Before I go back out there, can you do me a favor please?"

"Sure."

Terra chewed her lips, not knowing how well this might go. "Can you switch the connection off for a few minutes? I really need to pee."

"Sure…" There was little conviction in Dick's reply.

Terra sighed. "Fine. I'll do it my way." She closed her eyes and navigated her clothing blind, hoping the lens couldn't see through the thin veil of skin on her eyelids. She looked up as she peed, for extra caution. When she finished, she pulled her pants up and didn't open her eyes until she was ready to exit the cubicle.

The moment she exited, Dick clapped. "Great work. I'm impressed."

"Fuck you." Terra examined herself in the mirror. The door to the bathroom opened and two women walked in, both unsteady and a little drunk, and giggling as they linked arms. They disappeared into the same cubicle.

Terra adjusted her top and examined her makeup to ensure that she was in top form for the next part of their plan. As she did, Dick requested, "Since I did you a favor, I need you to do me one."

Terra stared at her reflection and nodded, unable to speak to Dick out loud with company present.

"When you hit the floor again, can you give me a full look at the casino? I want to take in everyone there."

Terra raised an eyebrow.

"Please?" Dick added, sickly sweet.

Terra gave a thumbs-up and headed back out onto the floor.

Michail eagerly waited at the bar and followed her with his eyes every step of her journey back. She sat on her stool as he commented, "I thought I'd lost you. Then I remembered there are no windows in the bathroom. No quick and easy escape." He closed his eyes, struggling with what he said. "I didn't mean it that way."

Terra smiled. "Is that a personal experience you often have? Lots of ladies running from you and escaping out the bathroom window?"

"You'd be surprised."

Terra placed a hand on his and tilted her head. "What do you say we get out of here?"

It was Michail's turn to raise his eyebrow. "Don't you want a chance to try and win some of your money back? The night is young."

"And we're not getting any younger." Terra swirled her fingers on the back of his hand. "Don't you agree?"

There was a fuzzy edge to Michail's eyes. When he stood and donned his coat, he swayed a little as though standing on a ship cruising over gentle seas. She linked arms as he guided her out of the casino. Eyes trailed them as they neared the exit.

"Is this a common occurrence for you?" Terra asked.

Michail blushed slightly. "I have to be honest and say that it isn't. I wish it were. You are very pretty."

Terra rested her head on his shoulder. Soon, they were back in the corridor with the flickering sconces.

Dick examined the room as Terra scanned with excruciating patience. He knew it might make her seem a little odd to be looking across the whole room when the man she was supposed to be interested in was waiting for her, but he had to know. He had to confirm that he'd seen what he thought he saw.

There was no evidence of Doug. There was no sign of him whatsoever. Dick wasn't sure if that was a good or bad thing. On the one hand, he didn't truly believe that Doug could still be alive, not after everything they had gone through. Enemy forces would have destroyed him on sight.

On the other hand, if Doug weren't there, that would pull Dick's mental faculties into question. He had always prided himself on his sense of reality and how his mind guided him to solve complex problems. Seeing ghosts was one step away from hallucinations and madness. If he fell that route, then his entire career would be over.

And then what would he do?

He thanked Terra as she sat with Michail. She worked quickly and efficiently, and soon they were in Michail's car and on the streets of Atlantica. Dick took a mild sense of satisfaction as he cranked the stick into drive and guided Terra's Escalade after them. He commented in her ear, "Let's see if this thing drives better with a real driver behind the wheel."

He wished he could see her face in response.

One problem that Dick encountered with his new micro-tech was that he had to watch their drive closely to follow Terra. She kept her eyes peeled on the road as they wound through the streets. Dick looked for landmarks that he recognized to guide him. One part of his mind was on the phone, another on the road, a third on Doug. That experience had knocked him, and he was still trying to recover.

Occasionally he would ask Terra to confirm a street name or direction. She did a great job pointing at landmarks and commenting to Michail, asking for information that he didn't have. What did Michail care for the Turkish takeout store on Friedman Drive? What business would Michail ever have frequenting a laundromat on the corner of Fourth? She worked with what she could, and soon they stopped somewhere Dick couldn't identify.

Dick slowed the Escalade as he awaited some indicator of where Terra had ended up. For the last few blocks it was difficult to tell, and instructions had gotten sparse. Dick watched Terra climb out of Michail's car and wrap her arms around her chest for warmth. They strode along the sidewalk toward a large building that pierced the sky. Terra was helpful and looked around at businesses whose fronts were closed and dark. One place jumped out at Dick, a 7-Eleven, one of the only companies still operating in this area at this time.

Terra's view moved toward a set of rotating glass doors leading into luxury apartments. Dick wasn't surprised that these Russian henchmen had pads of that caliber. Working for scum, while not honorable, would undoubtedly pay well. Terra glanced at the building name etched on a golden plaque, but Dick missed the detail as light reflected harshly on its surface and blocked his view.

Shit.

Dick switched away from the app and hopped onto a browser to search the local area for nearby 7-Elevens. While he trusted Terra to hold her own, he knew that he would get hell if he somehow lost her, and this mission was too important to lose a single thread now.

Three results popped up. Dick noted their addresses and headed for each in turn, navigating the darkened streets as he fixed his eye on the sky and looked for any sign of the looming tower Michail ushered Terra into.

When he tried to switch back to the application to see Terra's point of view, he got a blank screen. Small white text positioned in the upper left corner read: Connection lost.

Dick's throat went dry.

CHAPTER THIRTY-THREE

"Terra?" Dick's voice sounded distant and urgent. "Terra, if you can read me, know that I cannot see you anymore. Our connection is compromised. I repeat, I can't see through the lens. Give me some sign that you can hear me."

Terra stiffened. She stood in a golden elevator that rapidly rode the dozens of floors to the luxury apartments. Michail stood beside her, hands folded in front of him, occasionally throwing Terra a glance and a smile.

No music played. In the pregnant silence, Terra only hoped that the device stuck in her ear wouldn't compromise their intention. If she could hear Dick as clearly as she could, how much sound would leak out and reach Michail's ears?

"I'm glad we met," Michail offered. "It's been some time since I've brought someone back to my place."

Terra offered a coy grin. "I can't say I make a habit of this myself."

He turned, then his lips were on hers. Terra didn't know what else to do but kiss him back. The operation depended on her commitment to the role, and she played the part well.

His lips were dry and a little chapped. His skin was smooth.

There was a musky odor, and his breath tasted of liquor. He pressed his hips against her, and she drew back in the hope that he would identify the movement as a tease and not a repel. His kiss grew more desperate. Bile rose in her throat. When she had first thought about bringing justice to Atlantica, she had never once pictured a scenario like this.

Still, justice was justice, and sometimes you did what you needed to for the greater good.

She only hoped that she wouldn't have to "do" Michail.

The elevator *dinged* and pulled the Russian from his passion. He stared into Terra's eyes for a moment, then offered a hand. Terra took it and masked her disgust as playful silence. Her only solace in that elevator was that Dick's visual connection was dead, meaning he wouldn't have any video footage of their desperate make-out session.

"Come," Michail crooned as he fished keys out of his pocket and guided her to a door that faced the elevator. It was the only door on that floor, which would make this apartment enormous if Terra judged it correctly. She wondered how much a place like this would go for. AJS officers made a modest income, but it certainly wasn't in the region of the billionaires who made their piles of gold on the corpses of their enemies.

Michail moved slightly ahead of Terra. The elevator dutifully moved down to the lower floors, ready to ferry some other rich bastard who couldn't be bothered to use the stairs. He fumbled his keys in the locks while Terra waited.

"Problem?" she asked on his fourth attempt. She knew the plight of the drunkard trying to insert his keys in the lock. She'd been there herself on plenty of occasions, watching the lock dart away from the key every time she tried to position it in the hole. "Need a hand?"

"I've got it," Michail replied, although when he looked back at her, there was something in his eyes that she didn't like. A strange desperation that didn't make sense to her.

After his sixth attempt, Terra's Spidey-senses tingled.

This isn't his apartment.

"Michail?" Terra asked softly while taking a few steps back. Her hand moved to her hip, and her fingers grasped her gun handle. "Whose apartment is this?"

Michail turned to her with back bent and sweat beading his brow. His eyes lit up at the sight of the gun. He swallowed dryly, then opened his mouth to reply.

He didn't need to. The door swung open to reveal a man with a gleaming dome on top of his head, and a shark's toothy grin stretched across his face. Terra's pistol pointed directly at the man's double-barreled shotgun, and for a moment, they simply stared at each other.

"Come on in," the man crooned as he pumped the shotgun. "We insist."

Before Terra could respond, Michail had drawn his weapon.

Dick found the apartment building some fifteen minutes later.

Every second felt like a lifetime. The longer he left it, the more chance there was that Terra would be in danger. They had a rocky relationship at the best of times, but it had been Terra Kris who originally initiated Dick into the ways of Atlantica. Years back when he first arrived and needed help to solve his first case, Terra had his back.

In a sense. It wasn't a year later that she shot him in the ass.

When Michail's and another Russian's voices came through the audio feed, Dick knew he needed to speed up. He urged Terra to reveal the floor number and was pleased when her reply came through the receiver. The signal broke halfway through the number, and Dick wasn't sure if she had said "Twenty-seven" or "Thirty-seven."

A moment later, the line crackled and went dead.

Dick parked the Escalade and entered the building, then moved swiftly past the reception counter. He stared a moment at the elevator, then decided that it would be easier to lose any suspicious staff if he climbed the stairs.

By the tenth floor, Dick's breathing was labored. By floor twenty, he was struggling. The elevator rode past him, and he regretted his decision, but it was too late. He had to go on.

As he half-jogged up the stairs, he brought his cell to his ear and listened for Terra. The line was well and truly dead, which didn't bode well. If Dick hadn't heard the second Russian's voice before the line had cut, he might have imagined that Terra and Michail were fooling around and her earpiece might have come out. She might have turned it off on purpose.

But Dick knew that wasn't the case.

He reached floor twenty-seven and doubled over, taking a moment to regain his breath. He drew his gun, stood straight, then examined the door and the space around. There was no obvious sign of intrusion, although that didn't mean much. He pressed his ear to the door, but either the wall was effectively insulated against noise, or there was no one inside. Either way, that didn't help Dick one bit.

He examined the floor, hoping to find a trace of scuffling feet, anything that might suggest people had been here recently. The marbled floor was immaculate, not a speck of dust to be seen.

Dick grumbled, then turned to the stairs. He figured that he'd need to investigate floor number thirty-seven in case anything obvious was up there. Now was not the wrong time to barge into a stranger's apartment and scare the crap out of them.

Neither was now the time for subtlety.

Dick made it to the door that led to the stairs. He set one foot on the steps before a gunshot sounded behind him.

Suddenly, floor twenty-seven seemed like a safe bet.

Hmmm...maybe safe is the wrong word.

The bald man advanced on Terra as her gun flicked between the two.

The situation looked dire. One wrong move and she'd be a goner. Sure, she could take one of them out on the way, but she was outnumbered, and that was never a great position to be in.

"Inside," the bald man instructed.

Terra hesitated.

"Now," he insisted.

Terra's face hardened. "I'll have you know that I'm an officer of the law. You are currently threatening an officer bound by the duty of the Atlantica Justice System, and that is a federal offense. I must insist that it is you who comes with me."

The bald man smiled. Under his powerful demeanor, Michail paled in comparison. "Then we are at an impasse. I am currently standing in my home. The Atlantica Justice System protects me."

"The minute you shoot, it's over," Terra warned.

"The minute *you* shoot, you are beyond your bounds," the man crooned. "Come inside. Let us discuss this further."

Terra shook her head. "The moment I cross that threshold, I'm no longer safe."

He tilted his head, an empathetic expression on his face. "Oh, my dear. You think you are safe out there?"

The door to the stairs slammed open behind her, and a man rushed her way. Before she could do anything, strong hands gripped her shoulder and held her wrist at an angle where her pistol aimed at the floor. Terra grinned internally and allowed them to put her in such a position. She resisted precisely the right amount, knowing that she was in a situation in which power was key.

And the element of surprise was her only true weapon.

"Come," the bald man repeated and lowered his shotgun. "Let's talk."

He turned and entered the apartment. Terra resisted, but the man behind shoved her forward. He took her gun from her grasp, and as she crossed the threshold, the man barked instructions at Michail. "Remove her earpiece, won't you? She won't need that any longer."

Michail obeyed, unable to meet Terra's eyes. His finger clawed at her ear and produced the small black speck. He gave it a strange look, clearly not understanding what it was, and wiped his hands clean. "There's nothing in there."

The bald man sat in a chair and casually drank a blood-red cocktail. "Then you have lied to me."

"No, I swear it, she's bugged," Michail offered. He looked at Terra. "You are, right?"

"What was your first clue?" Terra retorted.

Michail couldn't meet her eyes. "Someone who spends a considerable while in the bathroom, only to return and spend time scanning the casino as if she were an IR scanner of some kind. It was obvious."

"You mean, you didn't fall for my charms?" Terra grinned.

"Oh, I did." Michail's ears burned. "I knew it was too good to be true."

"Don't be too hard on yourself, Michail," the bald man called. "Come, let us sit like civilized citizens. Let's get to the bottom of this bugging and work out what's going on."

A rough shove encouraged Terra to sit in a chair adjacent to the bald man. Michail and the other cronies stood on either side as the bald man examined her closely. "Tell me, Terra. Who are you working for?"

The question wasn't unpleasant. It was as if he was merely asking the time or directions to the nearest Costco.

"Your mother," Terra spat back, a pleased grin on her face. "Please, you think you can draw any information out of me? You have no idea what you're up against."

A flicker of annoyance passed over the man's face. Terra

enjoyed it but knew it could cause her trouble. If this man was who she thought he was, she needed to be careful moving forward. She only hoped that although the device rested somewhere on the cold, hard floor, Dick could hear her.

The bald man leaned closer and rested his elbows on his thighs. The overhead lights bounced off his immaculately shaved head as he studied her. "Oh, no, my dear. I believe it is you who doesn't know who they're dealing with. You said it yourself outside, you're in my domain now, and my domain is where I reign supreme." He motioned to the apartment. "This entire apartment is designed to accommodate the workings of the world of torture. Every surface in here is wipeable, every cupboard stocked with the devices that will remove any evidence a body had ever fallen to their doom in here. I work with monsters in this city, Miss. Monsters and the mad. I work in the dark crevices, places where you wouldn't think people could survive. I work alongside creatures who you could only dream of in your pitiful mind. You want to measure balls or enter a pissing contest, then fine, let's do it because there's not a shadow of doubt in my mind that I would win. People hear my name and cower. They hear my employer's name, and they dig their own graves. You may not yet know where you lie, but you will soon. So either talk or I'll find ways and instruments to extract the information I desire."

"Petrov, right?" Terra uttered the words so abrasively that Petrov flinched. "Sergei Petrov. That's you. Tell me I'm wrong."

Petrov leaned back. "So, you have heard of me?"

"In a sense," Terra replied. "I hoped to run into you. I have some questions, and I don't think your boy Michail is the one to answer them."

Petrov raised an eyebrow with an amused look. "And tell me, how is it you've stumbled across my name? I always like to know how far my infamy has stretched throughout Atlantica. There's a thin line to tread between a well-known name and a jail sentence. How far am I from that? Surely a cop can tell me that much?"

"Your name has certainly come up." Terra felt a growing sense of confidence that, as long as she could stall Petrov, Dick would be able to find her and help. "I wouldn't say that you were any of those things you described, though. A man working among monsters? You realize that I wipe the streets of your kind on a day-to-day basis? I'm an individual, but the AJS is a never-ending organization. Even if you kill me, they'll find you. They're already on their way."

She held his stare and hoped he wouldn't see through her bluff.

"What can they do, except stand outside the door and listen in?" Petrov replied with a flourish of his hand. "While Atlantica employs the AJS to maintain peace, it nourishes criminals and allows us to thrive. Not the petty criminal, mind, but the high-functioning felons of this world. Those with the capital to make a difference and pursue their goals and dreams. Where else in the world would I be able to hold you to ransom, while all the city can do is watch?"

"Yeah, it's a pretty fucked-up system. Still, it's fun bringing in guys like you. It's a game of chase. The hunt is the reward. You could kill me now, but the moment you leave that door, the AJS will be watching your back and waiting for you to slip up."

"I don't think so," Petrov retorted. Terra was impressed by his grasp of the English language. Although his accent was thick, the words came out as though he practiced them regularly. "We are more than one person. My employer would gladly end the trail and erase the evidence. He'd pay me good money to do so."

"Dexter Lockhart?" Terra responded.

Petrov's eyes narrowed.

She pressed on. "Surprised that I've picked up that name? I'm sure you are since it's not one that gets passed around all that much. What is strange, though, is how Dexter doesn't exist anywhere on our systems." Terra thought back to the research she conducted in the time between when Dick caught her up on his mission and the game. "As much as I've looked through our database and City Hall's information, there is no record of a living, breathing Dexter Lockhart."

"Your point?" Petrov asked.

"It's an alias," Terra stated. "He's hiding behind an identity, and only cowards hide. You might think that you have all the power and that you can sit in your ivory tower and have your minions do your dirty work, but those whose names rain down in legend do so with themselves at the center of the operation. Dexter Lockhart is a coward, and his name will be erased from history. Sergei Petrov will go down too, but for another reason altogether."

Terra grinned. "As the man foiled by a single AJS officer."

Her hand moved quickly to the pistol tucked in her boot. The guards on either side were slow in drawing their weapons, and Terra fired the first shot at Petrov's hand.

He reacted almost instantly. The bullet hit the shotgun, which clattered to the floor. He roared in rage as Terra kicked off the floor and pressed into the back of her chair. She toppled backward and out of the guards' grasp as she tucked into a backward roll.

She had scoped the apartment's layout on the way in and now dove behind the kitchen island counter. The pistol in her hand was small but deadly, and she leaned around the side to shoot the other guard in the shin.

The man howled and folded to the floor, his gun forgotten. Michail was nowhere in sight. Petrov's gleaming head poked out from behind the couch. His chair had toppled as he ran for cover.

Somewhere overhead, Terra heard a buzzer.

"I saw your ears prick up, AJS scum," Petrov announced. "That's my backup on their way. This apartment block is filled with my henchmen. You think I'd be stupid enough not to surround myself with comrades?"

"I'll refer you to my previous statement," Terra called over. "Cowards hide behind greater men. Ain't that right, Michail?"

There was no response.

"Just keep talking," Petrov called back. "Make the most of your final words before the cavalry arrives. Time will run out faster than you think."

It was then that Terra noticed the thin veil of pink mist creeping out from small black nodules spread around the bottom of the kitchen counters. The smell was sweet, but its intentions weren't. Terra yawned and realized exactly what was seeping through the holes.

CHAPTER THIRTY-FOUR

Dick hesitated outside the door as another shot rang out. One was bad. Two shots were worse.

Deciding there was no time to be tactful, Dick kicked the door. It shook in its frame. He reared back, kicked again, and the door crashed open.

He ducked by the wall and peeked inside. Terra was nearby, lying down in the kitchenette and surrounded by some kind of fog. Dick could only assume what was going on. He couldn't make out Petrov or the others at a glance, but he could hear Petrov's angry shouts.

"Nice of you to join us, Chambers!" Petrov shouted. "I had no idea that you were the cop's backup. Doesn't quite make for as happy a party as Terra promised, does it?"

Dick had no idea what he was talking about. Dick drew his cell phone while Petrov was distracted and thumbed in a number. He tapped on the keyboard and pocketed the phone again. With his back to the wall, he tried to find a way to scan what was happening in the apartment.

Terra crawled closer and whispered, "Dick. Behind the couch."

Dick couldn't get a good view. If he leaned out too far, he knew his face would make a great final destination for one of Petrov's bullets. In a bid for a better look, Dick noticed the gold plated elevator buttons across from him. He squinted and could make out a head poking above a tiny, distorted couch in the reflection.

Footsteps sounded in the stairwell.

Dick looked around for any other means of infiltration. There were no obvious signs that he could see. He fished into his pocket and drew out a small metal box. "Petrov. I'm going to give you one chance to surrender. Otherwise, this will not end well for you."

The footsteps grew louder. Dick's heart raced. If Petrov's goons got in on the action, they would outnumber Terra and him. It would all be over. He had to get on top of the problem.

Petrov fired a shot in response. Terra cried, "That shot makes this an AJS issue. Your bullet exited the room!"

Petrov laughed. "You're still in my quarters, little girl."

Dick saw movement at the stairs and knew he had to act. He hurled the metal box into the apartment, guessing at the right angle to catch Petrov. Someone yelled. Dick lowered his shoulder and dove toward Terra as three bullets sped over his head.

Another surprised yelp came when the metal box exploded in a burst of smoke. Thick reams of grey mist swelled inside the apartment. Petrov and his goon shouted. Several men appeared in the corridor.

Dick pushed himself to his feet but found Terra holding onto his wrist. "What are you doing? It's suicide."

"Trust me," was all Dick managed before he tore himself free and ran to the door. He didn't look back, didn't even check to see if Petrov had him in his sights. He shoved the door closed, then turned the locks. Bodies thumped against the wood.

Dick spun and dove toward a stylish table in an area that might have been used for dining. When he felt he was safe, he looked up to find that the smoke had grown denser. Soon Terra would be out of his sights, too.

Dick grabbed a chair, then ran back to the door. He braced the top of the chair against the handle and grabbed Terra to help her to her feet. The apartment was gone, now. Everywhere they looked they could only see smoke.

"Great plan," Terra commented dryly. "What if he runs out the front door?"

"We'll hear him," Dick replied softly. "Keep your voice down. We need to listen for him."

Something clattered on the far side of the room. People shouted outside. Objects banged against the door. Dick grabbed Terra's hand. "Come on. Follow me."

They covered each other as they crept their way forward. By the time they reached the couch where Petrov was, there was no one in sight. Dick's lip turned up as he glanced around, knowing they only had a short amount of time to clinch this situation.

"Divide and conquer?" Dick asked, his voice a bare whisper.

"Are you fucking crazy?" Terra replied.

Dick's eyebrow raised. "I thought you liked working solo?"

"When I can see where I'm going," Terra retorted. "Come on. This way."

"Why?"

Terra rolled her eyes. "Because I heard him go into another room."

Someone coughed, a little way ahead. They snuck forward, moving swiftly but silently until they reached a door. Terra looked down and indicated that Dick should open it. The banging on the hall door was louder now, accompanied by raised voices of the building staff trying to find out what was going on.

Dick tried the handle, but it held tight. He wiggled it, but nothing happened. "It's stuck," he muttered. "Maybe they have a lock on the inside?"

"Seems a strange way to operate. Try again."

He did, with the same result.

When he looked up, Terra was gone. He scanned around him but could only see the thick smoke from his mini-bomb. He was about to call for her when something rushed toward him. It appeared at first as a silhouette but coalesced into Terra's form.

She charged at the door, her face grim and set. Her body crashed against the wood and knocked it clean off its hinges. Dick's jaw fell, impressed by the strength in such a petite woman.

However, there was no time for appreciation as Terra drew her gun and shouted at a figure who knelt by a bed. The figure aimed two shots that went wide, and the next thing Dick saw was a spray of blood painting the wall behind the body.

"Terra! What the hell?" Dick exclaimed. "He's our key witness! We need him." Terra turned the gun on Dick. He raised his hands. "What are you doing?"

Terra shook her head. "Oh, relax, Dick. I'm not going to shoot you. The rest of the room is empty." She nodded to the dead body. "That ain't Petrov. That's his goon. Meaning that the only place Petrov can be is…"

"Behind you," Petrov growled and pressed a gun barrel into the back of Dick's neck. Dick didn't need to look to know that Petrov was using him as cover. "Game's over I'm afraid, detective."

Terra kept her gun pointed slightly to the side of Dick's head. It had been a long time since he'd been in a position like this, and he had to admit that he wasn't a fan.

"Well played, Petrov," Dick replied. "What are you going to do now? Just end it? Pop off my skull, then shoot the cop?"

"I'm considering it," Petrov stated.

Terra raised an eyebrow. "If that were true, you would have done it already."

Petrov chuckled. "There's nothing wrong with taking my time, is there? After all, this is my apartment. As long as I'm within these walls, I can do whatever I want." He eyed Terra and bit his lip. "Anything at all."

Terra fired a shot that passed so near to Dick that he felt its wake ripple in the air.

The bullet missed Petrov.

"Now, now, Miss," Petrov continued. "You really want to play this game? You want to see your boyfriend shot because you couldn't obey and listen?"

"He's not my boyfriend." Terra gritted her teeth.

"Oh? Hit a nerve, have I?" Petrov laughed.

A commotion sounded outside the door. The shouts increased in volume. Gunshots fired.

The gun pressed harder into Dick's neck.

Petrov drew a breath. "Ah, fuck it. Why shouldn't I end it now? You've been a nuisance for far too long, Chambers. Sniffing around in places where you're not wanted. A bloodhound covered in fleas who can't let shit go."

"That works out well," Dick replied. "Dogs love to sniff shit. Guess that's how I found my way to you."

Another gunshot sounded. Dick closed his eyes and prepared for the worst. When he opened them, he was still alive, Terra standing in front. Her shot found its place in the ceiling as plaster rained down on them.

Petrov still held Dick.

Smoke seeped into the room and slowly filled the space. Terra became blurry in Dick's vision. She moved forward.

Petrov moved the gun from Dick's neck and shot at her. The bullet skimmed her shoulder and tore the fabric of her shirt.

"Enough of this bullshit," Petrov stated. His voice carried a disturbing level of calm. "Say goodbye to your lady friend, Dick. It's certainly been fun watching you scramble for the truth. But I'm afraid that this is where your journey ends."

More gunshots sounded from outside. The door crashed open and people filed in.

Dick felt the gun press tighter as Petrov's finger tensed on the trigger. Terra screamed, "No!" as the report filled the room. His eyes were clamped shut, his teeth gritted. He never thought he would go out like this. He had always believed that his end would be spectacular, a showcase for others to follow his example. Maybe it would have been booze-related, or with a woman on his lap. He never imagined he would meet his fate in the hands of an enemy.

Petrov gave a strange gurgled chuckle. Something wet hit Dick's back. Dick waited for the pain to come, for the bullet to break through his skin and tear apart his mind. He prepared himself for the worst, to chase the light to the end of the tunnel.

But it never came.

The pressure on his neck lessened. He glanced over his shoulder and found Petrov staring in shock at the place where his arm had once been. Instead, blood fountained from the stump while his limb lay on the floor, the gun beside it.

Dick seized his chance and spun on the spot. He threw a haymaker at Petrov's head that caught him in the temple. The bald Russian's eyes rolled back as he dropped to the floor in one hit.

"Dick, watch out!" Terra shouted and fired several shots out the door. Dick made out the dim shapes of a dozen or so figures approaching through the slowly receding smoke. Their guns were raised, and they were all pointed at Terra.

Dick stepped in front of Terra and spread his arms. "Leave her out of this. Take me instead. Whatever you do, let her go."

The smoke eased as a figure with her dark hair pulled back in a ponytail and one grazed and bruised eye came into view. Determination stamped her face as she waved her comrades in and had them scan the place, including opening closets and checking beneath the bed for enemies. They all wore black leather jackets.

Relief flooded Dick's face. Maurine fixed Dick with a judgmental stare. "You really do like cutting it close to the wire, don't you?"

Dick shrugged. "I guess so."

AJS sirens sounded in the distance. Dick, Terra, and Maurine turned at their chorus.

"Come on," Maurine ordered. "There's not much time. We need to get going and fast."

"He's bleeding out!" Terra exclaimed. "We need to patch him first."

Dick grunted, then unclipped his belt. He hooked it around Petrov's bloody stump and pulled it tight.

Satisfied with the tourniquet, Dick lifted Petrov's body from the floor and carried him across his shoulders as they ran out of the apartment. Bodies littered the corridor outside, some unconscious, some undeniably dead. The Dead Devils guided Dick and Terra down the stairs and into the lobby below. Dick was thankful that the descent was easier than the ascent since his adrenaline was wearing off.

The Dead Devils were highly organized and held the receptionists at gunpoint while they flooded out of the building. When Dick, Terra, and Maurine were clear, they all piled out and left the pale-faced clerks to wonder what in the hell had happened.

When they made it to Maurine's vehicle, Dick and Terra hopped inside. They laid Petrov over their laps while Maurine cast a disapproving look at the Russian and made no secret about her concerns of getting the blood out of the upholstery.

Dick assured her that they'd find a way to fix it. He wasn't a stranger to clearing up dire situations. Terra urged Maurine to put the pedal to the metal. They screeched away from the apartment block, and far from the encroaching AJS squadron.

CHAPTER THIRTY-FIVE

Dick sat in the chair and patiently waited for Petrov to come around.

His wound was clean. his arm's exposed nerves and arteries had been fitted with a better tourniquet, and the worst of the blood cleaned up. It was a rudimentary job, but it would suffice to keep him lucid enough to answer Dick's questions.

Terra stood behind him with her arms crossed and a severe expression on her face. Maurine stood beside her, and Gilly sat at the back of the room. When Dick looked for a place to work his magic on Petrov, Gilly's place had sprung to mind since she was in her new apartment, but the old one would still be vacant. She looked away and busied herself with her cell phone.

Petrov's head rolled, and his eyelids fluttered open. When they focused on Dick, a sneer crossed his lips. He tried to lunge at Dick, but the rope held him firm. Then he remembered his missing arm.

"The tables have turned," Dick informed him around the lit cigarette between his lips. "Your men aren't around to save you now. You'll give me the information I seek, and we'll put you out of your misery."

"Shouldn't that be 'or?'" Petrov replied.

Terra interjected, "You can bargain for your life if you want to. The truth is that the minute this is over, I'm taking you into AJS custody. Your disruption at your place broke into AJS jurisdiction, and for that, I can have you taken in for some time, Mr. Petrov. We already have a laundry list of items to investigate, and threatening and shooting a federal officer is only one of them."

Petrov laughed, but his mirth quickly faded as pain took over. "I have no motive to talk to you, then. Get it over with. Kill me, or put me into custody."

Dick raised his eyebrows. "Oh, if it were only that easy." He reached into his inner jacket pocket and withdrew a passport-sized photo of a young girl with blonde hair. Her smile was wide, and her eyes were bright. "I found this in your apartment, Petrov. Specifically, I nabbed it from your bedroom as we were leaving. Never thought you'd find enemies at your doorstep, did you? Neither did you imagine I'd put two and two together."

Petrov glared at Dick.

"She's beautiful. Really. She has your eyes." Dick smiled. "What would your daughter say about you getting locked up for years at a time?"

Petrov's eyes betrayed him. He gritted his teeth. "What do you want?"

Dick moved closer as his eyes narrowed. "I want Lockhart."

Petrov burst into laughter, that hideous gargling chuckle of a man with too much phlegm in his throat. "You'll never get him."

"Bullshit," Terra exclaimed. "We got you, didn't we?"

Petrov gave Terra a sympathetic look with his dark eyes fixed on hers. "Compared to Lockhart, I'm nothing. Lockhart is integrated into this whole damn city. You want him; you'll have to fight through a whole ocean of defenses. Lockhart is out of your league." Petrov spat on the floor. "And if I give him up, I might as well consider myself dead."

Dick sighed, then drew his pistol. Terra held hers, too.

"What's it going to be?" Dick examined the photo again. "Man, I'd hate to have to give her the news that her daddy is gone."

Petrov growled. "I can't…"

Terra stepped forward. "Provide us with what we want to know, and I can offer you witness protection. It won't be easy, but I'm sure the AJS can make a deal. We have criminals living the quiet life all over town. You can be on that list. We can protect you until Lockhart is behind bars."

"Or dead," Dick added.

Petrov considered this, his face pained. "You'll protect Nadia, too?"

"We'll do everything we can," Terra replied. "That's a promise."

Petrov looked down at the floor. A wave of pain flooded through him as his tender arm throbbed. Dick fixed his eyes on Petrov while waiting and hoping for the smart response.

AJS sirens sounded in the distance. Petrov glanced at the window. Eventually, he sighed. "Fine. I'll tell you what I know. Let me call Nadia first."

Terra unlocked her cell phone. "Make it quick."

CHAPTER THIRTY-SIX

There was a knock on the door.

Dick rose from his slumber, his body so exhausted from the night's events that dreams hadn't come. He climbed the stairs and opened the door, knowing who was waiting for him.

"Why did you knock?" Dick asked.

"I didn't want to intrude," Terra replied.

Annoyingly, she looked as fresh as a daisy with only a few scrapes on her skin from the previous night. Her blue AJS uniform was form-fitting, and Dick had to fight not to stare.

Dick chuckled. "That didn't stop you before, did it?"

Terra shrugged. "Maybe I'm turning over a new leaf."

Dick welcomed her into the safe house and offered a coffee. She eagerly accepted, and for a while, they were both quiet. Dick's muscles were stiff as he hobbled around the apartment and cleaned up some of the clothes he had thrown around the room.

"I should start paying you rent," he quipped after catching Terra's eye as she watched him.

Terra's face grew serious. "Take all the time you need, Dick."

He raised his eyebrows. "You've changed your tune."

Terra took a seat. "Look, I know I've given you a hard time over the past few years—Lord knows you've given it back, too—but I can see that you're onto something big."

Dick nodded. "And I still have no idea what the end game is."

Terra sipped her coffee. "The end game is justice. That's what we both want, right?"

"Absolutely," Dick agreed.

Terra laid a hand on Dick's knee. He looked down at it but felt nothing more than the touch of a sister or a friend. "This game is big, Dick, and I want you to know that I have your back. I don't blame you for what happened yesterday. Missions come with risks, and this is the biggest undertaking I've been part of in a while. In the beginning, I wasn't sure I should associate with you off-duty, but even then I knew there was more to this than met the eye."

Dick nodded, unsure what to say.

Terra removed her hand. "Petrov is now in AJS custody. I've… modified the truth about how he came into my hands. Your name has been struck from the record. No questions required. You're free to continue your mission."

Dick smiled. "Thank you, Terra. It means a lot. I know it doesn't put you in a great position."

Terra's eyes narrowed in thought. "All my life, the only thing I've ever wanted was justice. To keep the peace. It's the only thing that's ever given me happiness. I'm damn good at what I do, but sometimes I feel like the AJS boxes me in, limits what I can do." She looked at Dick. "I've often thought of what life would be like on the other side. In the PI game, where I can play maverick and go wild."

"As I understand it, that's what brought you to this precinct in the first place. Why don't you?"

Terra nodded at her uniform. "Because I look amazing in blue."

They both laughed.

"In all seriousness," Terra continued, "you're a good guy, and you do great work. I only hope that you can take what you've gleaned and figure out the rest of this puzzle, because now that you've brought it to my attention, it's going to kill me, too."

Dick smirked, a twinkle in his eye. "There hasn't been a case yet that I haven't solved. I don't expect this one to be any different."

Terra left shortly after, ready to patrol the streets and respond to AJS calls as they came. As Dick watched her mount her motorbike, his thoughts wandered to all the people he'd encountered along his journey. Gilly, Maurine, the Dead Devils, Petrov...

And Doug Nevill.

So many questions uncovered. So many answers to find.

And all that Dick had to go on to make his next move was the location of a cemetery and the formerly deceased's name.

First, thank you for reading this book in 2021...Even though I'm eyeing the last few hours of 2020 like *I know you are going to try and @#@#%uck me, 2020. I'm looking out for your antics and will slap you into 2021 if you give me the chance.*

For those who read many of my other books and the author notes at the back, you know I'm going through a phase in my life that can be best described as 'older, not all that energetic.' I'm trying to learn to do something besides read, write, and think about publishing all day and all night.

In short, I'm studying all the different ways to cook, thinking somehow I might be able to cook these amazing meals...

With very little effort.

So, last night a celebrity chef had a commercial showcasing this new pasta maker. Now, I'm all about suggesting new kitchen gadgets, but after purchasing more than one of these 'amazing time slicing make-you-a-kitchen-god' items in my lifetime, I'm a bit jaded.

In short, I want to believe it can be real but have to check.

And MAN, did I want to believe the pasta maker was the real deal. Add two eggs, some flour, and something else (I can't even remember 3 ingredients) and give it 10 minutes, and poof, pasta from scratch!

It looked DELICIOUS!

(It was also 3:30 AM after a pretty fun night… Not the best time to be thinking logically, and this was without any alcohol… or very, very little.)

I wanted it!

It was $200.00… I wanted it a bit less. But my author brain kept telling me stories about how I would make lasagna so good, my wife would groan in ecstasy.

Wasn't it worth $200.00 to make that happen?

The TV didn't need to sell me, my own mind was doing a FANTASTIC job!

I jumped online… No, actually, that's a lie. I was getting tired, and I was in bed. I rolled over and grabbed the laptop and pulled it back to my lap to Google the product in a very smooth and slow progression. There was no jumping anywhere.

That's when reality hit. :-

Comments about breaking easily, hard to clean, and other issues sucker-punched my visions of chef-nirvana.

I closed my laptop and turned on my side, and went to sleep. I couldn't handle one more depressing kick in the stomach from this year.

Ok, I'll try to get back on track with author notes that have SOME relevance to the book I'm writing the notes for, but I just needed to get my pasta chef story out.

I hope you have a GREAT 2021, and let's all enjoy a better life as we come out of this misery.

Ad Aeternitatem,

Michael Anderle

CONNECT WITH THE AUTHOR

Connect with Michael Anderle

Website: http://lmbpn.com

Email List: http://lmbpn.com/email/

Social Media:

https://www.facebook.com/LMBPNPublishing

https://twitter.com/MichaelAnderle

https://www.instagram.com/lmbpn_publishing/

https://www.bookbub.com/authors/michael-anderle